Once a Scoundrel

CANDICE HERN

ONCE A SCOUNDREL

AVON BOOKS
An Imprint of HarperCollins*Publishers*

AVON BOOKS
An Imprint of HarperCollins*Publishers*
10 East 53rd Street
New York, New York 10022-5299

Copyright © 2003 by Candice Hern
ISBN: 0-7394-3593-0

Dedicated with thanks

to Louisa Pineault,
a fellow fashion print collector whose
knowledge of the prints and magazines
of the Regency period is breathtaking
in its scope and depth.
Her gracious generosity in sharing that
knowledge is deeply appreciated.

And to Elizabeth Boyle,
for kindly sharing her 1801 volume of
The Lady's Magazine.

Chapter 1

July, 1801

If he weren't so thoroughly drunk, he might never have got himself into such a fine mess.

Anthony Morehouse raked in the small pile of notes from the center of the card table and thought he'd better call it a night. Earlier that afternoon he had bested Lord Reginald D'Aubney in a curricle race, for which he'd won his lordship's favorite pair of matched grays, and had been celebrating the victory with his friends all evening. He'd lost count of the number of toasts in his honor. Clearly, he was too foxed to think straight or he would never have accepted such damned fool stakes.

It made him uncomfortable when a gentleman

began to put up personal possessions as collateral instead of money or vowels. Tony had never pegged Victor Croyden as that sort of desperate player, and yet he'd just won a piece of furniture from the man. Now, what the devil was he to do with this damned wardrobe or bureau or whatever it was he'd just won?

"Well, I'm for home," he said, and tucked the notes into his purse. He'd better take his leave before he won a matching set of chairs. He stood and had to grab hold of the table edge to keep his balance. Devil take it, he really was squiffed. "Care to share a hackney, Croyden? We can discuss this chest of yours and arrange delivery."

A burst of laughter from Croyden and similar hoots of mirth from the other men at the table caused Tony to look down and inspect his person. Was something amiss? His breeches gaping, perhaps? A wine stain on his neckcloth? Stockings puddling around his ankles? "What?"

"Really ought to pay more attention, Morehouse," Sir Crispin Hollis said. He was the only one not laughing too hard to speak. "It ain't a piece of furniture, you know."

"Course it is," Tony said. "Croyden said so. Heard him quite clearly. A chest or bureau or some such thing. Very fashionable, he said. It's all right here in his note."

More guffaws rang out in the card room and Tony began to become irritated. It was an idiotic thing to have won, to be sure, but he'd seen stranger stakes. Besides, he hadn't wanted to be rude and ask Croyden to stand down, even though he doubted the wretched bureau could possibly be worth the purse he'd staked. He was only trying to be civil, and look where it got him. All of White's was gathering around the table to see what the fuss was about.

"Better look at that note again," Sir Crispin said.

Tony fumbled in his coat pocket to retrieve his notes, but his fingers got all tangled up in the purse strings and the whole business was making him dizzy. He gave up. "Just tell me." Fearing he might take a header—not at all the thing to do in White's—he leaned on the table for support. "Have you bamboozled me, Croyden?"

"Not in the least," the man said, though his smile indicated otherwise. "Made myself perfectly clear. Thought you understood."

"Understood what?" Tony's celebratory mood had faded. Wished he hadn't drunk so much claret. Couldn't seem to think straight. Had a fuzzy sort of notion, though, that he'd been played for a fool.

"Understood my stakes," Croyden said. "The magazine."

"What magazine? See here, Croyden, I may be drunk, but I'm not that drunk. You staked some sort of cabinet and that's what I played you for. Said it was worth my purse. Took your word as a gentleman. If you've taken me in—"

"Nothing of the sort," Croyden said. He held up his hand to stop any accusations, though he did not have the look of a man about to be caught out in a dishonorable wager. In fact, he looked positively gleeful. "I put *The Ladies' Fashionable Cabinet* on the table and you won it. It's yours, Morehouse, fair and square."

"All right, so I won a piece of *female* furniture."

The players erupted in laughter once again. Tony was becoming seriously annoyed. "Well, what of it? It ain't all *that* comical."

The press of spectators surrounding the table had become oppressive, and the roar of their laughter made Tony's head ache. He lifted his hands, palms up, and looked around at his friends and acquaintances. "What? If the blasted cabinet is worth what he says it is, what is so damned funny?"

His friend Ian Fordyce took pity on him. He came to Tony's side and put an arm around his shoulders. "I think you'd better sit back down," he said. "And try to pay attention this time."

"Don't want to sit down. Want to go home and fall into bed. I'm done in, I tell you."

"I don't doubt it," Ian said, "but first you need to understand what you've won, old boy. It ain't a piece of furniture."

"It is, by God. If I've heard the word 'cabinet' once, I've heard it a dozen times."

"Yes, but it's not furniture," Ian said, his voice quivering with suppressed mirth. "It's a magazine.

The Ladies' Fashionable Cabinet. Do you understand me, Morehouse? It's a magazine."

Tony took a moment to allow this bit of information to work its way through the bleary pathways of his brain. He'd just won a magazine? A few sheets of printed pages against his entire purse? Could he have been that drunk?

No wonder he was a laughingstock.

"Let me make sure I have this right." Tony enunciated each word as clearly as possible, and tried to set his brain to listening with the same deliberate clarity. He glared down at Victor Croyden. "You put up a threepenny throwaway female ragsheet as stakes against my purse?"

"Not a single copy of the magazine," Croyden said. "The business. I owned the magazine, and now you do."

"Eh? What's that?"

"You are the new owner of the publishing enterprise started by my mother," Croyden said. "*The Ladies' Fashionable Cabinet.* And you're welcome to it."

Tony's knees seemed to have given out and he sank into a chair that somehow appeared at his back. "The devil you say. I played you for a goddamned ladies' magazine?"

"And won." Croyden was altogether too cheerful about his loss.

"Can't you just see it?" Lord Jasper Skiffington spoke in his loudest voice to the room at large.

"Old Morehouse here reporting on the latest fashions from Paris."

"Or waxing rhapsodic about Mrs. Radcliffe's latest novel."

"Or sighing over lovesick poetry."

"Or offering advice on the best method for removing unwanted facial hair."

"Or how to get stains out of muslin."

"Or how to treat the green sickness."

"Or how to fashion a headdress from a length of cheesecloth."

As each suggestion was called out, the laughter grew louder. Waves of dizziness swept over Tony and he thought he might be sick.

"Here, you'd better drink this." Fordyce had somehow managed to procure a cup of coffee and thrust it into Tony's hands.

He took a sip and grimaced. What the devil had he got himself into this time?

His head began to throb.

"Tell you what, Croyden," Tony said. "Play you another hand. You can try to win it back."

"No, no, Morehouse. You won it legitimately. It's all yours now."

It was a damned dirty trick, that's what it was. The man ought to be ashamed, taking advantage of a chap in his cups like that. Tony was still having difficulty wrapping his mind around the idea that he was now the owner of a ladies' magazine, but one thing was clear. It didn't smell right.

"Why are you so all-fired anxious to be rid of it?" Tony asked. "What's wrong with it? Besides being a female concern, that is?"

"Not a thing," Croyden said. "It's a decent little enterprise, in fact. Turns a tidy profit. It's only one of several publications I inherited from my father."

Tony took a long swallow of very bitter coffee and tried to focus his befuddled brain. He did seem to recall that among Croyden's many business enterprises, enough to taint him with a faint smell of the shop, he was in some way involved in the book trade.

"I have too many other publishing ventures of more importance to me," Croyden said. "Newspapers, political and literary reviews, court miscellany, as well as the usual books. And I'm very much involved at the moment in a new history of Greece. I'm afraid the *Cabinet* has never been of much interest to me. I don't have time for it."

Tony found himself looking at the man's fingers for traces of ink stains. He had not realized *how* involved Croyden was in the publishing trade, though truthfully he did not know the man well. Croyden was a good twenty-five or thirty years his senior, and they met only now and then at the clubs. "You say your mother started the magazine?"

"Yes, it was her pet project late in life. She somehow managed to coerce my father into financing it. As it turned out, she made quite a success of it. Since her death, my late wife's niece manages it.

Very efficiently, too. Keeps the thing running smoothly, so I am never bothered."

"Does the niece come with it?"

"Leave it to Morehouse," Sir Crispin said above another burst of laughter, "to get straight to the heart of the matter: a female."

"But a female who manages a magazine?" Fordyce said. "Liable to be a different breed than the sort you're accustomed to, old boy. Not susceptible to your usual, er, charms."

"Ah, but think of the challenge," Sir Crispin said.

Tony did his best to concentrate on the matter at hand and paid no attention to the subsequent bawdy remarks, however accurate, about his prowess with women. The important thing at the moment was the wretched magazine. He had no desire to get his hands dirty if he could avoid it. The only business he was interested in was one that ran itself and poured profits into his bank account. If Croyden's niece could make that happen, then he wanted her to stay on. "Well, Croyden?"

"I daresay that is up to you," he said. "She seems to enjoy working on the magazine and will likely stay on if you make no changes. I warn you, though, she can be hard headed. A bit on the bluestocking side, if you know what I mean. Likes to think she has a head for business." He chuckled and shook his head. "Silly woman. She's one of those frustrated old maids who thinks she can do a man's job. Never wanted me nosing about, but then I never wanted to interfere. A bunch of dotty old women and middle-aged spinsters writing about fashion and poetry and romantic stories." He shuddered visibly. "Leave 'em be, Morehouse, and you'll have no trouble."

Though still the worse for drink, Tony found his sudden ownership of a female publication had had a remarkably sobering effect. He wasn't altogether certain what was involved in running a magazine, but one rather horrifying notion did come to mind. "You never actually had to write anything for this . . . this cabinet thing, did you?"

"Write for it?" Croyden said. "Good Lord, I haven't even read the little rag in years. But it's very popular with the ladies. All you have to do, Morehouse, is sit back and collect the profits."

Tony hoped it would be as easy as that. "Where do I find this magazine of yours?"

"Of *yours*, you mean." Croyden chuckled again and Tony did not at all like the sound of it. "If you are talking about copies of the publication, you can find it at most of the large booksellers. Probably a good idea to have a look at one. If you are talking about the business, I put my niece's directions on the note. Except for the actual printing, she runs it all out of the house in Golden Square she shares with her brother. You might want to pay a call upon her tomorrow and take a look at what she and her gag-gle of silly old spinsters do. Then come by and I'll have my man of affairs draw up all the papers."

Tony's mind was much too befuddled to have a serious business discussion, so he cut it short and agreed to meet with Croyden the next day. When Tony had finished his coffee, Fordyce hauled him to his feet and dragged him outside.

"Slow down, Ian, I beg you. My legs still ain't working properly and my head's spinning like a top."

"Yes, I know. That's why I'm taking you out of there. Don't want to see you get into any more trouble."

"It was only one foolish wager, my friend. Better to win a magazine than lose my shirt, eh?"

"I wouldn't be so sure about that."

Fordyce hailed a hackney, which pulled to a stop in front of the club. He pushed Tony inside, called out directions to the jarvey, then climbed in and shut the door. An unpleasant odor wafted up from the straw at their feet, and Tony, feeling queasy again, tugged down the window to let in fresh air.

"You think this magazine's going to be trouble?" he asked.

"Bound to be," Fordyce said.

"Well, you're wrong there. I have no intention of holding onto the damned thing. What the devil would I want with a ladies' fashion magazine?"

"You going to sell it, then?"

"The very moment I have the papers from Croyden."

"Who do you know who'd want to own a ladies' magazine? Your mother?"

"Egad, no." The thought of his mother, posed languidly upon her chaise and dripping in expensive lace, being stirred actually to do something productive brought a smile to his face. "No, not Mother. Got a few ideas, though." In fact, he only had one, but he thought it might work. He'd sign it all over to the spinster niece. If she managed the whole business, she might as well own it. He suspected it would put Croyden's nose out of joint to have a woman in charge, but it wasn't his business anymore.

"I'll wager a monkey," Fordyce said, "that within a fortnight you'll be sorry you ever heard of *The Ladies' Fashionable Cabinet*."

"You're on." Tony said the words almost by force of habit. He almost never refused a challenge. Some, most especially his father, might suggest it was his greatest weakness. But as they drove back to his town house, Tony began to wonder if he had not just made yet another idiotic wager he would live to regret.

Edwina Parrish tied string around the package containing the page proofs for the next issue of *The*

Ladies' Fashionable Cabinet and handed it across the desk to the printer's apprentice. "I trust this will go to print tomorrow, Robbie?"

"We'll do our best, ma'am, if there ain't many changes."

"Not too many this time," she said. "But we do have an extra engraving and will need additional time for the hand coloring. The sooner we get the copies the better. Oh, and tell Imber we'll have another pamphlet for him by week's end."

"Yes, ma'am."

Just as Robbie left the room, Edwina's brother, Nicholas, entered. He settled into a chair across the desk from her and crossed one leg languidly over the other. It was their father's house, but he never came to town and had no objection to his daughter taking over the library for her magazine. Nicholas had never complained, either, though he would probably have liked to have the room for himself. He eyed the handwritten pages organized into neat piles in front of her. "Another issue put to bed, eh?"

"But for the final printing." Edwina collected the pages into a single stack and covered it with a blank sheet. She dipped her pen in the inkwell and began to write the date on the cover page. "Your article on Matilda of Tuscany is brilliant, by the way."

Nicholas smiled, bowed his head, and gave a little flourish with his hand. "Augusta Historica, always at your service. Did you manage to squeeze in your review of the new edition of *Essays on Practical Education*?"

"I did indeed." Edwina tied the manuscript pages together with a ribbon, and reached behind her to place the packet on top of a shelf filled with similar bundles, one for each month she'd edited the magazine. She leaned back against the chair and allowed herself a brief moment of pride that she'd steered another issue to completion. Once the printing was done, there was still the business of coloring, binding, and distributing, but she had others to rely on for those aspects of production. Edwina's main concern was the content, and she took pains to include high-quality essays, poetry, reviews, and short fiction. She wrote many of the book reviews herself, under the pen name Arbiter Literaria.

"The Edgeworths should be pleased with your review," Nicholas said. "Especially after the venom spewed by the *Monthly Mirror*."

Edwina stretched her legs beneath the desk. "I pray that for once in his life, Uncle Victor does not happen to pick up a copy of the *Cabinet*. Though I did not, of course, refer to the article in the *Mirror*, anyone who's read it will understand that mine is an attack on their review."

"Uncle Victor is too busy with the *Mirror* and all his other publications to give you or the *Cabinet* a second thought." Nicholas gave a wicked little chuckle. "The poor man has no idea what you've done to his mother's little magazine."

And it must stay that way. "So long as he sees a decent profit, he will keep his nose out of it."

"Speaking of profits, shall we take a look at the books tonight? I'd like to see if we can afford another pamphlet for Thurgood. His by-election is less than two months away."

"I think we can manage it. Pru brought in two new advertisers this week."

His brows lifted with interest. "Did she, by God? A good girl, Pru. Are they logged in the ledgers yet?"

"No."

"Good. Let's first see if there's a way to skim off some of the income for a new pamphlet."

There was always some cause or other needing their help, but they had little money of their own to spend. Their father was a bit of a scatterbrain where financial matters were concerned, and they could rely on him for nothing more than the town house. It was a shame there was not more, because Nicholas had plans—such magnificent, idealistic plans—but they required money. He made a little by writing articles for various journals, but not much. He'd taken almost everything he had and put it into a couple of speculative investments that he hoped would bring him a welcome windfall. But he never spoke of them, and Edwina suspected he'd lost a great deal. She knew their circumstances pained him much more than they did her.

The magazine was profitable, but those profits went directly to Uncle Victor. He provided Edwina a small salary as editor, and also allowed her to manage the books and to incur any minor expenditures she thought fit. Any major expense, though, such as hiring artists and engravers, had to be approved.

Since she kept the books, however, she could generally insure that Uncle Victor was aware of only those profits she was willing to document—so long as he didn't actually happen to pick up a copy of the *Cabinet* and notice an advertiser or two not logged in the ledgers. He had never yet questioned anything in regard to her running of the business, but Edwina never let down her guard.

"Is the pamphlet ready?" she asked.

"Not quite. I'm still working on it. The language needs some toning down." Nicholas gave her a sheepish grin. "You know how I am. I tend to get too passionate about these things, and that often serves to drive people away."

"Perhaps you ought to have Simon take a look. He has a way with words."

"Yes, and he's pouring them all into Eleanor's ears at the moment. He's too besotted to think clearly. Besides, he's still up at Tandy Hill basking in his newly wedded bliss. It would take too long to get something to him and back again."

"Well, I will take a look at it, then. You could probably use a feminine perspective. It might be a good thing to appeal to a female audience. Educate the women on the issues and they will in turn influence their men."

Nicholas reached across the desk and touched her hand. "I know the *Cabinet* is not the lofty public forum you had once hoped to achieve."

"It is enough, Nickie. I am content." It was true that she had once aspired to greater things. She had wanted to write grand philosophical works filled with new and radical ideas. But time—and loss—had softened her attitude and moderated her objectives. She no longer dreamed of great works, but only hoped to make a small difference.

"It is a challenge, after all," she said, "to maintain the innocent face of the *Cabinet*. So long as it appears to be the usual trivial feminine publication with fashion plates and sentimental poetry, no one will expect otherwise. I'd be willing to bet most readers do not suspect the true intent underlying some of its messages. Uncle Victor will suspect nothing, either, and will continue to leave us alone. We would not like him looking too closely at the account books, would we?"

A soft scratching at the door preceded the entry of Prudence Armitage, long a friend to both Parrishes, and Edwina's indispensable assistant editor. Her reddish-blonde hair was coming out of its pins, as usual, and her spectacles had been pushed to the top of her head.

"A letter has just arrived by special messenger," she said. A look of concern clouded her eyes as she approached the desk. "It is from Victor Croyden."

Edwina shot a quick glance at her brother, then took the folded parchment from Prudence. It was a bit unnerving to hear from Uncle Victor just when they had been speaking of him—an odd sensation, as though their conversation had been overheard. "Whatever can he want?" She could think of nothing that might have prompted this unexpected communication.

Edwina had a bad feeling about this. Had he finally discovered what she'd been up to?

She broke the seal and read. Her uncle's handwriting was cursive to a fault and difficult to decipher. But one thing was perfectly clear.

"Good God." She fell back against the chair, feeling as though she'd been punched in the stomach. "I can't believe it."

Nicholas bolted from his seat and came to her side. "What is it, Ed? Bad news?"

Ignoring her brother, Edwina considered what she'd read. A stab of anger, sharp and bright as a new blade, tore at her gut. "How *could* he? And without even a word to me." She jerked to her feet and began to pace the small, uncluttered area be-hind the desk. "I don't care if he is my uncle by marriage, it is a beastly thing to have done."

"What?" Nicholas asked. "What has he done?"

"All these years, all my hard work—it means nothing to him. You would think he'd at least con-sult me, as editor. Or, God forbid, offer it to me first. But, no. Oh, this is monstrous. Monstrous!"

"Ed, what are you talking about?"

"And now what am I supposed to do?" Edwina said. She continued to pace in agitated fury. Three steps, turn around, three steps, turn around. "Am I to politely stand aside? To pretend it doesn't mat-ter? To remain silent like a good little niece and do as I'm told? All because I'm a mere woman who cannot possibly have a head for business? Bah!"

"Edwina," Prudence said, "please tell us what has happened."

Edwina wadded the parchment into a tiny ball and flung it hard across the room. "It's all ruined, that's what. Everything we've worked for is in jeop-ardy. Hell and damnation."

Nicholas leaned on the desk. "For God's sake, Ed, if you don't tell us what the devil has happened, I am going to come over there and shake it out of you."

She stopped pacing and looked up into the anx-ious faces of Prudence and Nicholas. "He's sold the *Cabinet*. We have a new owner."

Chapter 2

ony glanced again at the note in his hand, thankful that at least the numbers were clear. If he had not vaguely recollected Croyden mentioning his niece lived in Golden Square, he never would have been able to figure it out from the chicken scratch that passed for penmanship.

He dismounted and tossed the reins to his tiger, who would keep the team happy by trotting them around the square while Tony made brief work of this little matter of business. It was a modest town house in a modest square, on the fringes of more fashionable neighborhoods. It seemed an appropriate setting for a spinster involved in an occupation barely on the fringes of respectability.

He checked Croyden's note once again. Blast the

man's handwriting, he could not be entirely sure of the niece's name. If he'd been told last night, he couldn't recall it. But then he'd been so thoroughly foxed, there might be a great deal he did not recall. It looked like "Paris" or perhaps "Partrige." Tony pulled out the copy of the magazine he'd purchased that morning: THE LADIES' FASHIONABLE CABINET: WHEREIN IS PRESENTED A POLITE COMPENDIUM OF INTELLIGENCE AND AMUSEMENT WITH A VIEW TO THE EDIFICATION AND ENTERTAINMENT OF THE FAIR SEX. At the bottom of the blue paper cover it said: PRINTED FOR V. CROYDEN, PATERNOSTER ROW." There was no mention of an editor's name, as far as he could tell. The authors of most of the articles used obvious pseudonyms.

It was not ideal to call upon a lady whose name one did not know for certain, but he'd been in stranger situations and would persevere. He grabbed the knocker.

Some minutes later, the door was opened by a young woman with flyaway reddish-blonde hair, spectacles, and a suspicious eye. Not your typical parlor maid.

"My name is Morehouse. I am here to see Miss Paris."

Her eyes widened and her mouth formed a perfect "O." She stared at him for a moment before speaking. "You must be the new owner of the *Cabinet.*"

So, the household already knew what had happened. Croyden had certainly lost no time in trumpeting the news. "Yes, I am."

"You'd better come in, then. We've been expecting you." The young woman turned and gestured that he should follow her into the hall. "And her name's Parrish, by the way, not Paris," she called over her shoulder.

Tony began to think she must not be a housemaid after all, but one of the magazine's spinsters. A handmaiden escorting him to an audience with the Queen Spinster. Lord, but he could not wait to be done with this.

The narrow hallway led past a dining room on the left and a stairway on the right. The woman entered an open doorway near the end of the hall. Tony followed her and found himself in a library or study crowded with worktables upon which papers and books were scattered about, though not in any sort of disarray. It was a busy room where work was obviously done, but there was a certain kind of orderliness about it.

Behind a large desk to the right of the door sat a woman bent over a page of cramped writing. She raised her head at their entrance, and Tony's breath caught in his throat as he found himself looking at one of the most beautiful women he'd ever seen.

She had black hair, very pale, clear skin, and perfectly arched dark brows over eyes almost as black as her hair. Her full lips were claret-dark against the fair complexion. Her coloring was so dramatic she had the look of being painted, like an actress in stage makeup. But as he stepped closer, he could see the coloring was perfectly natural. And perfectly breathtaking.

This was the Queen Spinster?

"Edwina, this is Mr. Morehead, the new owner of the *Cabinet*."

The Queen stood and offered her hand. "I am Miss Parrish, the editor." She stared at him curiously, and it was all he could do to step forward and take her hand. He was drowning in those dark eyes. "And you have already met my assistant editor, Miss Armitage."

"I am pleased to meet you, Miss Parrish, and Miss Armitage," he managed at last. And all at once he realized what he'd said and wrenched himself from the enchantment of her eyes. "Parrish? Your name is Parrish?"

"Yes."

He dropped her hand as though scorched. "Edwina Parrish?"

"Yes."

He stood back and studied her. He could see it now. How could he have missed that stubborn tilt of the chin, the determined set of her shoulders? "Well, I'll be damned. If it isn't the nemesis of my boyhood, all grown up and come back to plague me again."

Her elegant brows lifted in surprise, then she smiled. It was a lovely, slow-breaking smile that lit up her face, and almost stopped his heart. Lord, she was glorious. How had such a beauty managed to remain a "Miss" all these years? He knew she must be almost thirty.

"I thought there was something familiar about you," she said. "Anthony Morehouse? Dear heavens, is it really you?" She gave a soft chuckle and gestured that he should take a chair. "Morehouse, not Morehead. I never *could* read Uncle Victor's handwriting. My goodness, but it has been a long time. I'm surprised you remember me. It's been almost twenty years."

It suddenly seemed like yesterday to Tony. For many summers during his youth, a neighbor of his father's estate in Suffolk entertained visits from his granddaughter. Tony had spent many an afternoon romping and playing about the countryside with the headstrong girl. He hadn't seen her since her last visit, when he was thirteen, shortly before her grandfather died and the estate was sold.

She'd been two years his junior, but a more outspoken, unconventional, annoyingly clever child he'd never met. She had not been like other young girls, prim and prissy and meek, but seemed to have no sense of propriety whatsoever. She spoke her mind and did as she pleased. His father had said it was because her mother was an artist. A woman who publicly displayed her paintings of half-naked classical figures could have no notion of how real ladies behaved. The young Edwina—he'd called her "Eddie"—had no notion that girls were not supposed to do certain things, to excel at masculine activities, to display an unfashionable degree of learning. She took great pride in demonstrating her superiority in every endeavor, and he had hated her for it. More accurately, he had hated himself for appearing less than perfect in her eyes. A fellow wanted to show to his best advantage in front of any girl, even one as irksome as Eddie Parrish.

"How could I forget the girl who made me feel like the village idiot?"

"I did no such thing." The twinkle in her eyes said otherwise.

"Allow me to disagree. You challenged me at every turn. Always setting some wager on me."

"And winning, as I recall." She turned to her assistant, who stood scowling in the doorway. "We knew each other as children, Pru. We used to have footraces and such, and it seems that after all these years Mr. Morehouse is still grousing about losing a few."

"Do you still have the Minerva?" He hadn't meant to blurt that out, but after almost twenty years it still galled. In that last summer she'd been in Suffolk, he'd stupidly challenged her to a makeshift steeplechase—one he'd set up himself and had practiced enough times to insure his victory. When she had asked that the stakes be the tiny Roman head of Minerva, made of gilt bronze, that had been unearthed on his father's estate, he'd agreed without a thought. He had been so certain he'd win.

"Good heavens," she said, "you remember that?"

"How could I forget? My bottom was sore for weeks after my father found out I'd lost his most prized possession. He never forgave me." It had been but the first in a string of reckless acts that had kept him continually in his father's black books.

"Oh dear." She attempted a contrite face, but her eyes told him how amused she was that she'd caused him such trouble. "You never told me that. I thought it was yours, that you'd found it."

"Well, it wasn't and I didn't." But she was right. He had bragged that he'd been the one to find it. He was tired of being bested by her, and he had grasped at anything to appear superior. She *would* remind him of that folly. "Do you still have it?"

"I do, actually. I'm quite fond of it." She turned to Miss Armitage. "You remember the little Roman head, Pru?"

Miss Armitage's fair brows drew together in a puzzled frown. "The one you keep on the writing desk next to your bed?" She sucked in a sharp breath and blushed scarlet, a spinsterish blush at the indelicate mention of something so intimate as a bed. Her eyes darted nervously about the room. "It is unlikely I could forget it, is it not?"

Tony arched an interested brow.

"Unlikely indeed," Edwina said. She turned back to him and smiled. "It was the best thing I ever won from you."

"Hmph. You were long-legged and I was a late bloomer." So was she, apparently. How had that annoying, troublesome little girl grown into such a beauty? "It was stupid of me to accept all your challenges, knowing you would win. I'd beat you now, though." Lord, what a childish thing to say. What was wrong with him?

"I have no doubt of it. In fact, you have already done so." The amusement faded from her eyes. "You own the *Cabinet*, which by rights should be mine. I do all the work. I'm the one who's made it a success. I can't imagine why Uncle Victor sold it to you without ever bothering to ask if I might be interested."

"He didn't sell it to me."

Her eyes widened. "I beg your pardon? I thought you owned it."

"I do. But I didn't buy it. I won it."

"You what?"

"I won it in a card game. Thought it was a piece of furniture, but won it fair and square. I own it now."

"Damnation!" Her fist came down hard on the desk, causing the writing set to wobble and dance precariously toward the edge. "He lost it in a card game? How unutterably stupid. And so now I must work for you because you had the luckier hand? Oh, this is monstrous."

So, she was as hardheaded as ever. And as outspoken. A wicked little burst of glee swelled in his chest, and his original plan was discarded. He had a new plan, though. One that would pay her back for all those hopeless wagers of his boyhood, and still provide ample opportunity to keep this stunning beauty under his watchful eye for a time. It was devious. It was delicious. And he could hardly wait to put it into action.

"Well, well, well. It has taken almost twenty years, but I do believe I have bested you at last. I feel somewhat compensated, finally, for the Minerva."

Edwina wanted to fling herself across the desk and slap his face. How dare he be so pleased. He was not at all like the boy she once knew, who'd been so full of pride and determination, the one she'd tried so hard to impress. The years had turned pride into arrogance. But any man who looked as he now did probably came by arrogance naturally. No longer the skinny, freckle-faced boy, Anthony Morehouse had grown taller and broader, and sat there in his perfectly tailored clothes and roguish good looks like a golden god, a Mars to match the Minerva.

"It's not at all the same," she said, "and not at all

fair. You don't want the *Cabinet*. You probably know nothing about the publishing business. You simply want the profits."

"It is a profitable business, I am told. Of course I want the profits."

"But it's not fair." She paused, and tried to compose herself, to curb her petulant tone. "I should be the owner, but Uncle Victor would never have offered it to me because I am a woman. He does not believe a woman should own a business, though he seems to have had no objection to having a woman manage it successfully, putting more profit into his pockets. And now I am to put them into another man's pockets. Damn all of you!"

"Do not be so quick to damn me before you've heard what I have to say. I may have a proposition for you."

She did not trust the look in those silvery gray eyes. "You would sell the *Cabinet* to me?"

"Oh, that would be too easy. Considering our history, I believe a challenge of some kind is in order."

"What sort of challenge?"

"One in which the ownership of the magazine is at stake."

"Good God. I am to risk the magazine on a wager?" She ought to have guessed it would come to this.

"Just so. But I need to know a bit more about

this operation before I set the challenge. Perhaps you will allow me to review the account books."

A tiny spark of apprehension flickered in her breast. "Why?"

"I might want to set a percentage of profit increase as the goal."

"No. That is not a fair goal." She hoped her quick response had not piqued his curiosity. She must keep him away from the books for now, until she and Nicholas and Prudence had time to make the appropriate adjustments. "Profits depend on subscriptions," she continued. "Expenditures must be made to entice subscriptions, and profits will be down at first. You cannot expect an increase in the short run. I could never accept a wager based on profits."

"How about subscriptions, then? How many subscribers do you currently have?"

"Almost two thousand." She was proud of that number. It represented double the number of subscribers on the books when Edwina had taken up the editorial reins almost five years ago.

"Suppose I challenged you to substantially increase subscriptions," Tony said. "Would you consider that fair?"

Edwina pondered the idea for a moment. There were things she knew they could do to increase subscriptions. She and Prudence had often discussed the possibilities lately, and the new advertisers were a first move in that direction. She glanced across the room to where Prudence still stood, leaning against the doorframe. Edwina raised her brows in question, and Prudence nodded.

She returned her gaze to Tony. "Yes, I believe that would be fair."

"Good. Then I shall wager you the ownership of the magazine that you cannot triple the subscription numbers in three months."

"What?" The man was crazy. Edwina placed both forearms flat on the desk and leaned forward. "Triple? Are you mad? It is impossible."

A slow, lazy grin split his face. "You give up so soon, then? How unsporting of you. I suppose that means I win."

"You scoundrel. How hateful you are, all because of a few races I won as a child."

He cocked a brow. "Miss Parrish, you are no longer the intrepid girl you once were. The Eddie I knew would never walk away from such a challenge. You disappoint me."

Edwina blanched at the use of her childhood nickname. He was using every possible method to unnerve her, and damn it all, it was working.

"Set me a reasonable challenge," she said, "and I will accept your foolish wager. To triple the subscribers in three months is an impossible goal. No one could do it." And just to insure he did not believe she undervalued herself, she added, "Not even me."

He grinned and nodded his head in acknowl-edgement that she'd won the first round. "All right. Double, then. Two thousand new subscribers in four months. If you can do it, the magazine is yours. If you fail, I keep it, and you continue to work for me, or not, as you choose."

It was still a formidable challenge, one Edwina was not certain she could win. She had worked for years to double the original subscription number, and now she was to double it again in just four months? She would be mad to accept such terms. It was summer, after all, and many potential sub-scribers had left town for the country. But she knew he would not back down this time. It would be these terms, or nothing.

She supposed she could reject the offer, walk away and forget all dreams of ownership. She could continue to edit the magazine, at least until she learned how difficult it would be to work for Anthony Morehouse. She would have to curtail certain other activities while under his watchful eye, but she had been prepared for that as soon as she'd received her uncle's note. Any new owner would have necessitated the same caution.

But what if she won? She had never expected to own the magazine outright, could never have scraped together enough money to make an offer in any case. No, the best she could have hoped for was that Uncle Victor would pass it to her upon his death. Considering his opinion of women owning businesses, though, even that had been unlikely.

But if she won this wager, the *Cabinet* would be hers without spending tuppence. All profits would be hers, with no one to tell her what to do with them. No more hiding the account books. No more worries about being dismissed for printing articles with a republican sensibility.

It was too good an opportunity to pass up. Besides, she really did not believe she could continue working for the magazine if Anthony Morehouse was her employer. His presence was too unsettling.

She glanced briefly at Prudence, who gave a little shrug, then turned to face Anthony.

"I accept."

"Splendid!"

He smiled, and it set off a disturbing prickling of her skin. Good Lord, she wasn't ten years old anymore. She must get hold of herself.

"Oh, and one more thing," he said. "If I win, I get the Minerva back."

Edwina rolled her eyes to the ceiling. Was this all about the damned Roman head? Was it that important to him? The thing was, it had become rather important to her as well. But she would not lose it, because she had no intention of losing the *Cabinet*. "Agreed," she said, then stood, walked around to the front of the desk and offered her hand to Anthony.

He rose and took it, but not in a businesslike

handshake. Instead, he brought it to his lips, sending a tingling sensation up her arm. The look in
those disturbing gray eyes told her he knew he'd
rattled her, and it amused him.

"Excellent," he said. "Then let us record our wager properly." He reached into his breast pocket
and pulled out a tiny book bound in red leather.
"My betting book."

He flipped pages until he came to a blank one
more than halfway through, and then handed it to
Edwina. "Will you do the honors, please?"

She thumbed the filled pages and felt a pang of disappointment. The man was obviously a gamester.
She knew him to be a younger son. Is that how he'd
made his way through the world, by gambling? This
book, his betting book, seemed to have been used
only since the beginning of the year. Pages and pages
of wagers representing only six months. "My, but
you are a busy fellow, are you not?"

"What? Do I detect a note of disapproval? From
the very person who introduced me to the thrill of a
good wager all those years ago? Tsk tsk, Eddie. I
would never have expected that brazen child to
have turned out so tiresomely conventional."

"Horrid man."

Edwina dipped a pen in the inkwell on her desk,
and wrote out the particulars of the wager, after
first settling on November 1 as the date when the
objective must be met. She signed it and offered the
pen to Anthony. He leaned very close as he signed,

and she inhaled the scent of starch, bay rum, and the faintest hint of horse. It was a heady, masculine combination.

He straightened—surely that brush against her arm was deliberate?—and said, "In the meantime, it *is* my business, so I believe I should like to have a look at the account books."

Edwina's heart sank. She thought this danger had been averted. She must present a reasonable alternative, one that he would keep him away from the books, but would not make him suspicious. "I'd like to suggest a rider to the wager instead."

"Oh?"

"Yes. For the four months specified, you will not tamper with my management in any way."

"Hmm." His brow furrowed and he regarded her thoughtfully.

"No interference," she said. "No scrutinizing the accounts. No meddling in the day-to-day running of the business. If I am to win this wager, I must be allowed to continue to manage the business—every aspect of the business—on my own. Agreed?"

He gazed at her warily. "So long as I have access to the subscription numbers, I accept your condition."

Before he could change his mind, Edwina added the rider to the wager in his betting book. They both initialed it.

He stood before her, altogether too close, and

said, "It seems you and I are destined forever to be at odds in some fool wager. But we are no longer children. Let us seal this bargain properly."

And he pulled her into his arms and kissed her.

Chapter 3

Tony pulled the team to a halt in front of the modest portico of White's and passed the reins to his tiger. "Take it back home, Jamie," he said, and leaped down from the curricle. "I'll catch a hackney later."

"Yes, sir."

Tony took one more admiring look at the new team, courtesy of Lord D'Aubney, stroked the rump of the nearest gray, then headed up the steps to his club. He felt the need of a strong restorative after such a day. He'd just left Victor Croyden and now carried in his pocket papers that made him sole proprietor of *The Ladies' Fashionable Cabinet.*

His plan to retain ownership rather than sell it

might turn out to be one of his more stupid decisions, but one look at Edwina Parrish had knocked every last niggling doubt straight out of his head. He would keep the magazine because of her. Because she had tormented his boyhood and he wanted to pay her back in kind. And because she had grown into such a beauty he didn't think he'd be able to stay away from her.

Especially after that kiss. He would not have been surprised if she had hauled off and slapped him for it. The hovering Miss Armitage looked as though she wanted to do so. But Edwina had only looked amused. Nothing could have intrigued him more than the sardonic twinkle in those dark eyes, mocking him. Well, she would soon learn better than to mock his one true talent: seduction. Let her concentrate on the wager in his betting book. He had another more personal challenge in mind. For that, he would need to see more of her, and the *Cabinet* was the perfect excuse to clutter her doorstep.

He found Ian Fordyce sprawled in a large wing chair with his nose buried in *The Weekly Messenger*. When he looked up, Ian smiled and folded the paper.

"I must say, old chap, you are looking more the thing this afternoon. You must have taken care of that foolish bit of business from last night." He motioned with the newspaper to an adjacent chair. "Sit down and tell me how it went with the bluestocking editor. Was she properly agog when you offered to sell her the magazine?"

Before Tony could be seated, a waiter was on the spot to take his order. He asked for sherry, then sank into the chair and crossed his legs. "Didn't sell it," he said.

"What do you mean? I thought you—"

"Changed my mind."

Ian arched a brow. "But I thought you wanted it off your hands, wanted the poor old spinster to have it."

"She still might. I wagered her for it."

The second brow shot up to join the first, both almost disappearing beneath the brown locks combed forward in the latest Brutus style. "The devil you did!"

Tony grinned at his friend's wide-eyed astonishment. "I suppose some devil did make me do it, but yes, I wagered her for the magazine. I set her a challenge, to be more precise. She's got three months—no, wait a moment." He pulled the little betting book from his pocket and flipped to the last written page. "Four months. She's got four months to double the number of subscribers. If she succeeds, the magazine is hers."

Ian peered at him with narrowed eyes. "There's something smoky here, Morehouse. I know you never can pass up a good wager. But with a spinster editor? What are you up to? And what if you win and you're stuck with the damned magazine?"

"Oh, I intend to win."

"But why?"

"Let's just say I have a score to settle with Miss Edwina Parrish."

Ian heaved an exaggerated sigh. "I think you had better tell me the whole."

And Tony did so. He had Ian in whoops of laughter as he described one after another competition he'd lost to the young Eddie.

"I can see how you'd never wish to lay eyes on the wretched girl again," Ian said, his voice unsteady with suppressed mirth. "What a shock it must have been to find her now in your employ."

"Indeed."

And despite whatever grudge he might hold over her childhood triumphs, Tony hoped he might prove to be a better employer than her uncle. His meeting with Victor Croyden made it clear that the man had truly taken advantage of Edwina. Croyden had no personal interest in the *Cabinet* and was willing enough to allow Edwina to manage it for him. He even admitted that it returned a tidy profit. And yet he gave her little credit, and only a tiny salary. He clearly believed a woman wasn't worth the salary he might pay a male editor, and only paid Edwina what he did in order to appease his familial conscience. In fact, he didn't seem to think she deserved a salary at all, especially since his mother had taken none when she edited the *Cabinet*.

Yet, Tony suspected the magazine was not simply a hobby to Edwina, as it appears to have been for her great aunt. It was her work and she was proud of it. He also suspected she needed the money. The house she shared with her brother was not quite tumbling down, but it was a far cry from the May-fair elegance to which he was accustomed. From the little he'd seen, it appeared to be simply furnished with good-quality pieces. But he also noticed the occasional frayed bit of upholstery, a threadbare spot here and there on the carpets, a splitting in the silk draperies. And no servant to answer the door. The Parrishes were tottering on the edges of shabby gentility.

Though he'd agreed to keep his fingers out of the business for the duration of the wager, Tony was nevertheless determined to increase Edwina's editorial salary. If only to put Croyden's condescending nose out of joint.

"And so, because of all those public losses as a boy," Ian said, "you challenged her again, this time for ownership of the magazine?"

"I did. And I intend to win."

"You always do. Though I cannot for the life of me figure out why it is so important that you win this time."

Tony wasn't sure himself. Maybe it was because of the great walloping he'd received from his father when he'd lost the Minerva. Maybe because all those childish wagers had given him a taste for gambling and set him on a reckless course that had not let up for almost twenty years.

"I can't explain it," he said. "I just know that I'm determined to win."

The waiter returned with two glasses of sherry, along with a small tray of biscuits. Ian took his glass and raised it to Tony. "Here's to victory. I think."

Tony raised his own glass. "To victory."

Ian swallowed his sherry in one ungentlemanly gulp, burped, and leaned back in his chair with his hands resting on his belly and a contented smile on his face. He spent most of his time at one or the other of his clubs just so he could burp and belch and spit and curse to his heart's content, without worrying about offending the ladies. It amused Tony to think of the completely different mask Ian wore when in the presence of the opposite sex— thoroughly gallant and suave and charming. He suspected that one day Ian would fall top over tail in love, court the lady in his best gentlemanly manner, marry her, then shock her to the core when, after the novelty of marriage wore off, he belched at the dinner table and wiped his mouth with the tablecloth.

Ian reached inside his waistcoat and scratched his stomach. "If she was a childhood playmate," he said, "then she must be thirty if she's a day. Why not leave the poor woman alone? I'd have thought you'd rather run away screaming than spend more time than was absolutely necessary with a squint-eyed spinster."

"She's not exactly squint-eyed, Ian."

"Well then, she must be fat. Or skinny. Or hump-backed. Or Friday-faced."

"No, my friend. She is none of those things." Tony called to mind an image of her near-black hair and eyes; of her pale, milky smooth skin with the translucent quality of alabaster; of her full lips tinted by nature to a dark pink. Even her voice was pitched to match her dramatic coloring, a notch lower than most women. The slightly scratchy voice he remembered as a child had matured into an attractive sultriness. No, nothing about her was ordinary or plain. Nor remotely Friday-faced.

"In fact," he said, "she is quite startlingly beautiful."

Ian snorted. "Can't be. The words beautiful and spinster just don't go together. It's a what-do-you-call-it? An oxymoron."

"Well, it's true in her case. I tell you, Ian, she is drop-dead, heart-stopping gorgeous. That skinny little black-eyed girl grew into an extraordinary beauty."

Ian gave a soft whistle. He would know that Tony was not prone to hyperbole in such matters. "Then why has she never married? A prize like that doesn't remain unclaimed."

"Good question. I have no idea."

"It can only mean one of two things, you know."

Ian leaned over the arm of his chair and lowered his voice. "Either she's one of those women who are not available to men, and prefers the company of women, if you take my meaning. Or she is one of those modern, unconventional types who disdain marriage and take lovers at will, propriety be damned." He flashed a wicked grin. "Which do you suppose she is?"

Tony was momentarily flummoxed. He hadn't really considered either possibility. He certainly hoped the first was not true. What a glorious waste that would be. Though there was the ever-present Miss Armitage and her awkward reference to Edwina's bedroom. Were they perhaps . . . ?

No. He refused to accept that possibility. The second, however, was infinitely more interesting. Edwina had certainly shown no appreciation for propriety as a child. And she was most definitely too beautiful to have been ignored by men all these years. Despite their own past history, or perhaps because of it, a volatile, almost instant chemistry had flared between them. They'd both been aware of it, though she had likely welcomed it less than he did. It was why he'd been drawn to kiss her. And she had not objected.

Was she, then, a brazen Modern Woman who did just as she pleased?

He looked across to find Ian chuckling softly. Tony smiled and said, "I shall make it my business to find out, my friend."

*   *   *

Edwina stared at the page, crossed out what she'd written, and began again. After a few moments, she groaned in frustration, crumpled the paper into a ball and flung it into the basket at her feet, where it joined a dozen other failed attempts to put her thoughts clearly upon the page. It was no good. She simply could not concentrate on the review of *Memoirs Relative to Egypt* she was supposed to be writing for the next issue of the *Cabinet*. Something else entirely was on her mind.

At nine and twenty, she was much too old to be so affected by a simple kiss. She was no innocent, for heaven's sake. And she was accustomed to the admiration of men. She knew they often found her attractive, but it was of no consequence to her. She usually dismissed such attentions without a thought.

So why had this man, of all men, finally caught her interest? What was so different about Anthony Morehouse? Yes, he was handsome and charming and had an aura of seduction about him. But he was also the new owner of the *Cabinet* and poised to make her life a misery. He should be the last man, the very last man, who should draw her eye.

Perhaps it was simply a matter of who he'd once been—a good-looking golden-haired boy with a smile to steal a young girl's heart. He'd certainly stolen hers. But that was long ago when her head had been full of romantic dreams spun by her mother. Edwina had chased those dreams for years and handed out bits of her heart freely along the way.

Until eight years ago when all the dreams had crumbled and her heart had shriveled and died in her breast.

Was it pure sentiment, then, that made her susceptible to Anthony Morehouse? Her first love?

What foolishness. Thank heaven he had promised to keep his nose out of her business for the next four months. She would not be forced to see him, to remember those innocent days of youthful infatuation and romantic dreams.

She dipped her pen in the inkwell and began once again to compose the review of *Memoirs Relative to Egpyt*.

A scratching at the door was followed by the entrance of Lucy, the part-time maid who worked three mornings and two afternoons each week.

"Mr. Morehouse, miss."

Oh, no.

Lucy bobbed a curtsey and stepped aside as Anthony Morehouse strode into the room. She gazed dreamily after him for a moment, then uttered a quiet sigh before turning to leave. Edwina was not the only female, then, to fall under the spell of those silvery gray eyes. He'd no doubt been flirting with poor Lucy.

"What are you doing here?" she asked.

"And good morning to you, too." He actually grinned at her. "Do you mind if I sit down?"

"I do, actually. You promised to stay away."

"I promised no such thing." Without waiting for an invitation, he sat down in the chair opposite, scooted it closer, and leaned his elbows on the edge of the desk. "I can refer to the betting book if you like, but I can assure you it says that I will not interfere with the day-to-day business of the magazine for the next four months. It does not say that I must stay away."

"It was implied."

"No, it was inferred. By you. Not by me."

"Details. What are you doing here?"

"I thought to learn a bit more about the magazine, in a general sort of way. Not from a business perspective, of course, since that would mean examining the account books."

His eyes twinkled. A tiny tingle of apprehension skittered down Edwina's spine. Did he suspect something?

"But from an editorial perspective," he continued. "I'd like to understand how you decide what to print, who writes the articles, who designs the engravings, that sort of thing."

Edwina glared at him across the desk. "I can't see what possible interest any of that is to you, since for the next four months you have agreed to remain uninvolved. And after that, the magazine will no longer be yours to worry about."

He smiled, a sort of lopsided, quirky smile that reminded her of the freckle-faced boy she'd once known. "Ah, now that's the Eddie I remember. Confident to a fault. It makes the challenge that much more delicious."

"You, sir, are a scoundrel."

"So I have been told. Now, tell me about *The Ladies' Fashionable Cabinet.* I've read the current issue, and I can't help but wonder if some of the essays are not a touch too serious-minded for the average female reader."

"What?"

"Some of the fiction is good and the biographical sketches are interesting, but the poetry is uneven at best and the Busybody column is overly sentimental, though I suspect they reflect the tastes of the female reader. But the literary and dramatic reviews don't seem the sort to appeal to the female mind. Histories and letters and philosophy. Dull stuff, indeed, guaranteed to put your readers to sleep."

"Are you deliberately baiting me, sir?"

His eyes widened in feigned astonishment. "How so?"

"If you are going to insult the *Cabinet*'s readership and the general female population as a whole, you may see your way to the door. I have nothing more to say to you."

"My, aren't we prickly this morning?"

"The editorial content is my responsibility. It is no business of yours."

"You keep forgetting, Edwina, that it *is* my business. Quite literally."

She gave an ill-tempered little snort. "It is un-likely I should forget such a thing. I hardly need you coming around to remind me."

"Good. Then indulge me and explain a bit about the content. I have been perusing the latest issue of *The Lady's Magazine*, which I assume is your chief competition."

"One of them. What about it?"

"You must, of course, forgive my ignorance in such matters, but as an objective observer it ap-pears to me that *The Lady's Magazine* knows its audience well and aims all content to please the fe-male reader. The latest fashion news, for example."

Edwina rolled her eyes to the ceiling. "We have a fashion print in each issue."

"Yes, but only a line or two describing it. Who writes it, by the way?"

"Miss Armitage."

"Ah. I ought to have guessed. Terribly à la mode, that one. But only see what your competi-tion is doing."

He placed a copy of *The Lady's Magazine* on the desk and flipped through it. When he found what he was looking for, he swung it around for Edwina to see, jabbing his finger at the page. "Here are four, almost five pages given to what various ladies wore on the King's birthday. And another page on the latest Paris fashions. Now that is what I call ap-pealing to a feminine sensibility. I have it on good authority that ladies love to read about the latest fashions and who was seen wearing what."

Edwina pushed the magazine away. "It's nothing more than gossip, and I refuse to drag the *Cabinet* down to the level of scandal and innuendo found in other magazines."

"An admirable goal, to be sure," Anthony said, though his voice was tinged with a hint of sarcasm that set Edwina's teeth on edge. "But reporting on fashion is gossip only in the very broadest sense. Don't you think the average woman would enjoy reading about what the highest-born ladies in the land wore for the King's birthday? To know that the Duchess of Devonshire wore—let me see—'a petticoat of puce-colored crepe' so that she can dash out and have something made up in the same color and feel she is as fashionable as the Duchess?"

Edwina studied the man seated across the desk. Definitely a gentleman of fashion. A man who no doubt could distinguish puce from brown, crepe from sarsnet. His own clothes were expensive, expertly cut, and the tiniest bit flashy. Typical of a gambler, she suspected. His deep blue double-breasted coat sported very large brass buttons and was fashionably high-waisted, showing several inches of boldly striped waistcoat below. Not one, but three watch fobs hung beneath the waistcoat.

She realized how horribly dowdy she must appear to him in her simple muslin dress.

"I prefer," she said, "to leave that sort of reporting to *The Lady's Magazine*. Or the *Gallery of Fashion*. Of course I realize that fashion and fashion plates draw readers. That is why I continue to include them. But to give more space to such frivolous matters means less space for more serious content."

"The deadly dull literary reviews and essays?" He pulled a face. "My dear, you should take a closer look at the competition. There are no book reviews in *The Lady's Magazine*. No lengthy essays on current events in France, only brief reporting of the news. Lord, it's a wonder any ladies at all read the *Cabinet*. Take out the sentence or two on fashion, and perhaps the Busybody, and you practically have a gentlemen's magazine."

He'd gone too far this time. Now she was really getting angry. "Are you suggesting women can't appreciate the same intellectual stimulation as men?"

He lifted both hands in a defensive gesture. "With that look in your eye, I'd never dare suggest such a thing. I only wonder how you can ever hope to win our little wager if you do not write to the audience you hope to gain."

If he had set out deliberately to aggravate her, he'd done a good job of it. She held onto her temper with difficulty.

"I *will* win this wager," she said, "and not by lowering my standards. Along with a modicum of entertainment, our objective has always been to appeal to the minds of the readers. To stimulate them to read important literary works, not to dash off to the nearest mercer for a length of puce-colored crepe. I happen to believe there is a large audience of women who are pleased to read rational prose."

"I'll wager most of them wouldn't recognize rational prose if they saw it."

"Oh? And what will you wager this time? You have already put my future on the line."

He clucked his tongue but his eyes sparkled with merriment. "Pricklier and pricklier. But if you'd like to engage in another little wager, I have my betting book right here." He patted his breast.

"Must everything be a game for you? How disappointing to discover the young boy I once knew and admired grew up to be nothing better than a common gamester."

"But it is all your fault, Eddie."

"My name is Edwina. But you may call me Miss Parrish."

He pitched his voice low, with an undercurrent of sensuality. "Ah, but I fear you'll always be Eddie to me."

She looked into his eyes, beautiful eyes of silvery gray outlined in dark blue, and for a moment was lost in memories of her youth and other memories, of another pair of captivating blue eyes, full of promise, full of love.

She realized she was staring when his face broke into a slow, lazy grin. Damn. He'd rattled her again.

What was the matter with her? She gave herself a mental shake and called up the anger and frustration she'd been feeling only a moment before.

"And how," she said, "is your being a gamester all my fault, I'd like to know?"

"Isn't it obvious? My penchant for a good wager, a challenge of any kind, the thrill of the game began when we were children. When you continually claimed you could best me at something or other." He laughed, but there was a hint of self-mockery in it. "How could I resist?"

"It wasn't for the thrill of the game. You simply couldn't bear to be bested by a mere girl. It was pure competitiveness and stubborn male pride."

His expression softened. "No, it was just a boy trying to impress a pretty girl. And failing miserably."

Oh, dear. Did he have to be so charming?

"Even so," she said, "I hardly think I am to blame for your subsequent gambling. I saw your betting book. It is not an occasional thing with you, is it? It is your life."

"I confess that I cannot resist the thrill of risk, the danger of potential failure. I thrive on the rush, the thundering pulse, the tingly flush of anticipation. I have indeed made a life of it. A successful one, I might add, so you need have no regrets for setting me upon this course."

"But don't you worry about losing? About financial ruin?"

He waved a hand in casual dismissal. "In the first place, I never bet it all. I've never yet faced a wager worth *everything*. And second, I never lose."

"Never?"

He hunched a shoulder. "Almost never."

"You're that good a player, then?"

"No, I'm just astonishingly lucky."

Edwina placed her forearms flat on the desk and leaned forward. "Not this time. You will *not* win our wager."

"I will if you continue to waste so many pages on ponderous dissertations instead of lighthearted entertainment. You cannot expect to double the subscribers with your so-called rational prose."

"Oh, you provoking man. You wouldn't recognize rational prose if it reared up and bit you on the nose."

"Yes, I would. Could probably write it as well."

"Ha! Never."

"Shall we wager on it?"

Edwina groaned. "Do you never take anything seriously? Must you twist everything into a wager?"

"What venture is worthwhile without some element of risk? I propose a wager, a tiny, insignificant wager in the cause of rational, publishable prose. You will assign me something to write, something that you think is appropriate to your enlightened audience. You may choose the topic. If what I write is deemed worthy, I win. As simple as that."

"And I am to be the judge of its worthiness?"

"Hmm. You'd have to set aside your prejudices. That might be asking too much. Perhaps an impartial third party? One who is not told who is the author of the piece."

"It must be someone who knows what is appropriate for the *Cabinet*. I suggest Miss Armitage, my assistant editor."

"You think she can be objective?"

"There is no question of it."

"And you promise not to divulge the essay's authorship?"

She sighed in exasperation. "I promise."

"So, you accept my challenge?"

"I suppose so. Here, read this." She handed him the heavy book that was sitting on her desk. "I would like a review of it for the next issue. I will need it in three days."

He opened to the title page and cocked a brow. " 'Memoirs Relative to Egypt written in that Country during the Campaign of General Bonaparte in the Years 1798 and 1799 by the Learned and Scientific Men Who Accompanied the French Expedition.' Good Lord. Do you really expect that your readers will be interested in such a work?"

"Of course I do. Not only is it a study that should appeal to anyone interested in learning about other cultures, but anything related to ancient Egypt still holds fascination for the public in general. Even three years after Nelson's victory.

You see, Mr. Morehouse, I am not totally ignorant of what the public wants."

"So, I not only have to write something, but I must first read this tome? It is a formidable task."

"You set the terms. Have you changed your mind?"

"No, indeed." He closed the book and took it onto his lap. "The wager is on."

"Splendid."

If he won, she would have a review out of the way, and if he lost, she would have the satisfaction of telling him so. But what was in it for him?

"And what do you propose for the stakes?" she asked.

"Hmm. Let me think." He lifted his gaze to the ceiling and made a great show of tapping his chin with his finger, as though he really were thinking it over, though Edwina suspected he'd had something specific in mind all along.

"Ah, I have it," he said. "If I win, I get to see the Minerva."

Edwina leaned back and studied him warily. This wasn't what she had expected. "That's all? You want to see the Minerva?"

"I don't mean that you are to bring it downstairs for me to admire. I want to see it in its usual place. I want you to take me to view it where you normally keep it, where it sits right now."

The devil. He remembered Prudence saying she kept it in her bedroom. And so what did he think?

That she would take him by the hand, lead him upstairs, and let him seduce her? Did he really believe it would be that easy?

The provocative glimmer in his eye suggested he did.

Let him live on that hope. Edwina had a plan.

"All right," she said. "I agree. But let us make the terms and the stakes official by logging it in your little red book." She held out her hand in hopes he would allow her to log the wager, in her own words.

"A woman after my own heart. Here." He pulled out the betting book from his coat pocket. "You may do the honors."

She wrote:

Miss Parrish wagers Mr. Morehouse cannot pen a publishable review of Memoirs Relative to Egypt. If he wins, he is allowed to see the Roman head of Minerva in its usual place of display.

He read it, saw nothing amiss, and signed. Edwina sent up a silent prayer of thanks and tried not to smile too broadly as she added her own signature to the entry.

Anthony took the book and fingered its red leather. His gaze flickered to her mouth. Was he thinking to seal this new bargain with another kiss?

That would not be a good idea. Edwina rose

from her chair but kept the desk safely between them. "Three days, Mr. Morehouse. You have only three days to finish the book and pen a clearheaded, thoughtful, publishable review. I suggest you get to work."

He had risen when she did, and still looked hopeful that she might move from behind the shield of the desk. She would not.

"With such a prize in store," he said, "it will be no work at all, but only a pleasure. I shall return on Thursday ready to celebrate my victory."

"Do not be so sure, Mr. Morehouse. I bid you good day."

She smiled sweetly as he prepared to leave, biting back the gurgle of mirth that threatened to explode into full-throated laughter. He bowed and left the room. She waited until she heard the sound of the front door closing behind him before giving in to her amusement and bursting into laughter.

He might indeed win the wager. She had no reason to think him incapable of penning a decent essay. In fact she was perfectly prepared for him to do so. But it would be no victory.

Not for Anthony Morehouse, anyway.

Chapter 4

Tony sat back and smiled. He'd reread the pages he had penned for Edwina, and was excessively proud of himself. By Jove, it was good.

It had been years since he'd written anything serious. Since before he'd been sent down from Cambridge, in fact, when he still thought he might amount to something, when he was still passionate about learning, when he still hoped he might make his father proud with a first in Classics.

He had failed on all counts, of course, but had faced the world with an attitude of amused indifference as he went on with his life, seeking pleasure and risk at every opportunity. It was only in the occasional private moment when he allowed the weight of his failures to lie heavily upon his shoulders.

This was not one of those moments.

Tony felt quite puffed up with his own consequence, thoroughly cocky at having penned such an excellent essay. Even the dour Miss Armitage would have to agree. And when she did, the lovely Edwina would be forced to take him to her bedchamber. What a sweet moment that would be.

He had it all planned in his mind. Edwina would think he meant to seduce her, but he was never so obvious in such matters. He would not even touch her. He would speak softly and allow the intimacy of the bedchamber to infuse a hint of sensuality to their conversation, to provide a provocative suggestion of another sort of conversation altogether. He would make a slow survey of the room, running his hand along the edge of a dressing table or writing desk, perhaps picking up a personal item or two. A hairbrush. A quill feather. A scent bottle. His eyes would dart to the bed, then capture her gaze while his fingers caressed the Minerva. All the while he would speak only of the most proper and banal subjects.

He did not think it too presumptuous, or too arrogant, to believe he could well and truly befuddle Miss Edwina Parrish until she was unable to string three words together to make a sentence. He was very confident of his powers of seduction. Though it might not make his father proud to know it, seduction was the one area in which Tony truly excelled. And he had not misunderstood the look in her eyes when they'd last met. That curiously captivated look when she let down her guard for an instant and forgot to be annoyed with him.

She was interested. And that meant she would be receptive when he turned the full force of his charm on her. Maneuvering her into the bedchamber was simply the first step in a well-planned campaign. Soon enough, he would know the truth about her. Was she truly a Modern Woman, or simply a frustrated spinster who happened to be incredibly beautiful?

Or, heaven help him, was she that other type of woman Ian had suggested? No, he refused to believe that. She had been *interested*.

Tony blew away residual sand from the essay pages and stacked them neatly together. Edwina would never know he had already read the *Memoirs* and formed an opinion well before she had thrust the book into his hands. He made it a point to read every new publication having to do with Greece or Rome or Egypt. Though he'd not been allowed to complete his career at Cambridge, he had never completely abandoned his love of the Classics, or the fascination for ancient art and cultures drummed into his head from an early age. Sir Frederick would no doubt laugh to know his troublesome younger son had, after all, paid attention.

He looked up at the sound of voices. A rapping on the door of his study soon followed. Brinkley, the indispensable, unflappable gentleman who served as Tony's butler, valet, and housekeeper, held open the door for the two young men who strode past him.

"Mr. Fordyce and Lord Skiffington, sir." Brinkley discreetly scrutinized the second gentleman's attire, then rolled his eyes to the ceiling before he stepped away and closed the door.

"Hullo, old chap." Ian Fordyce removed his hat and plopped down into the most comfortable chair. "Missed you at White's last night."

Lord Jasper Skiffington remained standing. It looked as though sitting would be a somewhat difficult task in such a costume. He wore a waistcoat and jacket so short they reached only midway to his stomach, which meant his pantaloons had to be worn very high. In fact, it appeared Skiffy's pantaloons reached all the way to his armpits, and would not have been out of place among the French *Incroyables*.

"Deep play last night, m'dear," Skiffy said. "Very deep. Thought to have seen you there."

"Perhaps he had a more *interesting* engagement last evening." Ian wiggled his eyebrows suggestively.

"Nothing very interesting, I'm afraid," Tony said. "I had some rather dull business to take care of."

He pushed aside the essay pages, casually sliding

them beneath the blotter, but was stopped by a well-manicured finger upon the pages.

"And what's this?" Skiffy asked, and pulled the papers away from the blotter. "Something to hide, old chap? Not from your nearest and dearest, surely."

He took hold of the handwritten pages, but Tony made a grab for them.

"Nothing that concerns you, my friend." He took the pages, restacked them neatly, and placed them on the far side of the desk, away from Skiffy, and set a large paperweight on top of them.

Skiffy's mouth turned down in an exaggerated frown. "It must be something frightfully personal, Morehouse, for you to be so rudely clandestine among friends. A missive to a certain lady, perhaps? A secret correspondence?"

"I'm afraid not, Skiffy. It's only—"

"An essay on the *Memoirs Relative to Egypt*."

Hell and damnation.

Tony had been watching Skiffy and paying no attention to Ian, who had slipped from his chair and quietly purloined the essay. Tony reached for it, but Ian chuckled and passed it over his head to Skiffy.

"Egad, Morehouse, what's this?" His lordship leaned back and scanned the essay through his quizzing glass. "Didn't know you was interested in Egypt. Should have told me. M'mother just bought the most cunning crocodile bench from some new chap, a cabinetmaker on King Street. Could get you his direction, if you like."

"No, thank you, Skiffy," Tony said. "I'm not in the market for Egyptian furniture."

"You can't fool me," Ian said, and took the essay back from Lord Skiffington. "This is an essay. A bloody book review. It's for that damned magazine, isn't it? You're *writing* for the magazine."

"What magazine?" Skiffy asked.

"By God, I told you this whole business would be nothing but trouble," Ian said. "Now she's got *you* working for *her*. Writing for a ladies' fashion magazine, for God's sake."

"A what?" Skiffy said, his eyes wide with sudden interest. "A ladies' magazine? A *fashion* magazine?"

"It's not a fashion magazine," Tony said, the echo of Edwina's words ringing in his head. "It's—"

"Don't you remember, Skiffy?" Ian said. "Our friend here became the proud owner of *The Ladies' Fashionable Cabinet* last week. Won it from Croyden."

"Oh, I say. Forgot all about that business at White's. Had a cup too many that night."

"And now he's wagered the beautiful female editor for ownership."

Skiffy gave a shriek of delight. "Morehouse, you devil! A beautiful editor, you say? The spinsterish niece Croyden mentioned? Tell all, m'dear, tell *all*."

Tony opened his mouth to respond, but Ian cut him off.

"And it looks as though your lovely dark-eyed editor has taken the lead in this challenge," Ian said. "I can't believe you're actually writing book reviews, Tony. *Book reviews*!"

"Stubble it, Ian. If you must know, it's merely part of another little wager with the lady. And this time, I'm going to win."

"Oh?" Ian's face split into a grin. "And what will be your prize?"

"It's private."

Another shriek from Skiffy pierced the air and was followed by a sputtering chortle from Ian.

"Private stakes with a beautiful lady?" Skiffy asked, his eyes sparkling. "Oh, do tell. What shall you win? Something wonderfully improper, I have no doubt. A silk garter, perhaps? A corset busk? *A kiss*?"

"Come on, old man," Ian said. "Give us a look at your book. I have no doubt the wager is logged and initialed, all very proper. Hand it over."

Tony gave a resigned sigh. It was no use. They would wheedle it out of him one way or another. A tiny, almost imperceptible pang of caution made him want to keep everything about Edwina Parrish to himself, but he brushed it aside. Instead, he reached into his breast pocket, pulled out the betting book, and handed it to Skiffy, who stood closest. His lordship flipped pages, stopping to read once or twice and giving little grunts of interest. When he got to the last page he read it aloud, then looked up, his brow furrowed in puzzlement.

"Have you lost a screw, old chap? A roman head? You did this"—he pointed to the pages Ian was still holding—"only to see some musty old head?"

"Not simply to see it," Tony said. "You will note that I am to be allowed to see it in its usual place of display."

"And that is?"

"Her bedchamber."

Ian gave a bark of laughter, and Skiffy laughed so hard he had to sit down, and seemed not to notice the telltale sound of a ripped seam.

"This is quite good," Prudence said. "Excellent, in fact. Yes, I do indeed believe it is suitable for the *Cabinet*."

Edwina sighed. "Thank you, Prudence. I appreciate your opinion. I won't keep you any longer. I know you are anxious to meet with Mrs. Dillard about her advertisement."

Prudence nodded, slanted a quick glance toward Anthony, and left the office. She made sure, Edwina was amused to note, to leave the door conspicuously ajar behind her.

Edwina ought to have known the provoking man would pen a perfectly beautiful essay, with just the right balance of critical evaluation and personal insight. He'd also included astute comparisons to other works, indicating a greater familiarity with the subject matter than she had expected. Though perhaps she should not be so surprised.

He might be little more than a gamester now, but he had once been a studious young boy with a passion for ancient cultures. She remembered when he'd first shown her the Minerva. He'd been so proud and excited that it had been found in a riverbed on his father's estate. He had gone on and on about Roman Britain and the significance of the little gilt bronze head. He'd obviously done a great deal of study on the subject.

And so the core of that young boy lived on in the man, buried deep beneath frivolity and recklessness. But the essay showed he could still mine that core, could still be a critical thinker and appreciate academic study.

She experienced a tiny moment of smug satisfaction for bringing back the boy, if only for a moment.

Anthony was quite obviously feeling a touch of satisfaction himself. A cocky self-assurance oozed from every pore. He was exceedingly proud of himself. A broad smiled was plastered on his face as he sat across from her, altogether too comfortably ensconced in Nick's chair, one leg crossed casually over the other.

"And so you shall have an essay published in the

Cabinet. Congratulations. I suppose now you will be wanting an intriguing pseudonym?"

"Not at all," he said. "I am the modest sort, you see. I am perfectly happy to allow it be attached to your own handle, Arbiter Literaria."

"It's not entirely my own personal pseudonym, if you must know, but a general one many of us use for literary reviews."

"Ah. And here I thought I had discovered the distinctly elegant and eloquent voice of Miss Parrish in the Arbiter."

"Well, it is mostly me, in fact," she said, ridiculously pleased at his flattery.

Fool. He was obviously a practiced flatterer and seducer. She had plenty of experience with that type and should know better than to succumb to his easy charm.

"But others have used it from time to time," she continued. "As you will do now, apparently."

"By all means. I wrote only this one essay and will write no more. It is certainly not how I prefer to spend my time." A gleam of wicked amusement lit his gray eyes. "I will leave such matters to you ladies."

Edwina had forgotten that he still thought the *Cabinet* was written solely by a group of ladies, as it had been once upon a time. But now many others were involved. The Busybody was written by Simon Westover, Augusta Historica's essays were written by Nicholas, and other men within their particular circle of friends, including Samuel Coleridge, contributed from time to time under the guise of various pseudonyms. Other women, too. Women like Helen Maria Williams and Mary Hays and others whose sometimes radical politics generated much debate and public rebuke. Edwina had never dared let Uncle Victor know about the new contributors to the *Cabinet* or he would have felt the need to see what other changes Edwina had made. It would have been disastrous if he had asked to closely examine the account books.

At least she did not have to worry about Anthony in that regard. He had put his signature to the wager in that little red book, with the promise not to interfere with her management. Edwina supposed his gambler's code of honor would keep him away from the business records.

But not away from her. He showed up on her doorstep altogether too often.

"There is, however, one other small matter we have yet to discuss," he said.

"You wish to collect on your wager."

"That's what I like about you, Eddie. You always get straight to the point."

He rose from his chair. She stood and moved around to the front of the desk. Anthony walked across the room and gestured for her to precede him through the door.

When she made no move to leave the room but

simply leaned against the desk, he raised his eyebrows and said, "I believe we agreed that I could view the Minerva?"

"Yes, we did."

"Well, then, let us go see her."

"But there is no need to leave this room to do so."

He glared at her for a moment, then stepped back into the study. "I hate to disagree with a lady," he said, "but I am quite certain our agreement was that I would be allowed to see the Minerva in your . . . well, in the place where you keep it."

"Oh, I don't think so. Perhaps you should read the terms again to refresh your memory."

Anthony glowered at her, but then dug into his coat and pulled out the betting book. " 'If he wins, he is allowed to see the Roman head of Minerva in its usual place of display.' There you are."

"And here you are, sir. Here is the Minerva." She pointed to the desk.

He stepped closer and looked about, a wary frown furrowing his brow, then shook his head. "Where? I do not see her."

"She is right here, where she always is, in her 'usual place of display' for all the world to see." She picked up a copy of the *Cabinet* and pointed to the masthead, where an elegant engraving incorporated the head of Minerva. An exact copy of the one sitting upstairs in her bedchamber.

He clapped a hand to his brow and muttered something beneath his breath.

"I beg your pardon?" she said in the sweetest, most innocent tone she could manage.

"Piqued and repiqued. You tricked me, madam!" He scowled at her, though his eyes danced with laughter. Edwina thought she saw a flicker of admiration there as well.

"No, I simply outwitted you. Again."

The scowl quirked up at one end and transformed into the lopsided boyish grin that had stolen her heart so many years ago. "Maybe this time," he said. "But take care, for I shan't let it happen again. Next time, the Minerva will be mine for the keeping. Along with the *Cabinet*."

"We shall see about that."

"Indeed we shall. How *are* those subscription numbers coming?"

Edwina groaned.

Tony could not stay away. Not that he tried very hard to do so. He simply allowed his feet to point him in the direction of Golden Square before his brain had any say in the matter. Hardly a day went by that he did not find himself upon her doorstep. Today was no different. He slowed the team as he turned his curricle into the square.

It was pure foolishness, this eagerness to see her. Ridiculous in a man of his age and experience. He hadn't even tried to kiss her again. Instead, each day he took his place in the slightly worn armchair opposite the desk and just watched.

He loved to watch Edwina at work. She never interrupted what she was doing to accommodate his obviously annoying presence, but Tony didn't care. It wasn't the *work* he was watching, though he had to admit to a sincere respect for the efficiency with which she transacted the business of publication. He sat and observed, with no little admiration, as she dealt with printers and engravers and colorists and binders and distributors. Though he claimed his ubiquitous presence was for the purpose of learning the business, Tony could never have run such an operation himself, which made him wonder what he would do if she bolted when he won their wager.

He would just have to remove that possibility as an option. In the meantime, he simply watched. Watched *her*. Edwina's particular beauty was so unique and so striking he never tired of gazing upon it. There was the sultry voice, too. And the way she moved with such elegant grace.

Good God, he was becoming as smitten as a schoolboy. And what a joke that was—the same schoolboy and the same girl, all over again.

Well, this time would be different. History was not destined to repeat itself. He was no longer a gauche, half-grown boy. A gamester required self-assurance, and Tony had it in abundance. And he was not merely a gamester, but a winner. He was rich because of risks he'd taken at the tables as well as on the Exchange. He'd developed a glossy veneer of confidence that served him well whether playing at whist or playing at seduction. He had no doubt he could best Edwina Parrish this time, at any game they dared to play.

He left the curricle with his tiger, who was getting so accustomed to these visits that he boasted a regular routine of exercising the temperamental grays around the square and along Warwick Street and Brewer Street while he waited for Tony to return. Tony watched Jamie take the ribbons before turning toward the plain brick façade with its four neat rows of sash boxes. The only thing that distinguished it from the otherwise identical house to its left and the one to its right was the doorway with its typically Palladian white pilasters and pediment, and intricate fanlight above the door. It had a simple, understated elegance, rather like the lady who lived there.

He was shown in by Lucy, who blushed and batted her lashes and assured him Miss Parrish would be pleased to see him. He entered the study to find Edwina in her usual place behind the desk, her head bent as she made corrections to loose, printed pages. She looked up briefly at his entrance, then returned to her work.

"You again," she said. "I'm quite busy, as you see. Go away."

Tony ignored her petulant tone and strode into the room. He tossed his hat on a table, set aside some papers stacked on the armchair, and took a seat. "My dear Edwina," he said, "the warmth of your welcome never ceases to brighten my day."

"Those are page proofs," she snapped, and pointed to the papers he'd moved from the chair. "If you have put them out of order, I swear I will have your guts for garters."

Tony leaned over and picked up the pages. "No, no. Nothing amiss, I assure you." He placed the papers on the desk. "No violence is necessary."

"Hmph. Is there something specific you wanted? I'm very busy."

"Nothing specific. I just like to observe, as you know, to learn more about *my* business. What are doing, if I may ask?"

"If you must know, I am correcting page proofs for the next issue. And it is not going well."

"Oh? That explains why you aren't your usual cheerful self today. What is the problem?"

She gave an exasperated sigh. "Imber has mixed up the columns so nothing flows properly, and he's placed one of the engravings upside down. He is usually so competent. But we added one extra engraving this time, and more advertising at the end, and it seems to have thrown him off. Oh, this is maddening."

With so many pages printed on the uncut sheets, some facing one way, some facing the other, Tony didn't know how anyone could tell if the columns were mixed up. But Edwina seemed to know what she was doing.

"I hesitate to offer," he said, "but if I can be of any help—"

"You could leave. That would help. Imber's assistant will be here in a few minutes and I must finish with these proofs."

"Suppose I sit here quietly instead, while you finish the corrections."

"Why?"

"There is still much I'd like to know about your operation here. I thought we could have a nice chat, perhaps over tea?"

"There is other work to be done."

"Ah, but I'll wager you could spare a half hour."

She groaned. "Heavens, not another wager."

Tony laughed. "No, my dear. It was only a figure of speech. What do you say? I'll be silent as an oyster while you work, then we'll have tea. Agreed?"

She glowered at him, but finally said, "All right." She then went back to her work and ignored him.

Or pretended to. Tony slowly removed his yellow kid gloves, one long finger at a time, and could not help but notice when Edwina's eyes flickered up briefly. He smiled to realize she was not indifferent to him. He was not the world's most handsome man, but he did have a certain charm and knew how to use it. He placed the gloves in the upturned hat on the table beside him, and sat back to see how much he could discompose her without moving a muscle or saying a word.

She wore a simple muslin dress, as she usually did, with tight-fitting sleeves reaching almost to the elbow. The glories of her white bosom were left to the imagination by a striped muslin fichu crossed high in front and tied in the back. The dress, which had bits of white-on-white embroidery along the sleeve edges, had seen too many washings and was looking a bit thin. Even so, she wore it well, with a natural grace that would have made a feed sack look elegant. Lord, how he would love to see her in a fine ball gown, with a minuscule bodice cut low at the neck and with no lace or fichu to disguise her bosom.

Her fingers fiddled with her hair as she worked. Tony was pleased that she had not succumbed to the rage for cropped hair. Her face was framed in short black curls, a nod to current fashion, but the rest was gathered up in the back in some sort of complicated arrangement of plaits and combs, with two long, loose locks curling down her back and one hanging over her shoulder. That one was being twisted around her finger while she reviewed the proofs.

Would the whole glorious mass fall down her back if he released the combs? And how long would it be before he was allowed to find out?

He was jerked from such pleasant reverie by the entrance of Lucy, whose coquettish gaze drifted toward Tony before she spoke to Edwina.

"Robbie Vickers is here, miss."

A gangly, yellow-haired youth entered with a cloth cap crushed in his hands. Unlike Lucy, he seemed not even to notice Tony. His eyes, wide with adolescent adoration, were fixed on the woman behind the desk. Poor chap. Youthful infatuation was often a painful thing to bear, and this lad looked well and truly lost.

"I've come for the proofs, Miss Parrish," he said. His gaze dropped to the floor and he twisted the cap nervously.

Edwina gathered up the large pages and stacked them neatly in a pile. She glared at the stripling and jabbed a finger at the stack. "These will *not* do, Robbie. Tell Imber these proofs are a mess and will have to be completely redone."

"B—but, Miss Parrish," the boy said, clearly agitated to have somehow displeased the object of his worship, "there's no time. We can't possibly do a whole new set of proofs before going to press."

"Then you must find a way to make it possible," she said. "I cannot allow the *Cabinet* to go out like this."

She gestured for Robbie to step closer and began to point out several layout errors in such exasperated and outraged tones, the poor lad was rendered speechless. Finally, he took the pages, rolled them up, and placed them in a large bag he'd brought with him.

"I'll show these to Mr. Imber," he said, "and see if there's something he can do."

"There had better be," Edwina said. "Under no circumstances is he to go to print until he's delivered another set of proofs for my approval. Is that clear?"

Her tone brooked no argument, and she would get none from this poor lad.

"Yes, Miss Parrish. Thank you, ma'am." The boy turned on his heel and left as quickly as his long legs could carry him.

Edwina leaned back in her chair and muttered something beneath her breath.

"I can see you haven't changed much," Tony said. "As obstinate and bossy as ever."

She slid a glance in his direction and gave a disparaging little sniff.

He decided to use the occasion to prod a bit, to see what he could discover about Edwina Parrish. "Yes, just like the little girl I once knew. It is no wonder you never found a husband prepared to put up with such managing ways."

She bristled at his words. A brief shadow of uneasiness flickered in her eyes, and was as quickly gone. "I don't have to sit here and listen to your insults. Go away."

Aha. He had touched a nerve. Yet, some imp of mischief made him press on.

"Oh, but you promised me tea, as I recall," he said. "A perfect opportunity for you to fill me in on the last—what?—eighteen or nineteen years. You can tell me how your officious ways drove every man out of your life."

"You hateful man. I did no such thing!"

"Oh? And why, then, are you still unmarried?"

"It is none of your business, Mr. Morehouse."

Interesting. The subject had set her hackles up. Had there been a disappointing romance? A failed betrothal? A broken heart? She was squirming in her seat and would not look him in the eye. It was the first hint of vulnerability he'd yet seen in her.

"No, you are probably right. And my name is Anthony, you know. Or Tony. Whichever you like. We are old friends, after all. But you cannot blame me for being intrigued that such a beautiful woman has not been snatched up by some enterprising fellow with a discriminating eye."

"Do not try to distract me with flattery, sir. I've heard it all."

"I am sure you must have. Beauty such as yours does not go unnoticed. Was that what happened? You heard so many tributes to your beauty that you learned to distrust easy flattery? To distrust men?"

"What nonsense. I am not quite so delicate in my sensibilities, sir." She rose from her seat. "Excuse me while I run Lucy to earth and see about that tea."

Tony had stood when she did and watched as she

came from behind the desk, beribboned slippers peeking out from beneath the long muslin skirts, and the ends of the striped fichu scarf falling down her back from the high waist almost to the floor. She stood in the doorway and called out to the maid. The girl appeared almost before the words were spoken.

"Ah, Lucy. Would you be so good as to bring up some tea and biscuits?"

"Upstairs, miss? In the drawing room?"

"No, in here will be fine. I'll clear off a table."

Lucy's pursed lips expressed her disapproval of such an inelegant arrangement, but she bobbed a curtsey and turned to go.

"Oh, and Lucy," Edwina called out. "Not the good Bohea. The ordinary green tea will do."

"I am overwhelmed by such amiable hospitality," Tony said.

She turned to face him and there was a spark of amusement in her eyes. "I'm afraid my best manners, and my best tea, are reserved for those guests who have been *invited*. And for those who don't make a point of insulting their hostess."

"Then I am doubly grateful that you allow me to stay at all. Green tea in the study suits me perfectly. Will this table do?"

He removed his hat and gloves from the small table beside the armchair. He gestured toward the books and papers still neatly arranged upon it and arched an eyebrow in question.

"Fine," she said, and removed the papers to another larger worktable on the other side of the room.

Tony followed her with an armload of books. "And I assure you, I meant no insult earlier," he said. "I was simply curious about your unmarried state."

"I believe you are also unmarried?"

"I am." He grabbed another chair and moved it closer to the makeshift tea table. He would *not* face her across the fortress of her desk this time.

"And I suspect no one questions *your* decision not to marry."

"On the contrary. My mother questions it constantly." He held out the chair and she sat down. "Wants to see me settle down and fill a nursery. I would guess your mother wishes the same for you."

"My mother died when I was fifteen."

Her stark words stopped him. He still held on to the back of her chair, and reached down to touch her gently on the shoulder. "Oh. I'm so sorry, Edwina. I didn't know."

She shrugged, which had the effect of dislodging his hand. "It was a long time ago," she said.

Tony walked around the table and took his own seat in the armchair. "And your father?" he asked.

"I don't believe Papa has ever noticed that I haven't married. He doesn't notice much. The roof could fall down around him and he would simply put on his hat to shield himself from the debris and continue whatever he was doing. If not for the housekeeper, he would likely forget to eat."

"And so you live here with your brother."

"Yes, and quite happily, too. Don't assume, Mr. Morehouse, that you know my mind. I am, in fact, unmarried by choice."

"Indeed?"

"Though I have no doubt there are some who are put off by such a managing female as myself, my decision to remain unmarried is not based on lack of opportunity." There was the tiniest hint of humor in her eyes, as though she was laughing at herself. Or perhaps she was laughing at him?

"Everything I own I have worked hard for," she said, "and I've no desire to turn it over to a husband who might squander it or *gamble* it away. Nor do I have a desire to be forever dependent upon a man and his whims. There are more important things to do with my life."

"Like edit a ladies' magazine?"

"That is merely a means to an end. The profits allow us to do so much more."

Profits? What was she talking about? Her uncle had taken all the profits and given Edwina a mere pittance.

"That is," she continued, speaking very quickly and with a slight nervousness, "*if* we had access to the profits there is so much we *could* do. There are people starving because of the food shortages and heavy war taxes. Thousands of peasants have been forced off the land due to enclosures, and have been rounded up in the cities to work in factories. Yet the laborers are prohibited from demanding a fair wage by the wretched Combination Acts. While the government has concentrated on war, its people have suffered and been ignored. It is unconscionable."

Oh, Lord. She was a do-gooder. He ought to have known. "And you hope to right these wrongs?"

"We try to do what we can."

"We?"

"My brother and I. He has bigger plans, of course, and I am certain he will achieve them one day. But for now, we don't have the money for any sort of grand charitable gesture or sweeping reparation. We send clothing and blankets to factory families in the North. We help find work for displaced farmers near our family home in Derbyshire. And most importantly, we lobby politicians for reform."

Worse than a mere do-gooder, she was a reformer. "You astonish me, Edwina. Your words hint at republican idealism. Or do I misunderstand?"

"No, you understand perfectly. We had great hopes for France and the Revolution, but most of those efforts fell apart." A shuttered expression of regret, or perhaps sadness, came and went, quickly masked. "But the ideals and ambitions that fed the Revolution are still sound, and I support them."

Good God. The woman was a damned Jacobin.

Chapter 5

⸏⸏⸏

The entrance of Lucy with a tea tray precluded Tony's responding, for the moment, to Edwina's startling admission. It simply never occurred to him that the beautiful Miss Parrish might be a radical thinker. While he helped Lucy with the tray, Tony tried to reconcile the efficient editor of a magazine of light entertainment with the serious republican reformer.

It was not that he disapproved. He was not exactly a conservative thinker himself. If truth be told, he was not much of a thinker at all, as far as political matters went. Anyone who had lived during the past dozen years or so could not help but form some opinion on events across the Channel, first with the

Revolution and now with that upstart Bonaparte as First Consul, threatening borders throughout the continent. But Tony had been largely unaffected on a personal level, and whatever mild opinions he held were primarily those instilled by having grown up in a strict Tory household.

Sir Frederick Morehouse was a man of traditional, conservative English values, from his powdered wig to his buckled shoes. He was a stickler for convention. He hated the French on principle, simply because the English had always hated the French. And he was staunchly anti-Jacobin, fearing, as did many of his generation, a Reign of Terror on English soil. He was a loyal supporter of the King and of the government, so long as it did not fall into the hands of Whigs. The fact was, Sir Frederick had not allowed dissention in his house, and so Tony had never bothered to argue a single political point with him. There had been a time or two when he would have liked to do so, but since he was already his father's Great Disappointment, he decided not to press his luck.

Edwina poured the tea and handed a cup to Tony. "Does it bother you to know that I went to France in support of the Revolution?" she asked.

He took a sip of tea and set the cup back down without taking his eyes off her. "Bother me? No, why should it? It surprises me, that is all."

"Well, you may rest assured that those dreams

were . . . well, let us just say they were crushed by the Terror."

That shuttered look came into her eyes once again, briefly, and Tony thought there was a wealth of hidden meaning beneath those words. But then, she must have seen dreadful things if she had been in France during the bloody days of Robespierre's massacre.

"But you still retain your republican ideals?" he asked. "You still espouse reform?"

"My ideals are not as intact as they once were," she said, and shot him a wistful little smile. "But yes, I do support steady, wise reform. It is inevitable. The face of this nation has changed after years of fighting—and funding—a very expensive war. It is time to look inward. Our own people have been neglected for too long."

"Spoken just like a politician," he said, and then, out of sheer contrariness, decided to further taunt her. "You ought to have been a man, Edwina."

"I beg your pardon?"

He lowered his voice to a seductive tone and allowed his gaze to make a slow, deliberate survey of her body. "But I am eternally thankful that you are not."

She rolled her eyes and gave a disparaging click of her tongue. "And though my ideas appear to surprise you," she said, "yours, sir, are quite predictable."

"Oh?" Tony did his best to feign innocence. "How so?"

"You are completely unable to carry on a serious conversation with a woman without it degenerating into flirtation, innuendo, and seduction. You have no respect for a woman's intellect. And you certainly cannot even begin to comprehend the need for reform on behalf of those less fortunate than you. Clearly you have no thought beyond your own pleasure."

Tony winced at her last statement, for it was painfully close to the truth. He had never been a man overly concerned with serious matters. But neither was he a complete hedonist. He probably ought to defend himself. But that imp of mischief was still at work, and Tony had the irresistible urge to bait her.

"You are right, of course." He gave a sigh of pure ennui. "But I never saw the point in worrying over grand ideas and philosophical issues when there is so much pleasure to be experienced."

"Is that really all that matters to you?"

He shrugged. "Nothing much matters to me more than good food and drink, good friends, good women, a bit of sport."

"And gaming, I take it, is your primary sport?"

"It all comes down to risk, does it not? Anything with an element of risk is a manner of game, after all, whether it be a turn of the card, a roll of the hazard dice, a footrace with a pretty young girl, or a duel over a man's wife."

"A duel? Do not tell me you have engaged in dueling?"

"Once or twice."

Her mouth twisted in disgust. "How perfectly horrid. And perfectly idiotic."

"But it is the ultimate wager, betting one's life. The ultimate thrill."

Her eyes blazed with black fire. "You should be ashamed even to admit such a thing. How can you put your life on the line for such a frivolous cause while others risk their lives, or their freedom, in the cause of liberty?"

"You wouldn't understand." He waved his hand in a dismissive gesture. "It's a man's business."

She flattened her palms on the table and leaned forward. "Do you say such things merely to provoke me? It's almost ten years since *A Vindication of the Rights of Woman* was first published, and still we fight the same battles against narrow-minded attitudes such as yours."

"Oh, please." Tony raised his eyes to the ceiling. "You bluestocking types are forever bringing up the Great Wollstonecraft as if she were a damned oracle and the *Vindication* was Holy Writ."

"You wouldn't be so smug about it if you'd bother to read it."

Tony only just managed to stifle the reply on the

tip of his tongue. It seemed almost too easy, and yet he had an inspired notion for another wager.

"I know everything I need to know about that tiresome book," he said.

"Do you, indeed?"

"Yes, I do."

"Pardon me, but I don't credit secondhand reports and attacks in the *Anti-Jacobin Review* as valid sources."

"I'll wager I know as much about it as you do."

"Unlikely."

"Then you will accept my wager?"

"Oh ho, a real wager again," she said. "Not a mere figure of speech this time?"

"A real wager. You may quiz me on *A Vindication*, and if my answers prove I know as much about it as you do, then you must agree to go driving with me tomorrow in the park."

She glared at him skeptically, as though weighing the proposition from all angles. He could practically read her thoughts from the series of expressions flickering across her face. Did he really know something about Wollstonecraft? What were the chances he knew enough to keep her from tripping him up? And if he did, what was the harm in an innocent drive through the park?

He would swear she was thinking precisely that as she gazed at him over the rim of her teacup. He had demonstrated with his essay that he was not an illiterate numbskull. Did she guess that he had indeed read the famous *Vindication*? By God, she *knew* he just might win this game, and yet she was going to take the challenge. He would bet on it.

"Bring out your little red book, Mr. Morehouse. We have a wager."

Nicholas mumbled a greeting to his sister as he walked past the open door to her bedchamber, then returned, walking backward, to stand in the doorway.

"Well, look at you," he said.

Edwina was doing just that, as she studied her reflection in the dressing glass and adjusted her straw bonnet. "What do you think?" she asked. "Will I do?"

"Do what, exactly? In that gear you could do most anything, I'd imagine. You look very pretty, Ed."

She thought so, too. She wore a white cambric muslin dress, fitted close around the neck with a delicate ruff of Vandyked lace, and long, full sleeves with matching lace frills at the cuffs. Over the dress she wore a poppy red spencer jacket that tapered in front into two points adorned with tassels. The little jacket was from several seasons ago and was perhaps not as bright as it once was, but the color suited her. Edwina realized her rather unique coloring was not set off to its best advantage in pastels and muted tones. Plain white looked good on her, but when it came to color, she needed something bold and dramatic.

And that was the full extent of her fashion expertise. Or lack thereof. She liked color, but had little appreciation for texture or line. The current fashions that involved complicated draping and wrapping and fastening were simply beyond her. She never quite had the knack for putting things together in interesting and creative ways. Edwina had not inherited her mother's artistic eye. So she kept her wardrobe simple and could only hope that whatever she managed to put together did not offend.

But that aggravating man had threatened her confidence with his perfect tailoring, his beautiful waistcoats, and his ever-changing collection of watch fobs. What would he think of her simple, outdated costume?

"Where are you off to in such finery?" Nicholas asked.

"Out."

"I gathered as much. Out where? Or perhaps I should ask with whom?"

"I am going for a drive in the park."

"Good God. At the fashionable hour, too. This is indeed momentous. I cannot recall the last time you made such an appearance. And with whom will you be driving, may I ask? As your brother and erstwhile protector, I feel I should be allowed to know, don't you think?"

"Anthony Morehouse."

"No! You can't mean it." He stepped into the room. "Confess, Ed. Are you involved with that fellow?"

"Don't be ridiculous. Of course not."

"It could be dangerous, my girl. We are in a precarious position, what with him owning the *Cabinet* now. It would not be wise to let down your guard."

"I'm aware of that, Nickie. And you know how important the magazine is to me. You know I would never do anything to jeopardize that work."

"Forgive me, Ed. I do know that. And I do trust you. It's just that you have never shown an interest in any man since . . . well, in a long time. You've been away from the game for years, and Morehouse is a master player. As slick as they come. Don't let all that golden hair and roguish charm make a fool of you."

"Heavens, Nickie, you don't have much faith in my good sense, do you? I lost a wager with the man, that is all. And as payment, I must drive with him in the park."

"Another wager?" He shook his head and laughed. "Just like when you were children. I don't know who is playing off whom in this game of yours, but I think I will keep my nose out of it. Only first, tell me what he did to win this drive in the park."

"You will not credit it, Nickie, but he quoted

Mary Wollstonecraft to me as if he had committed *A Vindication* to memory. I even pulled a copy from the bookshelves and read along as he quoted certain passages word for word. I hadn't thought he could do it."

In fact, she had rather suspected he could, but not quite so thoroughly. When she had asked him to summarize in one sentence the main point Mary was trying make in *A Vindication*, he had replied without a moment of hesitation: "She believes that most women are fools because they have allowed the primary objective of their lives, and their educations, to center on how to please a man."

Edwina had never heard anyone put it in such bald terms, but that brief synopsis was actually spot on, and she had known in an instant that he had in fact read the book. Most detractors, who clearly had not read it, were outraged that Mary would dare to lash out at Man for making the life of Woman so miserable. But she was really more aggravated with her own sex for fostering, indeed for exploiting, the notion of females being the weaker sex. Anthony had understood the point completely.

Yes, Edwina had known the wager was set up for him to win, but she played along because . . . well, because he was a very attractive man and she saw no reason why she should not enjoy a bit of light flirtation. It *had* been a long time.

Edwina was not indifferent to men's admiration.

She simply had no inclination to deal with it. Normally she ignored it. Or rebuffed it, if it was rudely done. But she never let it affect her. Not since France. But now and then—rarely—a spark of interest surprised her and set off the tiniest pang of loneliness. Not for simple human companionship. She had that. But for something more. Something warm, something intimate.

Since Anthony Morehouse had first walked into her study, that rare spark of interest had been flaring brightly. Despite the fact that he hadn't become the man she had expected. Despite the fact that the bright, serious-minded boy she once knew seemed to have allowed all that was good in him to be corrupted. Despite the fact that he appeared to have made his way through the world on good luck and good looks. Despite all of these things, she'd discovered that the essential goodness of the boy still lay at the heart of the man. And she was as attracted to him now as she had been smitten as a schoolgirl.

"Take care, Ed," Nicholas said. "Morehouse is obviously more clever than we thought. Ah, I hear someone at the door. I believe the man has arrived. Allow me to escort you to him. And do stop fussing with that bonnet. You look very pretty. Any man would be proud to drive you in the park. But remember, Ed, you must try not to drop your guard. One slip and he may be on to us."

* * *

"You have made me a very popular fellow today, my dear," Tony said as he slowly maneuvered the phaeton through the crowded pathways of Hype Park. "At least I assume all those admiring eyes are not for my benefit."

"Perhaps it is your team that draws the eye," Edwina said. "I don't know when I have seen such a beautiful pair of grays."

"They are prime ones, aren't they? Won them off D'Aubney a few weeks ago."

"Fruits of another wager? I ought to have guessed as much."

"But I do not believe it is the grays drawing attention this afternoon," he said. "You look magnificent in that red spencer. Regal as a queen."

She shot him a skeptical glance, as though she did not believe his flattery. Could she really doubt her beauty?

"I feel rather queenlike," she said, "perched up so high above the rest. What on earth makes you want to drive such a dangerous-looking vehicle? Oh, but I have just answered my own question, have I not? You drive it *because* it is so dangerously high. The thrill of risk, I believe you said."

"That is one reason. There is, however, another reason, another thrill, that makes it worthwhile today. It is so high, it allowed me the pleasure of lifting you up into it. And I live in anticipation of the opportunity to lift you down again."

"Silly man."

But not so silly, in fact. Tony had indeed brought the high-perch phaeton precisely for that reason. He'd taken great pleasure in setting his hands about her waist, in getting a spectacular view of her long legs and the curve of her hip as he lifted her up into the seat. And catching a tantalizing glimpse of trim ankle and shapely calf when her skirts became momentarily tangled. He had already contrived a plan to get a closer look, if he was lucky.

And he generally was.

"You do not often drive or walk in the park during this hour, do you?" he asked.

"No, I don't. But how would you know that?"

"You are being admired as something new. A beautiful curiosity no one has seen before. Hold steady. We're about to be waylaid."

Sir Crispin Hollis was the first to approach and request an introduction. Within minutes, several of Tony's acquaintances had made their way to the phaeton to discover the identity of the lovely black-haired woman at his side. He had to quash a few remarks before the conversation took an unfortunate turn: Several men assumed Edwina was his mistress, simply because she was not in the first bloom of youth.

They were not the only ones who were under that misapprehension. Respectable ladies came nowhere near the phaeton. Tony began to think it had not been such a wise idea to put Edwina through such scrutiny. He had only meant to show her off a bit, to inspire jealousy among his friends by having such a beauty at his side. Unfortunately, he had not considered that it might be a disservice to her, that her respectability might be questioned.

Edwina chatted easily with the gentlemen surrounding the carriage. Her intriguingly husky voice added weight to the notion that she might be his latest paramour. She appeared unconscious of its seductive effect while she sat supremely elegant and composed on her high perch. Tony could not dismiss the pang of chagrin that he had forced this upon her.

Suddenly he saw an opportunity for rescue.

Only a few vehicles separated them from an elegant barouche carrying his sister, Sylvia, and her friend, Lady Walbourne. He waved at Sylvia, who scowled at him, gave a tiny shake of her head, and looked away. No doubt she, too, assumed the worst about Edwina.

"Excuse me, gentlemen," he said to the crowd at large, "but you must allow us to pass. My sister is just over there and I wish to introduce her to Miss Parrish."

He wasted no time in maneuvering the phaeton through the crowd, turning it in the direction the barouche had taken. Thankfully it was not High Season, when he would not have been able to move at all.

Edwina sent him a smile so warm his stomach did a little flip-flop and almost caused him to steer the carriage straight into a passing curricle.

"Thank you," she said in a throaty whisper. "I was beginning to feel a tad overwhelmed."

"I know. I do apologize. I hadn't meant—"

"For them to think I am your mistress? That I am not quite respectable?"

So, she *had* understood.

"I'm sorry, my dear," he said. "I hadn't expected that, though I suppose I ought to have done. If only you were hag-faced, they would have left you alone."

"If I were hag-faced no one would have thought me your mistress. Nor would they if I were ten years younger. But do not concern yourself. I am quite accustomed to men thinking I am something I am not."

She shot him a significant glance, just in case he missed her meaning. He did not.

"But I shall put things to right," he said, "by introducing you to my extremely respectable sister."

"What? You really do see your sister? I thought that was merely a ploy to get away."

"No, she's right here, trying her damnedest to avoid me." He edged the phaeton up close to the barouche and pulled the team to a halt. "Hullo, Sylvie. Didn't know you were in Town. What a charming surprise to run into you. And Lady Walbourne."

Sylvia turned to him and frowned, displeasure darkening her blue eyes. "Anthony." She acknowledged him with a nod but invited no further communication.

"You must allow me to present to you Miss Edwina Parrish. Miss Parrish, this is my sister Sylvia, Lady Netherton, and Lady Walbourne."

"I am pleased to meet you both," Edwina said.

Sylvia nodded, risked a tiny smile, and shot Tony a questioning look.

"You are no doubt too young to remember," he said, "but we knew Miss Parrish as children. Her grandfather owned Rosedale and she came to visit during the summers."

Sylvia's eyes brightened. "Rosedale? But that's the estate that runs right up against Handsley." She turned to Lady Walbourne. "It's where we grew up." Returning her attention to Edwina, she said, "Forgive me for not remembering you, but how lovely to meet someone from home."

"There is no reason you should remember me," Edwina said. "I was only at Rosedale a few times, but I remember it fondly. I knew your brother well"—she tilted her head in Tony's direction—"but I seem to recall that you were too young to tag along with us, and your older brother, in the way of all adolescent boys, wanted nothing to do with two children."

"Yes, that sounds about right." Sylvia's face

broke into a broad smile, and Tony knew the afternoon had been recovered.

"Do you stay in Town for the summer?" Sylvia
asked.

"Business keeps me in Town," Edwina said, and
slanted a glance at Tony, "but I do try to get back to
our family home in the Peak whenever I can. I prefer the country, in fact."

Hmm. Tony hadn't known that. And his wager
was keeping her in Town this summer. He seemed
to be doing everything in his power to make this
woman dislike him.

"I'm afraid I am here only briefly before I must
return to Netherton and the children." Sylvia lowered her voice to a conspiratorial whisper. "I only
came to do some shopping and visit my modiste
while the competition for her time is less fierce.
Since I leave in a few days, I fear I shan't be able to
invite you to call. But you must allow me to do so
when we return in the spring."

"Thank you, Lady Netherton," Edwina said. "I
would be honored."

"Good to see you, Sylvie," Tony said, "but we
must be on our way. Give my regards to Netherton
and the boys. And tell young Rupert I haven't forgotten he still owes me tuppence. I shall play him
for it when next I see him."

"Wretched man! Can you believe it, Miss Parrish? My brother has taught my seven-year-old son

to play Hazard. And now the boy plays for ha'pennies with all the stable boys on the estate. I really ought to bar the door when Anthony comes to visit, but the boys adore him, so there is nothing for it."

"I merely assist in providing the boy with a useful education." The grays began to dance impatiently and Tony took a firm grip on the reins. "We must be off, Sylvie. My team grows restless. Lady Walbourne, a pleasure."

"I shall wish you both a good day, then," Sylvia said. "Oh, and Anthony, you really should pay a call on Mother. She claims not to have seen you for months. Good-bye, Miss Parrish."

Tony flicked the reins and set the team to a slow trot. "I've had quite enough of this throng. Let us take one of the less frequented paths."

"Thank you again," Edwina said. "It was very kind of you to introduce me to Lady Netherton, and especially kind of her to suggest I might call upon her in the spring. She resembles you a great deal, you know. She's very pretty."

"The Morehouse coloring looks better on her. And she got the big, cornflower blue eyes, while I got only the paltry gray. Only think of the hearts I could have broken with those blue eyes."

"I suspect you've broken plenty of hearts with your gray eyes."

"Do you? I shall take that as a compliment,

whether it was meant so or not. What about you, Edwina? How many hearts have you broken with those dark eyes? Besides my own thirteen-year-old heart, that is?"

"I never broke your heart, Mr. Morehouse, nor anyone else's. I'm not a heart-breaking sort of female."

"You've been reading too much Wollstonecraft."

"Not as much as you, apparently. Why do I get the suspicion you studied up on her just so you could maneuver me into that wager?"

"A good gamester always knows when to play his hand." He tugged the reins gently and turned the team onto a new path.

"Speaking of hands," she said, "I don't suppose you'd give me a chance at the ribbons?"

He turned to her and smiled. "You wish to drive my highflyer? I don't think so. It is much too *dangerous*."

"This path is almost deserted. Even if I was not a skilled driver I would be unlikely to plow into another carriage. And as it happens, I am a very skilled driver."

"Have you ever driven a high-perch phaeton?"

"No, but—"

"Then you would surely overturn us or careen us off the path."

"I would not."

"Would you like to bet on it?"

She shook her head and smiled. "You never change, do you? Still a twelve-year-old boy at heart. Well, I have grown up. I was not looking for another wager. I just thought it might be fun to drive this ridiculous vehicle. But never mind."

"Come now, Eddie, I thought you were always up to any challenge. A gamester at heart, whether you admit it or not."

"I admit to no such thing. I suppose I have a bit of a competitive nature, but I like to win. Unlike you, I don't accept a challenge merely for the thrill of risking it all."

"Ah, but aren't you risking it all with our little wager over the *Cabinet*?"

She gave a little snort. "You forced me into that. I had no choice but to accept your terms."

"And yet you haven't even heard my terms for this challenge. It might be worth your while."

"I doubt it."

"Then you name the terms. Within reason, of course."

She turned to him. "And what does that mean?"

"That you cannot overturn our primary wager, or change the terms of that wager with a secondary one."

"But I may name anything else as stakes?"

He thought for a moment and considered how bad she could possibly make it. But since he didn't plan on losing, it hardly mattered.

"Yes," he said, "you may name anything. I call the challenge, you name the stakes."

"You tempt me, sir. But first let me hear the challenge. In detail, if you please."

"All right." He pulled the team to a halt. "See that clump of trees ahead, to the left of the deer pond? If you can make it there in . . . oh, let's say five minutes. If you can drive the phaeton to that spot within five minutes, by my watch, without veering off the established path or overturning the rig, then you win."

"Five minutes? It is to be a race, then? Not simply a test of my skill at the ribbons?"

"Driving skill includes managing a certain speed. What sort of victory would it be if you took half an hour to go such a short distance? The element of time, even one as conservative as I've suggested, gives an added spark to the challenge."

Her brow furrowed as she studied the path and the distance, clearly trying to determine if this was a fool's wager. Tony did not doubt, however, that she would accept the challenge. It was not an unreasonable objective. In fact, he had gauged it to be an easy victory.

"Do you accept the wager?"

She took a deep breath and said, "Yes."

"Excellent. And what stakes would you like?"

"If I win, I want to be allowed to hire another assistant editor to help Miss Armitage."

"Hmm. That doesn't precisely alter the terms of

the original wager, but it might make it easier for you to win."

"It would make my life less hectic whether I win that wager or not. There are only so many hours in the day, and the requirements of the magazine fill them all. Even this little outing is biting into production hours. I need help, but cannot fund additional staff on my own. You, sir, hold the purse strings."

"All right. If you win, you get to hire an additional editor. And if *I* win, I get to select the editor."

She sent him a quizzical look. "You have someone in mind, no doubt."

"Possibly. But the fact is, whether you win or lose, you get a new editor. I really do not see you how you can pass up such an offer."

"You're up to some trick or other, aren't you, to get me back for the Minerva? There must be something more in it for you besides getting the right to choose my editor."

"You're right. The editor is for you. There ought to be something for me if you lose. Something personal, I think."

She looked at him warily, though a glint of amusement lit her eyes. "Oh, dear. I'm not going to like this, am I?"

"I don't know. You might." He gave her his most seductive smile, and she actually laughed.

"What is it, then?"

"I want your stocking," he said.

Her eyes grew wide. "My stocking?"

"Yes. If you lose, I want one of your stockings. Not one neatly tucked away in a drawer in your bedchamber. I want one of the stockings you are wearing right now."

Edwina made a choking sound, somewhere between a groan and a laugh, as though she wasn't quite sure whether to be outraged or amused.

"And I suppose you'd want to take it off yourself as well," she said.

"No, no. Nothing so improper as that. But I do want to watch *you* take it off."

She laughed again, and he sent up a silent prayer of thanks that she was not one of those vaporish spinsters who fell into a swoon at any type of suggestive remark. He still wasn't sure if she was the sort of Modern Woman that Ian had suggested, but she clearly was not a prudish bluestocking either. Tony was determined to discover exactly what type of woman she was, and just how far he could push her.

"You, sir, are incorrigible," she said, still smiling.

"So I've been told. Are we agreed on the stakes, then?"

"I suppose so. Since I intend to win, it hardly matters. Now I suppose we must wait while you jot it all down in your little book?"

"Let us dispense with formalities this time, shall we? A simple handshake will seal the bargain."

He held out his hand and Edwina gripped it like

a man, as he ought to have expected. But he turned over their clasped hands and brought hers to his lips.

"Here's to victory," he said.

Chapter 6

"**A** bee!" he shouted.

Edwina recoiled as Anthony's hands fluttered in front of her face. She gripped the reins tightly.

"There he is. Look out!" Suddenly Anthony's hands were brushing at her bonnet, and before she knew what had happened, the bonnet had been knocked askew and covered her face. She couldn't see!

She involuntarily jerked on the reins and felt the team fidget uncertainly. She reached up with one hand to adjust the bonnet, but the team tugged at the reins and veered left, and she felt control slip away. Without a clue where she was going, but fairly certain it was not toward the specified goal, she slowly pulled back and brought the team to a halt.

"You wretched man." She reached up to set her bonnet to rights and felt Anthony take the reins away so she could use both hands. She untied the ribbon beneath her chin and pushed the bonnet back into place. "You did that on purpose."

"Did what? Set a bee on you?"

"I never saw a bee. You made that up to distract me so I would lose."

She saw now that the phaeton had veered off the path and come to a halt some yards before the group of trees that had marked her goal. She had indeed lost the wager. And it was all his fault.

"I assure you, madam, there was a bee. It was no doubt attracted to the flowers on your bonnet. I only meant to brush him away and keep you out of harm's way."

"The flowers on my bonnet are silk, sir, and of no interest to bees. You tricked me into losing."

"Now, why do those words sound so familiar? Wait a moment. It's coming back to me. Ah, yes. I believe I spoke those very words to you when you pulled that stunt with the Minerva."

"I did not trick you, sir. I outmaneuvered you. This case is not at all the same. You had to resort to clumsy efforts to blind me so that I would lose." She struggled to conceal a smile. "It does not seem at all sporting to me and shows no finesse whatsoever."

All of a sudden, the notion that he would go to

such lengths, such obvious trickery, to win her stocking caused her to give in to an irrepressible gurgle of mirth. She began to laugh.

His laughter joined hers, and it was a rich, melodious sound, full of pleasure. His gray eyes turned silvery, twinkling with merriment, and crinkled up at the corners in fans of tiny creases. He had the look of a man who laughed frequently, who took great delight in the unexpected little joys of life.

"I suppose you'll be wanting my stocking now," she said.

"I should think it is the least you could do after I saved you from a vicious bee attack."

"Vicious, was he?"

"Huge. Ferocious. I've never seen such a bee in all my life."

"I do not doubt it. Well, I am not going to argue with you. You will see that I can be a gracious loser despite the unfair tactics you employed. I still get my additional editor, do I not?"

"You do. And I will have your stocking now, madam."

"Here? Now?"

"Why not? No one is around. We are quite off the usual paths. I will have it now, if you please."

"Oh, you are the *most* provoking man."

Edwina reached down and pulled her full skirts over the knee farthest from his view.

"The other one, if you please."

She ought to have known that ploy would not

work. She readjusted her skirts, then slowly raised them over her other knee. He gave the tiniest intake of breath and she looked up to see his gaze fixed on her exposed leg.

And all at once she felt rather exhilarated, and rather daring. A little thrill ran through her that she could entice, even seduce if she wanted to, this exceedingly attractive man. It had been a very long time since Edwina had allowed a man's interest to interest her. She had almost forgotten how enjoyable a little mild flirtation could be. It made her feel young again. Invigorated.

She was going to have a bit of highly improper fun with Anthony Morehouse.

She bent down and removed her shoe, then hitched her skirt up slightly above the knee to reveal her garter. She made a slow business of untying it, then held it up and allowed the ends to flutter softly in the breeze.

"I'll take that as well," Anthony said.

Edwina looked at him. "That was not part of our bargain, sir."

"But you will have no need of it now, will you?" He held out a hand, palm up.

Edwina sighed. It was one of her favorite garters, but she dropped the length of embroidered silk ribbon into his hand. His fingers curled around it.

"You collect them as trophies, no doubt."

He smiled and said, "Proceed, if you please."

She began to roll down the top of the stocking

over her knee. Fortunately, she had worn a good silk pair today, pale pink with yellow clocking. Unfortunately, they had been quite expensive.

She watched Anthony as she slowly, slowly pulled down the stocking and exposed her bare leg to the cool afternoon air. His eyes never left her leg, and the look in them was so warm it was almost as though he physically touched her. She gave an involuntary shudder.

She continued the slow, deliberate peeling away of the silk, stroking one hand down the length of her leg to protect the delicate fabric. Anthony was breathing through his mouth, and the sound of it had become quick and slightly hoarse. Edwina smiled.

When she reached her foot, she almost instinctively hoisted it onto her knee as she did each night in the privacy of her bed chamber when removing her stockings. But that would not do here. Instead, she merely raised up onto her toes, pushed the stocking over her foot, and pulled it off. She allowed the pink silk to brush along the length of her leg as she pulled it up into her lap.

The cold floor beneath her bare foot jolted her from seductive game playing and back to earth. Lord, what had gotten into her? She quickly dropped her skirts over her knee and worked her foot back into its slipper. She looked up at Anthony and hoped to heaven she was not blushing. She crumpled the stocking into a ball and placed it into his outstretched hand.

He locked his gaze with hers while he brought the silk first to his nose, then to his lips. His mouth cocked up into a lopsided grin and he stuffed the stocking into an inside coat pocket, where she could see the embroidered ribbon of her favorite garter peeking out.

"Thank you," he said. "That was certainly worth doing battle with a vicious bee."

"I sincerely hope you will not be parading my undergarments about in public, sir, flaunting them before your friends in some sort of victorious display."

He lowered his voice to a seductive croon. "I have no intention of sharing them with anyone, I assure you."

He flicked the reins and put the restless horses at a slow trot as he steered the phaeton back onto the path.

"And you shall have your new editorial assistant within the week," he said in a more normal voice. "I know just the woman to help bring the *Cabinet* up to its full potential."

The tiniest prickling of alarm danced down her spine. "Who is she?"

"A good friend. Her name is Flora Gallagher."

Edwina's breath caught. "Flora Gallagher? *The* Flora Gallagher?"

"I am not aware of another woman by that name,

so I can only assume she is *the* Flora Gallagher."

"Well then, she will not be working for my magazine."

"Ah, but you are forgetting two very important points, my dear. In the first place, it is *my* magazine. In the second place, you have just lost the right to choose your own assistant."

"Then I shall have no assistant at all, thank you very much. I would rather work twice as hard than have that . . . that woman on my staff."

"Too late to change the game now, Edwina. You shall have a new assistant, and she shall be of my choosing. I choose Flora."

"You go too far, sir. That woman has no place in a respectable concern. Imagine if readers became aware that the notorious Mrs. Gallagher was associated with the *Cabinet*. We would be flooded with cancelled subscriptions. Or perhaps that is your plan? A neat maneuver to insure that I lose the wager for the *Cabinet*?"

"I am surprised at you, Edwina. I thought a woman of your intelligence and social conscience would not be so quick to judge the choices of one less fortunate than herself."

"Less fortunate? She is a notorious courtesan with a string of wealthy and titled lovers."

Including Anthony?

"And she chose that life rather than starve on the streets," he said. "Unlike you, she was not born to a position where many choices were available to her. I should think you would be pleased to help lift up such a woman into more respectable employment. I thought you were the champion of the oppressed. Where is your compassion now?"

Damn the man. He knew exactly how to play upon her weakest nature. She did indeed deplore the wretched life some women were forced to lead. She could not tell Anthony, but among other activities sponsored by the siphoned profits of the *Cabinet* was a school where such girls and women were taught to read and write, and were provided with rudimentary skills that would help them find honest employment.

But Flora Gallagher?

"You cannot tell me," she said, "that whatever small salary we may be able to pay her would compensate for . . . for all that other income she is accustomed to?"

"As a matter of fact," he said, "Flora has retired. She was unfortunately engaged in a profession that is not kind to women of a certain age. So she has removed herself from the lists, as it were, but not without first insuring that her future is secure. If I am not mistaken, Flora is quite a wealthy woman."

"Then why on earth would she be interested in working for a ladies' magazine?"

"Because she is bored. She has told me again and again that she wants something to do with her time, something useful. The *Cabinet* will be perfect for her. She can be your fashion editor."

"Oh, no. Not fashion again."

"Flora has a keen eye for fashion and is on intimate terms with all the best dressmakers in town. Her fashion advice could draw in new readers. New *subscribers*."

Damn it all, he was manipulating her again. He knew very well that she was having trouble increasing subscription numbers.

"As I have suggested before," he said, "a single fashion plate in each issue is not enough. Women want to read about trends, new fabrics, new accessories, new ways to dress their hair. Flora could handle all of that. In fact, she would probably enjoy nothing better."

"You are determined to undermine all my hard work, aren't you? All the years I've spent making the *Cabinet* into a fine publication with good, solid, rational content. And you want to destroy it by expanding frivolous topics that appeal to a woman's vanity rather than her intellect."

"You already include 'frivolous' topics. You have the small fashion section. You have sentimental poetry and romantic fiction. You have the Busybody, and I cannot imagine anything more frivolous than the advice she hands out. What difference would a bit more fashion make?"

"A big difference. It would tilt the magazine into a direction I have strenuously avoided. It would compromise all my objectives."

"It would bring you more subscribers."

"I don't care. It would not be worth it."

He gave her a sideways glance. "If you will not accept Flora, if you default on our agreement, then I suppose I shall simply have to be allowed to examine those account books you are so careful to keep from me."

She gave a quick intake of breath. "The account books?"

"It's that or Flora. If you default on one wager, then I should be allowed to default on another."

Edwina sighed in defeat. He had her, the devil. "All right. I will agree to bringing in Flora Gallagher. But under extreme protest."

He turned to her and smiled. "Good decision. Besides, I will wager you'll like Flora."

"Don't bet on it."

"He backed me into a corner, Pru. I had no choice."

"But . . . *Mrs. Gallagher*? Oh, my."

Prudence's blue eyes had grown round as saucers. She had said little more than "Oh, my," since Edwina had told her of the new "fashion editor" who would be coming by that morning with Anthony. She was clearly awed by the very idea of Mrs. Gallagher. Shy little Prudence would have no occasion to run into a woman like that.

The odd thing was, Prudence seemed not to be

outraged at having that woman thrust into their business. On the contrary, she seemed fascinated. Even a little excited.

"Well, we must make the best of it," Edwina said. "Mr. Morehouse is determined to foist a fashion editor upon us, and so we must learn to work with . . . that woman. But we must also be as discreet as possible about it. I will not have it bandied about that a notorious member of the demimonde is associated with the *Cabinet*."

"She *is* rather scandalous, is she not?"

"Indeed."

"She has been associated with quite a few gentlemen, I think."

"Yes, she has."

Prudence lowered her voice almost to a whisper. "Do you suppose that Mr. Morehouse . . ."

"Is one of her lovers? I believe it is quite possible. More than possible. It is almost certain." She had known it to be true the moment he'd mentioned Mrs. Gallagher as his *friend*.

"Oh, my."

"How else would he be acquainted with such a woman?"

"I'm sure I don't know. He told you she had retired?"

Edwina nodded.

"So perhaps he *once* was her lover but is no longer."

ONCE A SCOUNDREL   119

"Perhaps. It hardly matters, does it?" Except that it was one more reason she did not wish to have that woman on her staff.

"Well, at least it means that . . . well, that he is available. That is, not otherwise involved."

Edwina glared across the desk at her friend. "Pru, you are not getting ideas in your head about that man, are you? I hope you are not setting your cap for him."

"Me?" Prudence's voice came out in a squeak and she blushed scarlet. "And Mr. Morehouse? Heavens, no. Not him. I mean, not anyone else, either, of course."

Her blush deepened, spread to her neck and ears. She was clearly embarrassed. Was there someone she fancied? Quiet, unassuming Prudence who never went anywhere or met anyone new? Who could have caught her attention?

"What a foolish notion," Prudence continued. "A glorious creature like Mr. Morehouse with the likes of me?"

"You think him glorious, do you?"

"Well, don't you? He's so handsome. I mean, all that golden hair and those blue eyes. Although they're really more gray than blue, aren't they? And the beautiful clothes and the perfect manners. And all those elegant watch fobs. Yes, I think him quite dazzling, in fact." Prudence gave an embarrassed little giggle. She was not often so voluble. Maybe there wasn't someone else. Maybe she did indeed have a tendre for Anthony. "He is quite as beautiful as you are," she added. "What a striking couple you would make."

"Pru!"

"Well, it's true. And I am persuaded you are not entirely indifferent to him."

So *that* was what was on her mind. Not fantasies of her own after all. "My girl, you have been reading too many of Simon's romantic stories. I have no interest in Anthony Morehouse." It was not precisely a lie. She simply wasn't interested in him in the way Prudence thought. Not really.

"Oh, pooh." Prudence gave a wave of dismissal. "I've seen that look in your eye when you're with him."

"A look of pure aggravation most of the time."

"Well, I shan't press you about it. But if you ask me, he's a perfectly charming man who is obviously taken with you. It would do you no harm to let down your guard for once."

It was because she'd let her guard down that Edwina was now about to be saddled with a retired courtesan as her fashion editor. She had to admit, though, that it had been most satisfying to realize the effect she'd had on Anthony when she removed her stocking. She had quite enjoyed it.

It might be amusing to let her guard down again, once or twice. She was not a green girl, after all.

Prudence was right; it would do no harm. So long as she remained the one in control, she wondered how far she would allow their little flirtation to go.

Before she could ponder the answer to that question, voices in the hallway announced the arrival of Anthony and Mrs. Gallagher.

Anthony had been right about their infamous new fashion editor. Edwina liked her at once.

The upstairs drawing room, where they gathered for tea and cakes, seemed smaller than usual, through the sheer force of Mrs. Gallagher's personality. Her voice was not loud, but it was commanding in a way that was almost seductive. Something about her manner made one feel important and interesting and . . . cheered. Edwina found herself smiling throughout their conversation.

She could see how men were drawn to Mrs. Gallagher. Though not beautiful, she was strikingly handsome, even though her bright red hair owed none of its glory to nature and she wore more cosmetics than was necessary. She had an engaging smile, and she was beautifully dressed. Here was a woman who definitely knew a thing or two about fashion.

Flora, as she insisted on being called, had overwhelmed her and Prudence with profuse and repeated expressions of appreciation for the opportunity to serve as fashion editor for the *Cabi-*

net. But she was in no way cloying, and her enthusiasm seemed absolutely genuine. And she was full of ideas.

"I feel it is a very wise move," she said, "to expand your fashion coverage."

Edwina shot a speaking glance in Anthony's direction. "It was a difficult decision, but I feel *forced* to make changes in that direction."

"I can see how you would be," Flora said. "*The Lady's Magazine* has expanded its fashion reports and everyone I know reads them religiously. *The Lady's Monthly Museum* has two fashion plates to your one. Very little description, though, so it would be easy enough to best them in that regard. And, of course, there is the *Gallery of Fashion*."

"I have no intention," Edwina said, "of competing with that publication."

"Quite right," Flora said. "It is much too grand and caters to a very elite readership. You will want to appeal to the common woman—the shopkeeper's wife, the wool merchant's daughter. She is the one most interested in what the women of the *haut ton* are wearing."

Edwina sighed. "I suppose you are correct."

"Of course I am." Flora gave a rueful smile. "And that means including more than brief descriptions of plates reworked from French publications. Ideally, you must have original prints drawn from life. It is fine to know what the ladies of Paris are wearing this season, but it is quite another thing to know what the ladies of London are wearing, who made their gowns, where the fabrics were obtained, and so on. You will woo more readers with news of the gowns seen at Covent Garden or in Hyde Park than you will in describing the *élégantes* of Longchamps."

"Now, didn't I tell you Flora would be the perfect fashion editor?" Anthony rose to his feet, the movement causing his fobs to bounce against one another in a jangling chorus. "She obviously knows precisely what must be done. As owner of this operation, I give her my full support in this endeavor." He sent Edwina a look that clearly said he expected her to do the same.

"I shall leave you ladies to discuss the details."

Edwina rose to see him out, but he held up a hand to forestall her. "No need to disturb yourself. I know the way."

What he meant was that he would give Edwina no opportunity to bend his ear in private with complaints about Flora's ideas. He bowed to all three of them, then made a hasty exit.

"The blackguard," Edwina muttered.

"Oh, dear," Flora said. "I am guessing that none of this was your idea after all."

Edwina returned to her place on the settee. "Not exactly," she said and offered a sheepish smile. "I merely asked for some general assistance. Pru and I are quite swamped with work. It was Mr. Morehouse who insisted the assistance be in the form of a fashion editor."

"And so I have been forced upon you. Poor dear." She gave a musical little chuckle. "What a shock that must have been."

Edwina broadened her smile. "It was, actually. But I have been considering all that you have said. Do you really think we could substantially increase subscriptions if we added fashion reports?"

"Without question. Is that important?"

Prudence, who had been quiet as a mouse, choked on her tea. Flora turned to her and raised her brows.

"It is extremely important," Prudence said in a diffident tone. "Edwina will lose the *Cabinet* otherwise."

"What's this?" Flora gave Edwina a questioning look. "Lose the *Cabinet*? Perhaps I misunderstood, but I was under the impression that Anthony was the owner."

"He is," Edwina said. "Unless I can add two thousand new subscribers before November."

Flora groaned. "Do not tell me he has wagered you for ownership?"

"He has."

"A blackguard, indeed," Flora said with a shake of her head. "The boy is forever concocting some foolish wager or other. How utterly contemptible that he should play such games with you."

"My sentiments exactly," Edwina said. "But it is the only way I can ever hope to own the magazine outright. And I want that—and the control it would bring—more than anything in the world."

Flora regarded her thoughtfully. "Well, then," she said, "it seems to me Anthony is going out of his way to help you win this wager. For I will guarantee that if you add fashion reporting and more prints to the *Cabinet*, you will be more likely than not to reach your goal."

"I rather suspect Mr. Morehouse's intentions were to vex me as much as possible," Edwina said. She also believed he truly wanted to win their wager, just to pay her back for all those times she bested him as a child. And he wanted the Minerva back. He had made that very clear. Though his actions may sound helpful to some, she suspected he knew Flora's name would somehow, inevitably, become associated with the *Cabinet* and result in reducing rather than increasing subscriptions.

"However," she said, "I am forced to agree with you in regard to the fashion reports, as much as it pains me to say so."

"A magazine of fashion is not what you had in mind, is it?" Flora asked.

"Not in the least."

"And yet the title is *The Ladies' Fashionable Cabinet*."

"The title was already well established when I inherited the editorial reins from my great aunt. But we have worked so hard to improve the publication, to make it into something more than just a bit of throwaway amusement. Mr. Morehouse, however, will not listen. He does not understand."

Flora put down her teacup, rose from her chair, and came to sit beside Edwina on the settee. "But I believe I do understand," she said. "I have read the *Cabinet* for some time now. It is quite clear to me what you are trying to do."

"It is?" Prudence asked, her voice rising almost to a squeak.

"Yes, of course. The messages are subtle, but quite consistent. You want women to be strong, to think for themselves, to seek and receive proper education, and to take more control of their lives."

Edwina stared at Flora in open-mouthed astonishment. This woman, this infamous courtesan, had in one sentence precisely defined the objective of *Cabinet*. How extraordinary.

"Do not be so shocked," Flora said, as though reading her thoughts, "that a woman like me would catch on to your intent. I am more like you than you would think, Edwina. After all, we are both self-reliant women, doing what we can to take control of our lives. I have certainly lived my life on my own terms, have I not? I have never been tied to one man, but instead have used men in order to maintain my independence. You'd be surprised how many women who've chosen the same road as I have are on your side, my dear. We support the same reforms you do."

"Reforms?" Prudence darted a wary glance in Edwina's direction.

Prudence was not the only one thinking of the other activities supported by the *Cabinet*. But Flora couldn't possibly know about that. Could she?

"Granted," Flora continued, "you do not preach specific reform in the pages of the magazine, thank heaven. I fear you would have few readers if you did so. But social reform is certainly at the heart of what you publish, when you encourage education for women, when you encourage a certain level of independence. All I am saying is that a great many women like me agree with you. We just go about things differently." She gave a little laugh, tinged with self-mockery. "For example, we can subtly influence a man's opinions in ways his wife never could."

"I have always believed," Edwina said, "in the importance of educating women on social and political issues for precisely that reason—so they can in some way influence their men who, after all, have the vote."

She could not believe she was having this conversation with a renowned prostitute. It was almost bizarre.

"Just because women do not have political power," Edwina continued, "does not mean we have no power at all. We are not merely ornamental objects. We have brains. We must learn to use them."

"Brains," Flora said, "are not incompatible with beauty, as you so eloquently demonstrate, my dear. You have been most wise to include in the magazine at least a modicum of those less serious topics, like fashion, that help to entice women to read the rest."

"But you and Mr. Morehouse seem to agree that I must make further compromises in terms of content."

"Not necessarily," Flora continued. "You already accept the inescapable need, however distasteful, to appeal to that least attractive aspect of the female character: vanity. Now, all that is required is to escalate the seduction of your audience with a greater focus on fashion. It will bring in more readers, which will bring in more money. Once the revenues have increased, you could put them toward the more enlightened content you desire. It is the way of business."

"Oh, my," Prudence said. "That sounds so . . . so reasonable."

Flora laughed. "Do not sound so surprised, child. A woman in my position must have a head for business, or at least for strategy, if she is to survive. And it seems to me the best strategy in this case is to entice new readers with a little fashion, a little glamour, a brief glimpse into the lives of the *ton*. As they flip the pages, many of them will read the other content. Over time, they will subtly be converted to your way of thinking."

"Oh, Edwina," Prudence said, "I think Flora is absolutely right. Just think of how many more readers we could influence. It is so exciting!"

Edwina smiled. "All right. You are both extremely persuasive. Though in my heart I believe women are capable of being as delighted by the rational, I will allow a temporary expansion of the frivolous. As an experiment only. I will not, however, allow slander or gossip or scandal into the pages of the *Cabinet*. I do have my limits. You were saying, Flora, that we need more prints—"

"Original ones, not copies."

"—which means finding a new artist and perhaps even a new engraver. That will take time. And where are they going to find these fashions they will draw from life?"

"Leave that to me," Flora said.

"But in the meantime," Prudence piped up, "Flora could begin on the reports themselves, even if we don't yet have the fashion plates to go with them. Perhaps for the next issue?"

Edwina could not recall when she'd seen docile, quiet little Prudence so enthusiastic. Between the two of them—three, counting Anthony—Edwina felt as if she had been hauled into a fast-moving stagecoach barreling down the road to some unknown destination. She hated having things spin out of her control. The only thing to be done was to take charge.

"Yes, Flora," she said, "I think it is best that we

start right away. I will leave it to you, with Pru's help, to investigate new artists and engravers. We have an issue going to print this week. Imber, our printer, will want to murder me, but do you think you could create a report within the next day or so?"

"I will do my best. I am going to the theater this evening." She flashed a mischievous grin. "I shall take notes."

"Pru, we could pull the biographical sketch of Mrs. Montague and replace it with Flora's report. What do you think?"

"I think it's a splendid idea."

"All right, then. Let's get to work."

Two weeks later, *The Ladies' Fashionable Cabinet* lived up to its name for the first time in years. Flora's fashion report, under the pseudonym Vestis Elegantis, was slightly gossipy without being scandalous, included an amazing amount of detail on the various fashions seen about town, and was a huge success. Booksellers had reported all nonsubscription issues sold out within days, and every one of them had increased their orders for the following month. A stack of letters had arrived from readers asking for more fashion information, and a significant number of new subscriptions had been received. Edwina had moved one step closer to reaching her goal.

She turned to Flora, who was leaning over the desk to read the subscription list. "All right, I'm convinced," Edwina said. "Now, what else can we do to win this damned wager?"

Chapter 7

"You are, of course, coming to Newmarket with us, Morehouse," Lord Skiffington said. "I have the sharpest little gelding in one of the races, and have engaged Tibbets to ride him. It's a sure thing, I tell you."

"It sounds most intriguing, Skiffy," Tony said, "but I believe I will pass."

He had no intention of making the trip to Newmarket. Those one-day jaunts almost always stretched into three or four days of serious carousing, and he had no intention of being away from London that long. Away from Edwina and the *Cabinet*. If anyone were to ask, it was because he wanted to keep an eye on his new investment. In fact, he simply did not wish to be away from Edwina just now, when he was making such progress in his campaign to break down her defenses.

Skiffy leaned back and peered at Tony through his quizzing glass. "You're not coming?"

"Afraid not, old man."

His lordship looked around the table at the others who'd gathered at the coffeehouse after a long evening at a local gaming hell. "Quick, someone call a physician. The boy is not well."

"I have noticed of late," Lord D'Aubney said, "that Morehouse is often conspicuously absent from events and locales where one would normally expect to see him. Indeed I have been asking myself what could be the cause of such uncharacteristic behavior. Only one answer, of course, comes to mind."

"A woman," Ian Fordyce offered. He caught Tony's eye and winked.

"Oh, I say," Sir Crispin Hollis said, "it must be that dashing creature he's been driving in the park."

"A dashing creature?" Skiffy moved his chair closer to Tony. "You sly dog. Who is she? Another new highflyer to warm your bed?"

"Nothing of the sort," Tony said.

"It's that bluestocking editor, isn't it?" Ian said. "You've set her up as your mistress."

"I most certainly have not." *Not yet, anyway.*

"But she's the one," Ian persisted, "you've been driving in the park, is she not?"

"I've driven her once or twice." He had actually managed to get Edwina to agree to another drive with him without requiring a wager to do so. After that business with the stocking, he simply had to see her again, alone, away from the trappings of the magazine. They had actually spent a very pleasant afternoon together, with only a minimum of teasing and wrangling and sniping. They had spoken mostly of their days in Suffolk as children, and he also had allowed her to ramble on about her favorite issues of reform and education. He was trying to contrive an occasion where he could take her out in the evening, but the right situation had yet to present itself.

"You've been driving with the bluestocking?" Skiffy asked.

"Wasn't a bluestocking I saw," Sir Crispin said. "Nothing of the sort. The woman was an out-and-out beauty. A real picture. Not a young chit, either. And with the voice of a siren, as provocative as a rumpled bed. Thought she was Morehouse's mistress until I saw him introduce her to his sister."

"Miss Parrish is a respectable lady," Tony said, "so take care what you say about her."

"Oh, Lord, Tony." Ian took a long swallow from a tankard of ale and wiped his mouth with the back of his hand. "You've gone and done it, haven't you? You've lost your head. You're smitten with the woman."

"So what if he is?" D'Aubney asked. "If the woman's a beauty—"

"She is that," Sir Crispin said.

"—then what's the problem? He isn't going to marry the bird, after all." D'Aubney turned to Tony. "Are you?"

"God's teeth," Tony said. "Can't a fellow engage in a bit of flirtation without answering to the lot of you?"

"I told you that magazine would be nothing but trouble," Ian said. "The woman's put you under some sort of spell. She's probably got you doing more work on the damned ragsheet, hasn't she? I tell you, she's playing you for the fool, my friend. You really ought to stay away from her until . . . well, until everything regarding the magazine is resolved."

"If I had a woman like that," Sir Crispin said, "you couldn't keep me away from her."

"A real stunner, eh?" Skiffy asked.

"Yes, indeed," Sir Crispin said. "Where the devil has she been hiding?"

"She has not gone out much in Society," Tony said.

"Why not?" Skiffy asked. "Most women, especially pretty women, thrive on being seen in Society. Is there a scandal in her past, or some such thing?"

"Not that I know of. The London social scene simply does not interest her, I think."

"You did say she was a bluestocking," D'Aubney said.

"To the tips of her toes." Tony would not mention she actually wore very pink stockings, like the one neatly tied up with a silk garter and tucked away in a drawer in his bureau.

"She quotes Wollestonecraft," he said, and a collective groan rang out around the table. "And preaches reform."

"Well, there you are, then," Skiffy said. "She may be a beauty, but no man could stand a woman like that for long." He gave a dramatic shudder. "Never could stand a talker. A little moan now and then, perhaps even a tiny scream at the right moment. But chatter takes the wind right out of my sails, I tell you."

Bawdy laughter filled the air, and the conversation took a more ribald direction. No one mentioned Edwina again, but Ian shot one or two knowing glances at Tony.

His friend was right. Tony was smitten. He just hadn't quite decided yet what sort of smitten it was. He liked Edwina enormously, and he respected her. He did not always agree with her view of the world, and often enjoyed baiting her with opposing opinions just to hear her reasoned arguments. There was an honesty about her he admired. Her idealism, her passion for reform, her concern for factory workers and education for the poor were all quite genuine. Listening to her had caused him to question his own views more closely.

Edwina had made him realize that he had gone through life as most other men of his class, following the path set by his father and his grandfathers, never really thinking beyond what was accepted and normal for a man of his social standing. For the first time in years, Tony found himself seriously scrutinizing his opinions and considering alternatives.

It was an unfamiliar experience, to actually like a woman, a beautiful woman, for herself and not for whatever pleasure he might have from her.

Truth be told, though, he hadn't changed all that much, because he wanted that pleasure as well. Sometimes he would close his eyes and conjure up an image of those long, elegant legs, the sight of which had very nearly taken his breath away, and dream of them wrapped tightly around him. Oh yes, he wanted pleasure from her, and he suspected she might be interested in a bit of pleasure herself. After all, she had shown herself to be no prude. She had stripped off her stocking in broad daylight and handed it to him.

That gave him hope, and he had a few more ideas about testing those waters again. He could not afford to waste time on a trip to Newmarket. And yet . . .

"Tell me about this sharp little gelding of yours, Skiffy. A sure thing, you say?"

* * *

The next afternoon found him back in Golden Square once again. When he walked into the study, he found Edwina, Prudence, and Flora bent over the desk, chattering all at once and completely oblivious to his entrance.

Tony began to wonder if he would ever have a moment alone with Edwina again. It was his own fault. He had only suggested bringing Flora into the operation as a means of aggravating Edwina, which he took a wicked pleasure in doing. But his scheme seemed to have turned against him. The women got along together like a house afire.

He leaned against the doorway and watched in silence for a few minutes as the three ladies discussed something about fashion plates. Edwina smiled and laughed and touched Flora's arm once or twice. They had obviously become close friends. How close, he wondered? Had Flora told her about their past relationship? And what difference would it make if she had? Edwina would know he had not lived thirty-one years as a monk.

He was not ashamed of his liaison with Flora. It had been something of a coup for a young man of twenty-five to set up so infamous a mistress, even though he suspected she had never been entirely faithful to him. But he had loved her, and he knew she had an affection for him as well. She had taught him much about life and love and intimacy. Even after their affair had ended, they had remained friends and saw each other often. He hoped he had done right by her by bringing her into this business.

Finally, Edwina looked up and saw him.

"Do come in, Mr. Morehouse."

"Anthony, my dear." Flora offered her cheek for his kiss. "How lovely to see you. We have exciting news."

"Do you?"

"You will not credit it, Mr. Morehouse," Prudence said, "but Lionel Raisbeck has agreed to be the artist for our new fashion plates."

"Raisbeck?" He looked from one woman to the other, and found each with a gleam of triumph in her eye. The man was a fashionable portrait painter and a member of the Royal Academy. No wonder they were so pleased.

"He is a friend," Flora said, "and could not resist my passionate appeal."

Tony caught her eye and wondered just how passionate an appeal it had been. Flora's face gave nothing away, however, and he would not ask.

"This is certainly wonderful news," he said. "I think. How much is it going to cost me?"

"Now, that is one of the most remarkable things of all," Edwina said. "He has agreed to work for the normal rate of half a crown per design. So we will get beautiful engravings and no doubt increase our subscriptions without spending an additional shilling. You see, Mr. Morehouse, I am going to win our little wager after all."

"Don't be so sure of that. Have the numbers increased since the last issue with Flora's report?"

"Indeed they have," Prudence said. "We have received over thirty new subscriptions this week."

Edwina frowned and looked away. She would not be pleased that Prudence had revealed her hand. Despite her show of confidence, she was nowhere close to winning.

"As many as thirty?" Tony said. "What a thrilling success for you. Why, that leaves only one thousand nine hundred and seventy more to go."

"Horrid man," Flora said, but gave him one of her more radiant smiles. "You must excuse us, my dear. Prudence and I have business to attend to."

She removed a straw bonnet and India muslin shawl from a hook on the wall and handed them to Prudence, then picked up her own more dashing bonnet from a table. "We must be off," she said.

"What sort of business?" he asked.

"Oh, Mr. Morehouse," Prudence said as she tied the bonnet ribbons beneath her chin, "it is very exciting. Flora has arranged—"

"Come along, Prudence." She took the young woman by the arm and steered her through the door. "We must hurry. Edwina can regale Tony with the details of our next triumph."

With a jaunty wave Flora was gone, tugging the sputtering Prudence along at her side. Tony struggled to conceal a smile. If he was not mistaken, Flora had just deliberately manipulated a moment of privacy for him and Edwina. He had not admitted the depth of his interest to her, though she could hardly fail to notice his attraction for Edwina. He wondered if Edwina had said something to Flora. Had she perhaps admitted to her own attraction for him? Had Flora maneuvered that awkward exit on Edwina's behalf?

The stunning possibility shot an unexpected surge of euphoria through his body.

The feeling ebbed slightly when Edwina moved to her usual position behind the bastion of her desk. He suspected it gave her a sense of invulnerability, of command, to have the great protective bulk between them.

What was she afraid of?

Tony moved a stack of papers and perched himself on the edge of the desk. She pulled a face, glowering at the intrusion of his hip and thigh into her private territory. She said nothing, however, but quickly lowered her eyes and pretended to be busy with some documents.

"Prudence certainly has become the gregarious little creature," he said. "She always seemed such a shy little mouse. What a change. Perhaps she is merely getting accustomed to my presence."

"It is Flora's influence. She has taken Pru under her wing."

Tony chuckled. "I cannot imagine a more unlikely association. But Flora can sometimes be quite irresistible."

Edwina looked up at him, her elegant brows lifted in mild inquiry. "Indeed?"

He ignored the implied question and flicked a piece of lint off his coat sleeve. "So. Tell me of this additional triumph. First Lionel Raisbeck. What else?"

Her expression softened, and her eyes lit up with a sort of banked enthusiasm, as though she were not quite sure of this next triumph. Or not quite sure if she should share it with him.

"Flora has been talking to some of the better modistes," she said. "She has suggested the fashion plates be drawn from their own models, with each modiste getting credit for her designs."

"That sounds like a fine idea, but where is the particular triumph? Don't other magazines do the same?"

"Hardly ever. The modistes are almost never mentioned. But the triumph is that in exchange for that bit of free publicity, the modistes have agreed to allow Flora an advance look at any new dresses being made up for some of the most fashionable ladies of the *ton* for specific elegant occasions. That way she can describe them in much more detail than she could from simply viewing them at a distance. She believes those details will set the *Cabinet* apart from other publications."

"Leave it to Flora to come up with such a tidy little quid pro quo arrangement."

"And by starting now, the process will be in full

motion by the time the Season begins and the really important gowns are worn. I must confess it is truly a marvelous idea."

Her sheepish smile showed how much that confession cost. She had not wanted so much space to be given over to fashion.

He returned her smile. "Didn't I tell you she'd be good for the magazine?"

"You did and she is. I was furious with you, of course, but I do like her. She is a most unusual and fascinating woman."

"She is that."

"Perhaps you will not be so fond of her when you realize how much her efforts will help me to win our wager. Pru only mentioned the subscriptions that came in the mail this week. She did not include the increased volume of bulk subscriptions from several booksellers. Those numbers count, too."

"Don't get overconfident, my dear. You still have a long way to go and I am determined to get back the Minerva. But I wouldn't worry too much. When you lose the wager in November, I shall still be more than willing to keep you on as editor." He flashed her a wicked grin.

"Odious man!"

"Egad, what's he done now?"

Tony looked over his shoulder to see Nicholas Parrish lounging in the doorway.

"He is only teasing me again," Edwina said and gave Tony an exasperated look.

Nicholas walked into the study, skirted the desk, and sank into the armchair opposite, never taking his eyes off Tony.

"As long as it is only teasing," he said, "I will not call the man out on your account, Ed."

Edwina laughed, but even though it was meant facetiously, there was a hint of seriousness behind the remark. Tony had the distinct impression the man did not like him. Whether it was because of Tony's new role as his sister's employer or because he mistrusted Tony's intentions toward her, Nicholas definitely acted the role of protective brother whenever they encountered each other.

"No need for pistols at dawn, Parrish. I am merely reminding your sister that she has a long way to go before she can have any hopes of winning our wager. I fear she does not appreciate my little reminders."

Nicholas continued to glare at him through narrowed eyes. "No, I suspect she does not."

"Oh, but Nickie, we have had such news," Edwina said, drawing his attention away from Tony at last.

She proceeded to tell her brother about Raisbeck and about Flora's scheme with the modistes. Nicholas was visibly impressed with the notion of such an accomplished artist drawing figures for the *Cabinet*. But it was when Edwina explained Flora's plan that his eyes finally lit with genuine enthusiasm.

"And I assume Pru is tagging along," he said, "in order to solicit supplemental paid advertising?"

"She is indeed."

"Good Lord. Think of all that additional revenue."

The siblings shared a significant glance, which reinforced Tony's notion that something was going on at *The Ladies' Fashionable Cabinet*, something involving profits and those account books he was supposed to keep his nose out of. And what was Nicholas's role?

"The future is certainly looking brighter," Edwina said. She stood and stepped from behind the desk. "I'm going to go downstairs and see about making us a pot of tea. The good Bohea this time," she added, and sent Tony a teasing glance. "And perhaps some of Mrs. Gibb's cream cakes in honor of all the good news. I will meet you both upstairs shortly."

When she'd gone, Tony pushed himself off the desk and straightened his coattails.

"You'll never be able to sneak up on someone with all that metal clanking at your waist," Nicholas said, and then rose from his languid slouch in one graceful move. He had the same fluid grace and dark good looks as his sister.

"I'm not the sneaking-up sort," Tony replied. He adjusted his watch chain and allowed the fobs to jingle. "I rather prefer to announce my presence with a flourish, so to speak."

"Nice set of fobs," Nicholas said. "That one in particular, with the lock of hair. A sweetheart's?"

Tony fingered the locket fob with the curl of blonde hair beneath glass. Was Nicholas worried that Edwina might have a rival for his affections?

"It's my mother's hair, actually."

"Ah."

Nicholas stepped past him and moved toward the door. Tony stopped him with a brief touch on the arm. "Look here, Parrish, if you're going to act the protective brother and question my intentions toward your sister, you can save your breath."

Nicholas stared for a moment, then his face split into a wide grin. "Morehouse, I would not *dream* of interfering with Edwina's personal life. She would have my head if I tried. If she decides to become involved with you, that is her business."

"Well, then. Good. Although I must say yours is a somewhat unconventional attitude, is it not? I believe most brothers would not be so blasé about it."

"We are not, as you must know, the most conventional of families."

"I knew your grandfather when I was a boy. He was fairly upstanding, as I recall."

"You must tell me about him someday. I never did know him well. I didn't have the advantage of summers with him like Edwina. But I know he disapproved of Mama."

Tony recalled what his father had told him about

Edwina's family all those years ago. "Because she was an artist?"

"That, and her rather cavalier disregard of convention. She had a somewhat overwhelming personality, an artist's temperament. Brilliant, passionate, single-minded. Life with Mama was a bit chaotic. We never knew what she was going to do next. Her every thought was for her art. She was always seeking something new, would do anything, go anywhere to find new sources of light. She was forever chasing light. It's how she died."

"How so?"

"There was a huge storm, and she wanted a close look at the effects of lightning in the sky. Papa tried to stop her, but she would not be deterred. She climbed up to the top of the highest peak in the district and must have been taking shelter beneath a tree. By the time we found her, she was dead. The tree had been struck by lightning."

"Dear God."

"It was a difficult time. Papa withdrew completely. Edwina took it the hardest. But she recovered and went her own way, eventually into another sort of chaos."

"France."

"Yes, France. But my point is that even if Mama had lived, Edwina would still have led an unconventional life. Mama taught us from the cradle that we must discover our own passions and go after them. Edwina has always done so. She's been doing precisely as she wants since she was a girl."

"I had a taste of that pigheadedness when we were children." Tony gave a chuckle. "She hasn't changed much, has she?"

"Actually, she has. She's never been quite the same since our time in France. Oh, she's as pigheaded as ever, but she's much quieter. No longer as impulsive or rebellious. Hates disorder of any kind. Always wants to have things under control."

"So I've noticed."

"Which means she will brook no interference from me. Especially where men are concerned."

Interesting. It suggested there had been men in her life. She might after all be one of those women who eschew marriage and have no scruples about taking lovers.

Tony cleared his throat. "Have there been many occasions, then, where you have refrained from interfering?"

"Look, Morehouse, Edwina may be the most independent-minded woman I know, but she is also very beautiful and often the object of male attention. Men have been sniffing about her skirts since she was a girl. But to tell you the truth, she generally sends them packing. She wants nothing to do with them." He narrowed his eyes a bit as he looked at Tony. "She has not been interested in men for a very long time."

Oh, God. What was Nicholas trying to say? Was Edwina that *other* sort of woman after all? The sort Ian had alluded to?

"There are other things much more important to her than romance," Nicholas continued. "The *Cabinet* means everything to her. It has been the center of her life for years now. If you expected a brotherly warning, it is only this: Do not underestimate her dedication to the magazine. Don't insult her by assuming it is a frivolous diversion. It is a serious business to her."

"Are you hinting that I should forfeit the wager and give it to her outright?"

Nicholas cocked his head to one side as he pondered the question. "No," he said at last. "I don't think you should. Strangely enough, your idiotic wager has allowed her to see a broader picture of what she might do with the *Cabinet*. This business with Flora Gallagher, for example, is certain to give her a larger audience. That is what she has always wanted, but she has been too cautious, unwilling to compromise more than was absolutely necessary. Your damned wager may be the best thing that's ever happened to her." He grinned. "But don't tell her I said so."

"I am pleased to hear you say that, Parrish. I had begun to hope that my impulsive challenge was not entirely a bad thing."

"So you won't mind if you lose?"

Tony was about to offer his usual quip about never losing when it came to him in a sort of blinding flash that he wanted to lose this time. In fact, without ever admitting it to himself, he had been doing everything possible to make sure he lost. He had justified Flora and the fashion reports as simply a matter of improving the business. The truth was, he was hoping her efforts would increase subscriptions. Not for the business. For Edwina.

"I'm rather hoping I do lose," he said. "The *Cabinet* should belong to Edwina." He flashed a grin to her brother and echoed his words. "But don't tell her I said so."

"Then all those exclamations of frustration I hear from her every time you come by—"

"Are the results of my teasing, nothing more. It's all a part of the competitive nature of our relationship. Simple conversation between us does not come easy. We banter and spar and bait each other. But it is not serious, I assure you. I have no designs on the magazine." It was true, even if he had just this moment realized it. "I know how important it is to her."

"Then, by God, she had better win that wager, Morehouse, or there will be no living with her."

"Though she may not realize it, I'm doing my best to see that she does." Tony clapped a friendly hand on Nicholas's back and headed with him up the stairs to the drawing room, a new amity between them.

As conversation flowed onto other topics, there was one thing still troubling Tony—something Nicholas had said that Tony could not get out of his mind.

She has not been interested in men for a very long time.

He thought of her comfortable spinsterhood, her closeness to Prudence, her easy friendship with Flora, the way she touched Flora's arm or shoulder so casually.

So, was Tony the first man to interest her in a while? Or was she simply toying with him, when she in fact had no real interest in him, or in any man?

By God, he was going to find out.

They had a surprisingly pleasant afternoon over tea. Edwina had always sensed a sort of tension between Anthony and Nicholas, but that no longer seemed to be the case. The three of them had laughed and joked with astonishing ease.

But Nicholas, always restless, had not lingered long, and excused himself after only one cup of tea and one cake. Anthony, on the other hand, showed no inclination to leave. He was comfortably ensconced at one end of the settee, one arm draped carelessly over the back.

"Tell me about the Minerva," he said.

"What do you mean?"

"How did she come to be emblazoned on the masthead of the *Cabinet*?"

"Oh. Well, she has always been special to me, symbolic of so many things. I became enthralled by the Classics as a girl. Ultimately, I came to dream of republican ideals based on the example of Rome. It's what finally drew me to France. All along, the Minerva was sort of a personal symbol to me, a symbol of myself as a warrior against tyranny and oppression."

"A warrior?"

"With my pen for a weapon. She still inspires me, which is why she is on the masthead." And why Edwina would fight to the last subscription to insure she did not lose the Minerva to him.

"You've spent so much time fighting your various battles," he said, "that you've had no time for a life of your own."

"I have a life."

"A life alone."

"Not entirely alone."

"But without a husband and children. You have taken Mary Wollstonecraft's views too literally, I suspect. She scorned women for spending their time learning to please a man, so you have scorned that aspect of life altogether. Why else would such a beautiful woman still be unmarried?"

"We have had this discussion before, sir."

"I think it is because you never took the time to

learn how to lure a man's interest. You've probably never even been in love."

She flinched. "You're wrong. I have been in love."

"With a man?"

Edwina gaped at him. "What a question."

"Do not worry, my dear. I would never hold it against you if the great love of your life had been a woman. I would think it a terrible waste, from a purely selfish perspective, of course. But I would never condemn you for it."

How difficult it was not to laugh! Was this what he thought of her? That she was a woman who rejected men because she preferred women? No doubt he was simply baiting her again. Perhaps she would take the bait this time and play with it a little.

"How terribly civilized of you, sir. You are more open-minded, more sophisticated than most."

He lifted an eyebrow. "Open-minded enough to know that a woman like you is generally receptive to any new experience. Like learning to take pleasure in a man."

"A woman like me?"

"Unconventional."

"Ah. You would make me conventional, then?"

"Not all convention is to be disdained, my dear. How fortunate to have Flora at hand. You might learn a thing or two from her."

"What sorts of things?"

"Perhaps she could teach you how to please a man."

He was still baiting her, but she was compelled to jerk back on the line. Some character flaw within her wanted him to know that she was not the sort of woman he was painting, that she was not a dried-up spinster with no feelings or desires.

"What makes you think I don't know how to please a man?"

He laughed. "Edwina! Unless you have been leading a secret life as a lightskirt, what else is one to think? You are the consummate bluestocking, a thirty-year-old spinster—"

"Twenty-nine."

"—who prefers the company of women. You seldom leave the house. You have books instead of lovers. You have projects instead of children. You have no romantic attachments that I am aware of. Hell, when I kissed you that first day there was only laughter in your eyes, not desire or pleasure."

"You seemed pleased enough when I stripped off my stocking for you."

"Pure showmanship. And I suspect it is the first time you have ever done anything so wicked in your life. Instead, you stay in your own little world, coiled up like a hedgehog, afraid to allow anyone too close. Except, of course, Prudence. And now Flora."

"I am not allowed to have women friends?"

"I would not be surprised to learn there is more

than simple friendship between you and Prudence."

"Indeed?"

"At the very least, you spend more time with her than going out into Society to meet and mingle with gentlemen."

"And all this means that I cannot possibly know how to please a man?"

"You've been a spinster for almost thirty years, my dear. If you ever knew, I suspect you have forgotten."

"Would you like to bet on it?"

His eyes widened with interest. "A wager?"

"Yes, another wager. That seems to be the only way we can make a point with each other. I will wager you that I *do* know how to please a man."

His splendid gray-blue gaze slid over her like a caress. She considered for a moment that she had made a terrible mistake.

"You intrigue me, madam. And might I assume that you have some specific stakes in mind?"

"I do, actually."

"Tell me."

"Now that we have secured Mr. Railsbeck to draw our fashion prints—for no additional cost to you, I might add—it is important that we have the best engraver to bring them to life. I should like to hire Benjamin Jarvis. He is the best there is, but he is expensive. Uncle Victor would never allow us to use him. If I win the wager, I want your approval for the extra cost to hire Jarvis, for the fashion prints and any other prints we decide to publish."

"It's always the *Cabinet* with you, isn't it? All right, then. You may have your Mr. Jarvis, *if* you can prove that you do know how to please a man." His gaze narrowed. "But how will you prove it?"

"I will demonstrate, sir. On you."

Chapter 8

She slowly rose from her chair and came to stand in front of him. Tony could have told her she had won already. He would not do so, of course. He had pushed and teased in hopes of an actual demonstration such as was apparently about to take place. But the fact that she put a wager on it gave him an even bigger thrill.

He shifted his position to relieve the tightening in his groin.

"Don't move," she said.

She stood close enough that the full white muslin skirts of her dress brushed against his knees. She stretched like a cat, lifting her arms and placing her hands behind her head. Her arched back pulled the fabric of her bodice tight against her breasts.

He had always admired the elegant grace of her movements. But he had never seen her move like this.

Tony swallowed hard. His neckcloth suddenly felt too tight and he reached up to adjust it.

After a moment, thinking she was simply posing, he realized she was unpinning her hair. The complicated arrangement of coils and plaits soon fell loose, accompanied by the pinging of dozens of hairpins dropping to the floor. She brought the mass of tangled black locks over her shoulders and began to comb her fingers through them, starting at the scalp and slowly pulling through the length to the ends—over and over, until the tangles were out and the plaits undone, and soft black waves almost covered her face. Then she dropped her head back and shook her hair so that it floated about her like a dark cloud.

Tony's breath had become shallow.

Edwina moved closer so that their knees touched. She nudged his legs apart and moved between them. When she looked down she could surely see the signs of his arousal. She looked into his eyes with a knowing smile. She had won, and she knew it. She could stop now.

But she did not.

She wriggled closer and lifted one knee onto the settee, between his. She lowered herself in such a way that he was forced to shift sideways. Finally, he was practically prone, with one leg stretched out along the back of the settee, one foot still on the floor. His head rested on a loose cushion placed against the settee's carved wooden arm. Edwina sat between his legs.

"Now, Anthony," she crooned, her voice never huskier, "let me see what I can do to make you more comfortable."

It was the first time she'd called him Anthony. But he couldn't think about that right now. He couldn't think about anything right now.

She began to work on his coat. It was double-breasted, so she first unbuttoned the right side, then the left, and then slid her hands underneath and pulled it open. She placed her hands flat against his waistcoat and looked into his eyes. Hers were heavy-lidded and dark as night, pulling him like a mesmerist to tumble into their depths.

She leaned over and brushed her lips against his, her breasts rubbing against his chest. Tony could bear it no longer and brought his arms up to enfold her, but she pulled back.

"No, Anthony. I need no help from you. Lie back and allow *me* to please *you*. Relax."

He dropped his hands and tried to relax, but it was difficult, when every nerve was twitching with desire.

She slid her hands up over his waistcoat, and her deft fingers began to undo the neckcloth Brinkley had tied to perfection earlier that morning. She loosened the knot, and Tony lifted his head slightly so she could unwrap the length of it. When it hung lose over his shoulders, she took the ends and tied them behind her neck. As she pulled tighter she was forced closer and closer until her nose brushed his. He arched up to kiss her, but she turned aside and simply rubbed her soft cheek against his and nuzzled his ear. Her tongue flicked at the lobe, then took it in her teeth and tugged gently.

The room had grown uncomfortably warm.

With a quick twist of her hand, she pulled away the neckcloth and flung it aside. The buttons of his waistcoat were next. One by one they came undone, and again her hands slid beneath and pushed aside the fabric. Her palms rested flat on his chest and he could feel the warmth of them beneath the thin lawn of his shirt. She next unhooked the single button under the collar and exposed the top of his chest. He gave a sharp intake of breath when she traced a slow finger from his chin, down his throat, and as far as the opening would allow. When she bent to kiss the bare skin of his chest, he could not stifle a soft moan.

Edwina sat back and gazed at him with a look worthy of the most skillful courtesan. Without taking her eyes from his, she reached up and unhooked a brooch at the center of her bodice and dropped it to the floor. The fichu it had held now hung loose. She took one end of it and slowly pulled. It came away to reveal a beautiful expanse of white bosom.

He had somehow forgotten how to breathe.

She leaned forward so that the smooth skin of her bosom was pressed against the bare skin of his chest. He closed his eyes and it was as if they were naked together. It was almost unbearable. She began to kiss his neck and he dropped his head back to allow it. She traced a path with her tongue all the way to the middle of his chest. As she was bent over him, his arms instinctively came around her.

Again, she pulled away. "Anthony, Anthony. You know you are not to help. Put your hands behind your head and close your eyes."

He did as she asked. She began kissing his neck once again, but this time her hands reached up for his. She brushed something against them. Something soft. He thought it must have been the fichu because he felt the lace along its edge. She dragged it along his fingers and over the sensitive skin of the underside of his wrists.

She wriggled up and up until her glorious bosom almost covered his face. He rubbed his cheek against the soft mounds and nuzzled the creamy flesh with his nose. He began to plant a kiss in the valley of her cleavage, when suddenly the fichu was pulled tight over his wrists and his eyes flew open.

She had tied his hands to the arm of the settee!

He had known Edwina was a woman who liked to be in charge, but he'd never expected this.

"Now you will not be tempted to help," she said. "Are you hungry, Anthony? No, don't speak." She placed a finger over his lips. "Of course you are hungry."

Edwina got up from the settee, leaving him bound and bereft, but returned with a cream cake in her hand. She sat beside him again, nudging her hip against his very obvious arousal. A trickle of perspiration ran down his temple and over his jaw.

She took a bite of cake, savored it audibly, and allowed a bit of cream to remain on her upper lip. Her tongue came out and slowly curled up to remove the spot of cream, then it darted to the corners of her mouth to flick away bits of crumb, and finally licked her lips in a long, slow circle.

His heart beat wildly in his chest. His ears rang with its thumping.

She dipped her finger in the cake and came away with a dollop of thick cream. She brought the finger to his lips and allowed him the exquisite bliss of licking away the cream. When she didn't take her finger away, he took it into his mouth, circled it with his tongue, and sucked. Edwina's eyes closed and she made a tiny sound of pleasure that was more erotic, more arousing than anything she had yet done.

She pulled the finger from his mouth and transferred it to her own, sucking on it while gazing into his eyes. She leaned forward so that her face was inches from his own. At last, he thought, she is going to kiss me. But she did not. She turned her head so that her long hair fell over his face. It was thick and soft and smelled of carnations. She brushed it back and forth over his face and neck and chest. Dear God!

When she began to trail kisses along his collarbone, he started to squirm, pressing himself against her in a slow grind. He was on fire for her. She slowly, slowly worked her way up his throat and chin and finally—finally!—her lips hovered over his. He lifted his mouth to hers, but she backed away slightly.

"Anthony."

He could feel her lips shape his name. Only a breath separated them.

"Anthony."

The deep, husky purr of his name on her lips, the soft breasts crushed against his bare chest, the cloud of sweet-smelling hair all combined in a sensation of pure erotic desire that left him senseless and panting.

"Anthony." She spoke against his mouth, lips touching but not yet kissing. "Have I pleased you?"

"Oh God, yes."

He lifted his mouth to cover hers, and she was gone. She rolled away, stood up, and shook out her skirts.

"Good," she said. "I win."

Edwina retrieved her fichu—it wasn't tied that tight; he could have broken free at any time—and bent to pick up her brooch. She grabbed a few hairpins that had landed in the vicinity, and walked to the tea table. The fichu was quickly pinned back in place, but she decided there was nothing to be done about her hair. So she poured herself another cup of tea and returned to the chair she had occupied earlier. She took a long restorative swallow and looked over the rim of the cup to see that Anthony had not stirred.

"Well, sir. Do I get my engraver?"

He gave a great noisy sigh and sat up. His shirt still gaped open to reveal the muscular planes of his golden chest.

"Madam, you may have anything you want. Anything at all."

She smiled secretly and took another sip of tea. She needed it. Pulling away when she did had been an effort of sheer will. Her body had been thrumming in a way it hadn't done for years. She had been tempted to give in and take the seduction to its limit, but that would have been a huge mistake. She had only needed to prove a point. And she had done so.

But oh! the temptation had been fierce.

Anthony began to put himself to rights. Edwina sipped her tea and watched.

"Might I hope," she said, "that you no longer think me a dried-up old spinster?"

He looked up from buttoning his waistcoat. "My dear Edwina, after that demonstration, I am fairly certain there is not a single part of you that has dried up. Quite the contrary, in fact."

She was glad he returned his attention to his buttons and couldn't see the blush that heated her cheeks. It was the shimmer of pure feminine triumph that warmed her blood.

Tony rose and went to stand before the mirror above the fireplace. His collar was still open, revealing the strong column of his neck and the smooth, honey-gold skin of his throat. The intimacy of watching him, even in only slight *déshabillé*, brought about a sudden pang of longing so strong it took her breath away. For an instant, the face in the mirror was that of another man, equally fair, equally handsome. She blinked, and the vision was gone.

Edwina took another swallow of tea and shook off the strange feeling of disorientation. She returned her attention to Anthony's attempt to repair the damage she'd done to his pristine appearance.

He buttoned the collar of his shirt, adjusted the points, and wrapped the long neckcloth around it.

"Brinkley will give me the fisheye when he sees the mess I am about to make of this cravat."

"I am sorry to be the cause of your valet's displeasure." Her lips twitched into a smile.

His eyes caught hers in the mirror. "He will get over it. As for me . . . well, that is a different matter altogether."

He made a casual knot in the neckcloth, adjusted the ends, and pulled up the collar. Finally, he rebuttoned the fine bottle green coat, tugged down his waistcoat so just the perfect amount showed below the coat front, and made one final adjustment to the neckcloth. He turned to face her. His eyes twinkled with the wicked amusement she'd come to expect, but this time it was tinged with a hint of that sensual desire she'd seen earlier when she'd been pressed close against him.

"I believe it is time for me to leave," he said. "I would hate to wear out my welcome."

She rose to see him out. He walked up to her and reached out to touch her hair, which still hung loose about her face and down her back.

"Beautiful," he said, and moved his hand to cup her chin. "Very beautiful. Thank you, Edwina, for allowing me to know that you are not ignorant of the joys to be shared between a man and a woman."

She smiled. "It was my pleasure, sir."

"Was it? I thought it was all for my pleasure. In fact, I am certain of it." He brushed the pad of his thumb against the corner of her mouth. "Now it is my turn to please you."

He took her face in both hands, leaned closer, and kissed her.

Dear God. She had tried to avoid this. She had known what would happen. The touch of his mouth against hers sent intense sensations surging through her body. She had not wanted this. But, oh my . . .

His lips were soft and the kiss slow and gentle. Intoxicating. She instinctively moved into it, and he responded by sliding one hand down her neck, beneath her hair, and around to her nape. His lips never stopped moving, shifting, encouraging.

Her body seemed to become boneless, and suddenly her hands were on his shoulders, hanging on, clutching for an anchor. And his arms were enfolding her, pressing her tightly against him. Her lips parted, and he came inside. She twined her arms around his neck as his tongue and lips slowly deepened the kiss, sending waves of sensual excitement coursing through her veins.

Desire flooded her, filled her up, and wrested away all vestiges of control. He tightened the embrace and threaded his fingers in her loose hair. She melted against him and opened her mouth wide to his. Ripples of sensation spiraled through her as he set up a sensual dance of lips and tongue.

He brought the kiss to an end as gently as it had begun. Both hands were buried in her hair when he pulled back and gazed deeply into her eyes.

"Ah, yes," he said in a hoarse whisper. "That is the look I want to see in a woman's eyes when I kiss her." He cradled her head in his hands and she was lost in the silvery depths of his gaze. "The last time I kissed you, there was only laughter in your eyes. I must have made a better job of it this time."

Edwina had no words to reply. He had stolen all her wits with that kiss. He smiled, drew a thumb along her jaw, and released her from his embrace. She grabbed the edge of the tea table behind her for support.

"I will see myself out, my dear. I believe my hat and gloves are still on the hall table."

"Yes."

"Thank you for a most . . . enlightening after-noon."

"Yes."

He bowed over an elegant leg, turned, and left.

Edwina sank down into her chair and tried to compose herself. How foolish that she had not been able to manage a single coherent sentence. He would know how thoroughly he had discomposed her with that kiss. More so than she had unsettled him earlier. Everything was a competition with him, a challenge. He would have wanted to best her in this, too.

And he had done so.

She was still shaken by it. Damn. She hadn't wanted this. She had never wanted this wild, chaotic feeling again. This tempest of confusion, this jumble of sensation was the last thing she ever wanted to experience again. She could not govern it, and that frightened her.

If it was simply a matter of the physical, even

sexual reaction, she could have controlled it. She *had* controlled it earlier. It had been difficult, but she had done it. It was more than physical, though. The whole afternoon had left her emotions in a state of total disarray.

And she hated that.

She had set out only to play a game of flirtation, to challenge him with a little gamesmanship of her own. But it had not turned out as she'd expected. Even while she was "seducing" him, she knew it was not completely a game. Now that he'd kissed her like that—surely not out of competitiveness alone, but with pure passion—her feelings for him had taken a new turn. Her stomach was knotted up with confusion and excitement and anxiety and wonder. She feared to put a name to it. But she was certain of one thing.

She hated the feeling.

And, God help her, she loved it.

What the devil was she going to do about Anthony Morehouse?

Tony soaked in the bath Brinkley had prepared for him after his return from Golden Square. His arms dangled limply over the edge of the copper tub. His valet's mouth had puckered up in disapproval when he saw the sadly rearranged neckcloth, but he said nothing more than to suggest a hot bath. No doubt he'd assumed much more had taken place that afternoon than a bit of harmless dalliance in Edwina's drawing room.

Harmless? The way his heart had raced, he'd been damned near apoplexy. Lord, what an afternoon.

He pondered all that had happened, reliving every tantalizing detail, as he relaxed in the warm bath. Edwina's "demonstration" had not entirely surprised him. A woman of her beauty and her age must surely have had some experience of physical passion. He had hoped to tease her into a decent kiss, if nothing else. Her thoroughly erotic performance, though, had been more than he could ever have dreamed. The woman had the makings of a sorceress.

And he was completely willing to fall under her spell. If only he could contrive an opportunity for further demonstrations.

One thing he ought to have expected was the way she had taken total control of the situation, never allowing him to make a single peremptory move. Edwina Parrish was definitely a woman who liked to be in charge. He wondered what it would be like to make love to her. Would she allow him to participate at all?

Though she had provided a compelling and provocative display, it had not actually given him the proof he sought, the proof that she could desire a man. It only proved she knew how to make a man desire her. He had suspected the truth, but had not been one hundred percent certain. Her brother's words still rang in his ears.

That was why he'd kissed her. He'd wanted to be sure, to remove that last niggling doubt.

And he had done so. Her response to his kiss left no uncertainty as to her nature. She could desire a man. She could even desire him, if she would only loosen up a bit.

He wondered what had brought about this powerful need of hers to be in full command of every situation? Nicholas mentioned how she had changed since going to France during the Revolution. Had something happened there? Something specific and personal? Or was it simply a matter of watching the Revolution turn on itself, when its violence consumed its own leaders? For someone who strongly supported its principles and ideals, it must have been devastating to witness such an outcome at close hand.

Tony closed his eyes and replayed their kiss in his mind. Her infernal control had slipped a bit then, to be sure, and she had grown pliant in his arms. He rather suspected her response had even stunned *her* a little. Though she had let down her guard for a moment, freed herself from whatever self-imposed discipline was at work, it had been involuntary. There had been pleasure between them, incredible pleasure, and yet Tony did not believe it pleased her. More likely, it scared her.

Poor Edwina. There was a passionate nature beneath all that control. Probably inherited from her mother. It was a shame to so deliberately restrain it.

Tony was doing everything he could to insure she won their wager for the *Cabinet*. But as he recalled her pliant body in his arms, he was surprised to discover there was something else he wanted to do for her. Something she deserved equally as much.

He wanted to set her free.

Free from those unnatural restraints on her emotions, her feelings, her passions. Free from that powerful need to keep her defenses up at all times. Free from whatever chains bound her heart. He wanted to give her the freedom to let go, the freedom to live.

He wasn't sure why he wanted to do this for her. Not because her beauty shot raw desire through his veins. It was more than that.

He cared for her. He liked her. He had a special sort of affection for her, perhaps because he'd known her as a child, and he wanted to do this.

Though she was contemptuous of his gambling, there was something to be said for it. Living so often on the knife edge of risk fired his blood, fueled every moment with a sense of immediacy, made him feel alive. Perhaps the best thing he could do for her was to teach her how to find some of that excitement in her own life. By letting go. By letting down her defenses. By accepting that it was all right for someone else to take charge now and then.

He finished his bath and Brinkley helped him

into the evening clothes he'd laid out. He had nothing special planned for the evening. He probably ought to find a woman to slake the restlessness, the hunger brought on by the almost-seduction of the afternoon. But he knew he would not. The hunger was not of a general nature, easily assuaged by a convenient bed and a willing female.

He wanted Edwina. No one else would do.

Most people believed him to be a libertine of sorts. He'd done nothing to encourage that reputation, but there it was. Probably had to do with his well-known liaison with Flora all those years ago.

The fact was, though, he was what you might call serially monogamous. He never got involved with more than one woman at a time. He seldom indulged in one-night flings. He preferred to get to know a woman, to spend time with her. Some associations where shorter in duration than others, but he was always faithful while they lasted.

And even though he was not—yet—having an affair with Edwina, he found he wasn't interested in anyone else at the moment. So instead of female companionship, he went in search of good friends and good play.

The evening began at White's, as it so often did. Before he could make his way to the tables, he ran into Victor Croyden in the coffee room.

"Evening, Morehouse. Playing whist tonight, are you?

"I thought I might see about a game or two."

"Hoping to win a gentleman's magazine this time?" Croyden cackled at his own witticism and slapped Tony on the shoulder.

"Think I'll stick to the usual blunt," Tony said. "Easier to deal with."

"Ah. Having problems with the *Cabinet* ladies, are you?"

"Not particularly. In fact, it's turning out more profitably than I'd expected."

Croyden's eyes widened with interest. "Oh? How so?"

"Made a few changes. Subscriptions are up. Hope to see them doubled by November."

"Doubled?" Croyden chuckled. "I would not expect such an increase if I were you. But then, you don't have any experience in these matters, do you?"

"None whatsoever. But I am learning. And I have every faith in your niece's ability to turn this enterprise into a huge success."

"Edwina?" He clicked his tongue. "A word of advice, Morehouse. Never depend on a bevy of old women and spinsters to do a man's job. If you really want to make a profitable venture out of the thing, you're going to have to bring in someone else to run it."

"Oh, I don't think so. Miss Parrish is doing an excellent job. In fact, it is due to her efforts that the subscriptions are likely to double in so short a time. She's expanding the fashion reporting. Brought in new writers and artists, and new advertisers. Revenues are increasing."

"Oh? Revenues up? I wonder, Morehouse, if you have not got in over your head with this business. A bit out of your element, eh? I might be interested in buying it back. Or we might play for it again. What do you say?"

"If I were going to sell it to anyone," Tony said, "I would sell it to Miss Parrish. She is responsible for its success. It ought to be hers."

"Sell it to Edwina? Are you mad?"

"I don't believe so. In fact, I am seriously considering giving it to her."

"Well, if that's not the most damned fool thing I ever heard. Got a screw loose, Morehouse, and that's a fact. A woman shouldn't be allowed to run such a business."

"Seems to me a woman's been running it for years. All you ever did was collect the profits. And now that those profits might be growing, you want the thing back. Well, you can't have it, Croyden. I'd give it to Edwina before I'd sell it back to you."

Croyden puffed up like a pouter pigeon, scowled, and sputtered incoherently. Finally, he made a curt nod and left without another word. The bastard.

Tony turned to find Ian Fordyce standing close behind him. He took Tony by the elbow and steered him to a private corner with a pair of unoccupied chairs.

"What's got into you, old man?" Ian asked as he

sank into one of the comfortable wing chairs. "You've let this magazine—this *woman*—take on too much importance in your life, I think. I told you there was nothing but trouble ahead."

"There's no trouble, Ian. I just don't like that fellow Croyden and the way he tries to take advantage of his niece."

"Awfully protective of her, are you not?"

Tony laughed. "Edwina Parrish is not a woman who needs protection, I assure you."

"But there's something going on, isn't there? Damn it, Tony, you haven't fallen in love with the woman, have you?"

Had he?

"I don't know, Ian. Maybe. I don't know."

It was true. He hadn't bothered to put any sort of definition on his feelings for her. He didn't love her. But he might be a little bit *in* love with her.

"Maybe?" Ian clucked like an old hen. "Good Lord. You're done for, old man. Well, they say she's a beauty."

"She's stunningly beautiful." Especially with her hair down and her eyes glassy with desire. "But it's not just that. I like her. She's quite unconventional. Doesn't care a fig for Society or propriety."

"Much the same could be said of you, my friend. Perhaps you feel a kindred spirit in her."

"No, we're not at all alike. Her motivations and objectives are as far removed from my own as they could be. She flouts Society because she seeks to reform it. She cares about factory workers and displaced farmers and education for the poor. I only wish I could claim such selfless compassion. It's true I've been flouting Society most of my life, but that's only because . . ." He paused. He had almost said "because of my father." But that didn't make any sense. Why would he say such a thing?

"Because," Ian said, finishing the thought for him, "you've been doing it so long, it's second nature to you. I remember when you were sent down from Cambridge over that gaming hell you'd set up in your rooms. You wore expulsion like a badge of honor, as if it was your defining moment."

"It was, in a way. It proved my father had been right about me all along."

Ian smiled. "Lord, I remember how furious he was. But you rather liked being the bad boy. You were so damned good at it."

A waiter strolled by with glasses of brandy on a silver tray. They each took one. Tony warmed the glass in his hands.

"To tell you the truth," he said, "I never really enjoyed making my father angry. It just seemed inevitable. I was never going to be the son he wanted."

"And so you have found in Miss Parrish another who has placed herself outside the accepted standards of polite behavior?"

"Possibly. Though her disregard for convention is born out of principle and a completely different sort of upbringing. I do not believe she set out deliberately to be rebellious, as perhaps I did. It is simply her nature—independent, confident, generous, unapologetic. It's all a part of who she is.

"Listen to yourself, Tony. You're in love with her."

He shook his head. "I am smitten, to be sure. Infatuated. Definitely in lust."

"I've known you for too long, old man. I see the signs." He tossed back the brandy, gave a little shudder, and set the empty glass on the candle stand beside his chair. "But what about all those wagers between the two of you? Is that still going on?"

Tony thought of the afternoon's wager, and a little shiver of recollected desire shot through his body. He countered the fire with a long swallow of brandy and allowed its soothing warmth to calm him. "It is still going on. But it's different now. At first, it was a matter of goading her, taunting her, challenging her because of all that humiliation she heaped on me when I was a boy. I wanted that damned Minerva back. But now . . ."

"Now you want more. You want her."

Tony looked at his friend and sighed. "God help me, Ian, I do."

"Is she going to be just another challenge for you, then? I know how you love the thrill of the game, but what if your luck runs out this time? Are you prepared to fail with Miss Parrish?"

"I don't know. And I don't completely understand the stakes, so I can't yet define failure. I have begun to believe, though, that she might be willing to take me as a lover."

Ian eyed him skeptically. "Is that what you want? Is that *all* you want from her?"

"Maybe. I don't know."

"I wish I had a guinea for every 'I don't know' you've uttered tonight. If you didn't care about her, there would be no question. All this uncertainty leads me to believe that you do care. I think you simply haven't yet admitted it to yourself."

"And I think you should mind your own business."

Ian grinned. "Ha! Now I know it's serious. But I'll not badger you about it. I'll leave you in peace to sort it out."

But Tony didn't really want to sort anything out. He liked to keep things simple. He wanted her. Badly. That was simple enough. But only in his bed? Or did he want more? Did he want her in his life? Did he want her heart and soul as well as her body? And what about her? What did she want? What if he helped to free her from all those invisible chains that bound her, and she flew right out of his life on her new wings?

Lord, so many questions and so few answers. Damn. There was nothing simple about it at all.

Chapter 9

"**H**ave you taken Anthony to bed yet?"

Edwina looked up from the drawings spread out on the dining-room table. "I beg your pardon?"

"I shouldn't pry, of course." Flora gave a self-deprecating smile. "But that never stopped me. I have a great fondness for him, you know. And it's clear as a midsummer's day you're attracted to each other. I just wondered if that attraction had led to the bedroom yet."

It was no use objecting to such an improper subject of conversation. She had learned that Flora was very frank in discussions of a personal nature. No subject was too intimate or too private. Almost paradoxically, though, she was also the soul of discretion. Edwina had often teased her about publishing her memoirs. Flora had claimed that though she had nothing to be ashamed of in her own life, she would never stoop to discuss the private lives of the men she'd known. That would be disrespectful and dishonorable. Flora had a bone-deep sense of honor. It was one of the things Edwina liked most about her. She didn't probe for information so she could gossip elsewhere. She simply asked outright what was on her mind, proper or not.

"I am not sleeping with Anthony," Edwina said. "It would be foolish to do so. He is my employer. For the moment. He holds my future in his hands, you may recall."

"Bah! A silly little wager that you are bound to win. You should not let that get in the way of life's pleasures."

Edwina was glad Flora and others were so confident of her victory in the wager with Anthony. She would never admit it, but she did not always share that same confidence. Subscription numbers were slowly increasing, but not at the rate needed to reach her goal by November. Much as it pained her to consider it, she just might be working for Anthony Morehouse for a good, long time.

"It would not be wise to become intimate with him, Flora."

"Well, then, perhaps *after* you've won."

Edwina laughed. "Recollect, if you will, that I am a respectable spinster. I am not like you, Flora. I do not hop into bed with every attractive man who comes along. No offense meant, of course."

"None taken. But you have hopped once or twice, have you not?"

"Flora!"

"You must have done. I mean, look at you. You're quite the most beautiful creature I think I've ever seen. You must have to beat men away with a stick. But surely there have been one or two who got in the door. I realize you're a spinster, though God knows why. But that doesn't mean you're a virgin. Good Lord, you're blushing. Don't tell me you *are* a virgin?"

"It is not right to speak of such things."

"And here I thought you were an enlightened woman. Well, you don't have to say anything. I have been around many more years than you, my girl, and I have learned a thing or two along the way." She picked up one of the drawings and studied it closely.

"Spinsters, for example," she continued, and picked up a second drawing to compare to the first. "There are the ones who titter and twitch around a gentleman because they have no experience of men and are intimidated by them. Then there are those who hate men, for whatever reason. Perhaps because they've been passed over by them. These sorts scowl and hiss and generally scare the life out of any man who comes near them."

She put both drawings down and regarded Edwina with frank appraisal. "Then there are the spinsters by choice, who have had a taste of life, but decide not to commit theirs into the keeping of one man. You are of this last type, I believe."

Edwina shrugged. "I am definitely unmarried by choice."

"I thought as much. And the way you act around men, especially Anthony, tells me that you are neither hateful of them nor intimidated by them. You have experienced men, or at least a man, and so you are comfortable with them, comfortable with your reaction to them, even if that reaction is sexual."

Edwina thought of her reaction to Anthony's kiss. She was not at all comfortable with it. She had expected that after so many years the sensations would have dimmed. Instead, she had begun to believe that physical desire intensified with age. It seemed to have done so with her.

"You ought to be a writer, Flora. You have a grand imagination."

"Oh, you disappoint me, my dear. You will not admit to anything, will you? You will maintain your appearance of respectable spinsterhood. I had rather hoped to hear a story of grand passion. Or two."

"There is nothing to tell." Nothing she wished to tell.

"Well then, perhaps there will be, soon enough." Flora smiled suggestively.

"I am not interested in taking Anthony for a lover."

Flora's eyes widened in disbelief. "Why ever not? Good God, do not tell me you are holding out for marriage? At your age, my dear?"

Edwina chuckled. She was approaching thirty and yet you'd think she was near the end of her life, the way everyone seemed so concerned about her age. "I am not looking for marriage, either."

"Then you are a fool, my girl, if you will not have him for either a lover or a husband. It would be criminal to let such a lovely man get away, especially when he is so obviously attracted to you. You could do much worse than to take Anthony Morehouse for your lover. He knows how to treat a woman."

"Is he . . . are you . . . ?" Edwina felt a blush heat her cheeks and couldn't bring herself to finish the question she was dying to ask. She looked away and gave her attention to the drawings.

"Is he my lover?" Flora asked for her. She shook her head. "No. He was, several years ago. It turned out we made better friends than lovers. Anthony needs a woman who can commit to him and him alone. I was not able to do that."

Edwina puzzled over this information. It seemed a paradox of sorts that a man who lived through the uncertainties of gambling would seek the certainty of a committed relationship. Or maybe he needed it to keep him anchored in some way. That did not also mean, though, that he himself promised fidelity in return.

What did it matter? All she wanted from Anthony was the *Cabinet*. She was not seeking a commitment, or anything else personal from him. A single kiss, no matter how explosive, did not constitute a promise.

"I was just another one of Anthony's rebellions," Flora said. "He made certain our liaison was very public so that his father would be sure to hear of it. He had earned Sir Frederick's ire so often without trying that he had begun to do so deliberately, I think. Poor Anthony. He could never please that man."

"Well, he *is* a gambler. That would displease any parent, I should think."

"Except that it was his father who pushed him into it."

Edwina's brows shot up in astonishment. "Anthony's father encouraged him to gamble?"

"No, of course not. But Sir Frederick is a very formidable man with very traditional values. Hates frivolity or recklessness. And the French. And Fox, of course. Anthony took a few missteps when he was young and the man never forgave him. He thoroughly crushed the boy's dreams of doing anything useful. Anthony is simply living up to, or perhaps down to, his father's expectations. And I was a part of all that."

Flora made it sound as though cocky, confident

Anthony thought himself a failure. That he sought ways to fail in order to prove his father was right about him. It was hard to believe. Edwina had assumed he was simply another one of those self-absorbed pleasure seekers who filled London's ballrooms and clubs and gaming hells. She would like to have learned more, but she already felt intrusive.

"I beg your pardon, Flora. Your relationship with Anthony is none of my business. But these drawings are. Now let us decide on which ones to use for the next issue."

"You'll want a morning dress and an evening dress, of course. The first to give the readers something they might actually aspire to wear. The second to give them something to dream about."

"They're all so lovely." Edwina sorted through the half-dozen drawings done by Raisbeck from live models. "Not so stiff and formal as our previous prints."

"And the faces. Just look at those faces. You can tell Lionel makes a living painting portraits. You should allow him to paint you, my dear."

"I have no need for a portrait. Though I do love his work. This one in particular." She held up a drawing of a woman in a promenade dress. "You can practically hear the swishing of her skirts as she moves."

"Perhaps, then, you should model for one of the fashion prints."

Edwina chuckled. "I would need someone to dress me properly, then. As you see, I have little sense for fashion and no style whatsoever."

"With your looks, my dear, who needs style? But if you ever want advice, I'd be happy to oblige. If you were going out for an evening with Anthony, for example."

"I cannot imagine such a circumstance. He has taken me driving a few times, that is all. Now, which one of the evening dresses would make the best fashion plate?"

"Has he kissed you?"

"What?"

"You said you have not been to bed with him. I'd be sorely disappointed in the boy if he has not yet kissed you."

"If you must know, he kissed me the first time we met. I mean the first time since we were children."

"Good for him. Always was quick-witted. That's why he's such a successful gambler. Never misses an advantage. So, has he kissed you again?"

"Really, Flora!"

"Lord, you are skittish. As if talking about such matters would be the least bit shocking to me. Recollect who I am, my dear."

"It's just . . . very personal. I'm not comfortable speaking of such private matters."

"Silly notion, between women. Between friends."

"All right. Yes." She blurted it out before she could stop herself. "He kissed me again."

"And?"

And her mind had been in an almost perpetual state of confusion ever since. Thoughts of Anthony and his kiss had interfered with her work altogether too often. Her mind wandered, her skin tingled and flushed at the memory, her stomach tied itself into knots of anxiety. She felt rather foolish, as though she were sixteen and had just been kissed for the first time.

She had so far been helpless to keep such silliness under control, and that made her nervous. It was not like her to be so undisciplined. For almost eight years she had imposed a strict restraint on her emotions, her passions, her life. She would never again be the victim of impassioned chaos.

And yet, there was something so seductive about it, about the way she'd felt after Anthony's kiss. He had been the first man in all that time to bring about those quivery, legs-turning-to-jelly feelings again. Probably because he'd been the first man bold enough to just walk up and kiss her, as he did that first time, sneaking through a tiny chink in the armor before she even knew it was there. He'd almost stripped the armor away entirely the second time, and she had let him. Fool! It would be much too easy to succumb to those feelings again. And much too dangerous.

Which is why she'd avoided being alone with him again, always keeping Prudence or Nicholas in the room with them. He had invited her out driving several more times, and she had gone once, having run out of excuses. But she made sure he kept to the public areas and never veered off into any remote corner of the park. He was always the perfect gentleman in public, though he whispered teasing comments about getting her alone and inviting further demonstrations.

"And?" Flora asked again, dragging Edwina's thoughts back to the present. "Did you enjoy his kiss?"

Edwina sighed. "Yes, I did. But enough of that. We have much to do. Choose one of the evening-dress drawings, Flora, and let's get on with it."

"This one."

"Fine. Now we can send these to Keech for engraving. But we still have a problem to deal with. Because of increased subscriptions, we will need almost three thousand engravings to be hand colored. Imber has said his small staff can no longer handle the volume. He suggests coloring only a small portion and selling those issues for a higher price. But frankly, I'd prefer to have them all colored. It would be such a bother to keep track of which subscribers got color and which did not."

"No, no, they must all be colored," Flora said. "Your old plates were colored. You cannot offer simple line engravings now, even if they are of better quality. Besides, you cannot expect to continue increasing your subscriptions without hand-colored plates."

"I agree. But it looks like we will have to hire our own colorists. Perhaps Pru can help find them."

"Now that one is a different matter, is she not? She could stand to be kissed. By that handsome brother of yours."

Edwina's head jerked up. "Nicholas? Kiss Prudence? Don't be ridiculous, Flora."

"Not at all ridiculous. The girl can hardly see straight when he's in the room. Of course, he barely notices her, which is a pity. I shall have to teach her a few tricks to catch his eye."

Edwina stared at her. "Prudence? Interested in Nicholas? Surely not."

"Use the eyes in your head, my girl. She's top-over-tail in love with him, poor thing."

Edwina was stunned. She had never noticed anything of the sort. Prudence was her friend. How could she have failed to notice something so important? Was she so absorbed in the *Cabinet* and her own personal interests that she paid no attention to those close to her?

"Does Prudence know where to find colorists?" Flora asked.

"I don't know." She was still unsettled by the notion of Prudence being in love with Nicholas, and her mind wasn't yet back on the business at hand.

"Where does one find them? What sorts of skills are required?"

Edwina shrugged. "I suppose they must have

some ability with water colors and be able to paint carefully and neatly. They are usually young women who do piecework here and there and are paid by the sheet. We can't pay them much, I'm afraid. But I suppose we could place an ad in one of the dailies."

"Could they work here, do you think?"

"Here?"

"If you could provide the materials, the paints and brushes and such, I believe I could hire you a group of colorists who would be willing to work cheaply and would appreciate the work."

"Truly? Well, I don't see why they couldn't work here. It would only be a few days a month. And we seldom use the dining room for dining anymore. We could certainly turn it into a workshop." She smiled at Flora. "Why not?"

"How many do you need?"

"Perhaps a half dozen?"

"Consider it done."

"Oh, Flora, you are a wonder. If we get these drawings to Keech right away, he could probably have the engravings printed next week. Do you think the girls could be here on Thursday?"

"I'll have them here with bells on."

"Miss Parrish be in the garden out back. Shall I take you to her?"

"Thank you, Lucy, but I can find my own way."

Tony nodded toward the coalscuttle in her hand and the dirty cloth draped over her arm. "Looks like you're busy enough."

She gave him a saucy look, bobbed a shallow curtsey, then disappeared down the stairs to the lower level. Tony stepped into the entry and was placing his hat on the hall table when he became aware of voices coming from the dining room. Female voices.

"They ain't supposed ter be red, ye stupid cow."

"She said they was pink."

He cocked an ear to listen while he tugged off his gloves.

"Yeah, but 'oo'd want prissy pink slippers when they could 'ave red ones?"

"Better make 'em pink, Sadie."

"Wot color was this ribbon supposed ter be?"

"I made mine yeller."

"T'ink I'll make mine green."

"Yer sure them slippers can't be red?"

"Make 'em pink if yer wanna get paid."

"We could put red stripes on 'em."

"Cor, red-striped slippers. That'd be summink. Wot I wouldn't give fer a pair o' them."

"Yer can't give wot yer don't 'ave, Madge, an' I figger as how y'ain't got much o' nuffink to give wot ain't already been took."

Cackles of coarse laughter filled the air. Tony peeked in the doorway of the dining room. He was brought up short by the sight of six scruffy women who looked for all the world like they had just stepped out of the back alleys of Covent Garden.

Their clothing was faded, patched, and worn, with pitiful little scraps of tattered lace or ribbon added here and there in an attempt at adornment, or to disguise frayed edges of sleeves or necklines. Two of them wore corsets over their bodices. One wore a cloth bonnet with crushed feathers on the side.

"Yer want striped slippers, Madge? Git yerself some toff from up west an' work a pair orff 'im."

"Ha! Don' I wish."

"Now wot yer be wantin' wiv slippers, anyway? Wouldn't last a week on the streets."

" 'Ere now, wot's this?"

He'd been spotted.

"Cor lumme, Madge, would yer look at this? It's yer West End toff in the flesh. Look at all them fancy sparklers danglin' at 'is waist."

"Ooh, ain't 'e a pretty one."

"A sight prettier'n yerself, Sadie."

"Wun't mind smokin' dat pipe."

"I'd share me mutton wid 'at one any day."

"C'mon in, dearie. We in't gorn to bite."

Tony wasn't so sure about that. "Perhaps later, ladies," he said. "Good day."

A burst of shrill laughter was followed by a buzz of excited chatter as Tony hurried down the hall to the garden entrance beyond the study.

What the devil was going on here? He felt like

he'd wandered into a madhouse. Or a cheap brothel. What were six old bawds doing in Edwina's dining room?

He stopped at the open door to the garden. He'd never been in the back rooms of the house, and so had never had a view of the garden. It was tiny, hardly bigger than a snuff box, but just as decorative. A strict formality had been forced onto the small space. The sides were defined by tall, clipped yew hedges that acted as walls. The back was enclosed by a stone wall shared with the neighboring houses, and was here covered with espaliered pear trees in full fruit. Gravel paths split the garden into quadrants, with a central octagon in which a small statue of Diana held court above a lush mound of periwinkle. Geometrical patterns of low, ruthlessly clipped box enclosed beds of herbs and late-summer roses in each quadrant. It was orderly, rigid, and neat as a pin.

Edwina was bent over one of the far sections, pulling weeds and flinging them into a basket at her feet. Tony watched her, unobserved, from the garden door. She wore a green apron over a white muslin dress and a broad gypsy hat of chip straw. She looked charmingly rustic, and he savored a moment of private scrutiny.

The sun was bright and the sky clear, a good enough reason to send anyone outdoors. A slight breeze moved the muslin of her skirts and lifted the apron ties at her back. She straightened, one gloved hand on her hip, spied another offending weed, and bent to remove it. She reached for it, couldn't get to it, and stretched farther, bending low from the waist and thrusting her nicely rounded bottom into the air. Bracing herself with one foot slightly behind the other, she tugged. The plant was stubborn and she tugged harder, stretching the fabric of her dress taut across her shoulders. The weed gave up its roots at last, sending her bobbling backward slightly. She straightened, tossed the weed into the basket, lifted a hand to her hat, and searched the ground for another weed. She found one, and the routine was repeated.

Tony had been struck by her beauty from the first moment he'd laid eyes on her. There were times—when the light fell on her in a certain way, or she tilted her head at a certain angle, or she looked up quickly with an unguarded expression—when she still had the ability to leave him breathless. She faced away from him, but even so, he experienced a pang of pure desire as he anticipated seeing her face when she turned: the pale skin set off by the elegant arch of black brow above large, deep-set eyes, extraordinarily dramatic in their inky blackness, the full lips so deep a pink they looked painted.

He loved to look at her, didn't think he could ever tire of it.

But at the moment, more than her beauty was on his mind. He was about to have a moment

alone with her—one of the few since that remarkable afternoon of seductive games and passionate
kisses. He continued to invite her for drives in the
park, though he'd been accepted just once. Not
only had he wanted those opportunities to have her
to himself for a short time, but also just to get her
out of the damned house. As far as he could tell, she
seldom left Golden Square.

Part of his new campaign to teach her to be free
was to get her out of the house. It would do her no
good to learn to fly if she never left her cage. He
wanted to take her out in the evening, to the theater
or the opera or a grand Society ball. Anything. He
had considered another wager, but she was becoming wary of those tactics. Besides, he wanted her to
go with him of her own accord, not because she'd
lost a wager. And so he kept his eyes open for an
appropriate invitation, one she would not be likely
to refuse.

In the meantime, he had this private moment.

The sound of his boot heels on the gravel alerted
her to his presence, so he could not sneak up behind
her and steal a kiss. She smiled to see him, though,
and that gave him confidence.

He walked right up to her, dipped his head under
the brim of her hat, and kissed her on the mouth.
He kept it simple and quick, but it was still very
sweet.

The delight shining in her eyes was even sweeter.

"You, sir, are a rogue."

"So they tell me. But you looked too pretty to resist in the midst of your pretty little garden. I did not know you were a gardener, my dear."

"I find it rather soothing to work among the plants and flowers. And I like to be outdoors. I come out here to read sometimes when the weather permits." She nodded toward the low stone benches placed at the end of each gravel path.

"It's a lovely garden."

"Do you think so?" She looked about her and shrugged. "I realize it is not in the current taste. But the space seemed too small for the rather wild, natural style that is so popular. It needed more tamed plantings."

"And you are keeping them tame, I see." He indicated the basket at her feet.

"I fear I am rather ruthless when it comes to weeds. I will not allow their disorderly presence to spoil the harmony of it all."

"Speaking of disorderly, what the devil is that group of old tarts doing in your dining room?"

Edwina laughed. "They are rather . . . vivid, are they not? That, sir, is your new staff of colorists. They are providing the hand coloring for our new prints."

"Do I detect the work of Flora in this?"

"Yes, she asked to hire them when I told her Imber could no longer handle it. The volume is too great, you see."

"Is it indeed? So you are inching toward winning our wager, it seems."

"More than inching. We are making great strides. We have just under three thousand subscribers now."

Tony's eyes widened in surprise. "Three thousand? Egad, I am in danger of losing the Minerva. I shall have to take steps. But tell me about these . . . colorists."

"They are all women Flora once knew, long ago before she became more successful. Can you believe that she actually kept in touch with them over the years, looked out for them in a way? Most women in her position would never have looked back."

"Flora is indeed a rare and extraordinary woman."

Edwina studied him from beneath the brim of her hat. She knew, he realized. Flora must have told her. Well, she was bound to find out sooner or later. Theirs had been a rather public liaison, after all, so what did it matter if Edwina knew about it? Still, he could not help but wonder just exactly what Flora had said.

Tony had been very young, after all, when she had become his mistress. He had not been gauche and inexperienced, precisely, but he'd known little of refinement, subtlety, or finesse. Surely Flora would not have revealed what a clumsy lover he'd been at first.

"Yes, she is quite remarkable," Edwina said. "And when she thought to provide a bit of respectable daytime employment for these women, how could I object? In fact, I am delighted to do what I can to help them stay off the streets. She did, though, make sure to bring on only those who had some skill in painting."

"But not in following directions, I fear."

"I beg your pardon?"

"From what I overheard, some of them may be taking liberties with the specified colors. Red slippers, for example."

"Red slippers?" She chuckled softly. "Oh, dear. Perhaps I had better take a look. Come along, Anthony, and I will introduce you to the 'Crimson Ladies.' "

Edwina removed her apron and gypsy hat and hung them on hooks in a small potting shed just off the entrance to the house. She shook out her muslin skirts and fluffed her hair a bit—for his benefit?—before leading him back into the house.

The chatter from the dining room met them the minute they entered the hall. But when they approached the open doorway, he saw that each woman was bent over a sheet of printed figures, carefully adding color as they talked.

"How are things progressing, ladies?" Edwina asked.

They all looked up at her words, though most eyes fell on Tony. He felt he was being mentally undressed from six different directions. It was most unsettling. He stepped behind Edwina.

"We be gettin' a lot done, miss." A dark-haired, buxom woman of indeterminate age seemed to be the spokeswoman for the group. "See 'ere."

Edwina walked in and picked up several completed sheets from a large stack, each sheet with two engravings printed upon it. "Oh."

Her voice, and her expression, registered uncertainty. Tony could see why. Not a single sheet appeared to be identical. The shawls and sashes and ribbons and slippers and bonnets and gloves were all neatly colored in a variety of bright, bold colors. Primrose yellow and fiery orange. Deep violet and bright apple green. And red. Lots of red. Tony had to suppress a grin.

Edwina gave a resigned shrug of her shoulders and smiled. "Well, they are beautifully painted, and certainly are colorful."

" 'Fraid we might've mixed up some o' the colors," the leader said, pushing back a lock of brown hair that had come loose from the untidy knot at her nape. "Couldn't 'member wot yer said 'bout some, and none of us can read good 'nuff to make sense o' that writin' yer give us."

"Oh, of course," Edwina said, and looked chagrined. "Forgive me. I hadn't thought about that. I believe what we should do next time is to have one set already colored, and you ladies can simply copy it."

"That'd be good, but 't'were more fun this way. Got to use our 'maginations, like."

"Figgered them pale colors wouldn't catch nobody's eye," a full-bosomed redhead offered. "Brightened 'em up a bit."

"You certainly did," Edwina said. "I think they are quite charming." She shot a skeptical look at Anthony.

"I agree, Miss Parrish," he said as he stepped into the room. "Bright colors are much to be preferred, I think."

"Ladies, may I introduce to you Mr. Morehouse? He is the owner of the *Cabinet*."

"Is 'e now?"

"This pretty man?"

"Well, don't that beat all."

Edwina smiled and gestured for him to come closer. He stayed where he was.

"This is Madge." She indicated the dark-haired leader. "She has agreed to act as group supervisor, which frees up some of my time, for which I am most grateful."

"Good afternoon, Madge."

"Afternoon yerself, darlin'." She eyed him up and down suggestively. "Long time since such an 'andsome devil paid me fer work." She winked at him.

"Honest work, Madge," he said.

"Ay, an' I thank ye fer it, too. Gettin' too old fer night work."

"And this is Ginny," Edwina said, indicating a slightly younger and prettier woman with a head full of frizzy brown hair that stuck out in all directions.

Ginny smiled and batted her lashes, then reached her hand down into her corset and adjusted her breasts, lifting them higher. "Hey there, 'andsome. I i'nt too old fer night work, if yer interested."

Tony grinned and hoped to heaven his cheeks weren't flaming red.

"This is Polly," Edwina said, unable to keep the twinkle of amusement from her eyes. "She's our face painter. She has such a way with faces we asked if she would do them all. Only see what a beautiful job she's done."

"Only paintin' wot that Raisbeck feller already drawed," Polly said. She had limp blonde hair, pale rheumy eyes, and a stick-thin body that looked as if it had not seen a healthy day in many years. She was likely much younger than she looked. "Such pretty faces. It be a true pleasure to paint 'em. An' to git paid, too. Almost don't seem right."

"Don't be daft, girl," Madge said. "O' course it's right."

"Indeed it is," Edwina said. "You're providing a special skill, Polly, a valuable skill. It's a real art to be able to blend the flesh tones just right, to add a blush to the cheek without it looking harsh. Your sweet faces will set these prints apart from those of any other publication. Of course you should be paid."

"They are indeed beautiful," Tony said. "It's a pleasure to meet you, Polly."

The girl tittered behind her hand and looked away.

"This is Bess," Edwina said, indicating the woman seated beside Polly, a blowsy pink-cheeked redhead as round as Polly was thin. She smiled and revealed deep dimples and a missing front tooth.

"How d'ye do, sweet cakes?" There was a touch of Irish in her voice.

"Good afternoon, Bess."

"And this is Marguerite." Dark ringlets arranged in a youthful style framed a face that had grown coarse and hard. But there was a twinkle in her brown eyes.

"That's a beautiful name," Tony said.

"Me muvver were French." She thrust her bosom high and fluffed her ringlets so they bounced about her cheeks.

"Har!" Ginny exclaimed. "The closest 'er ma ever got to France was when she were 'it in the 'ead wiv a empty brandy bottle tossed out of an 'ackney by some flash cove."

The women cackled with laughter.

" 'Er name's Daisy," Madge said with a wicked grin. "Tries ter make it soun' fancy, like. Mar-gur–reet. Just a Frenchified way o' sayin' Daisy."

"I can call meself whatsoever I bloody-well please, and I like Marguerite, thank you very much."

"It is a pleasure to meet you, Marguerite," Tony said.

Marguerite nudged Bess in the ribs and said, "See? This one be a proper gent."

"And finally," Edwina said, still smiling, "this is Sadie."

She had a long, plain face with a prominent beaky nose, and dirty blonde hair piled high on her head. Her thin chest was wrapped in a muslin fichu that had once been white but was now gray and stained.

"How do you do, Sadie?"

"A lot better fer 'avin' a look at yer phiz, pretty boy."

"You are each doing a wonderful job," Edwina said. "Madge, come to me when you're all ready to quit for the day and I will pay you before you leave. Now, we will let you ladies get back to your work."

Edwina left the room and Tony followed. When he reached the door, he turned and gave a smile and a wink to the group in general. Shrieks of laughter and a string of bawdy suggestions rang out behind him as he made his way down the hall and into Edwina's study.

He closed the door behind him, leaned against it, and began to laugh. Edwina's laughter joined his as she sank into the chair behind her desk.

"That was cruel," he said at last. He walked to

the desk and hitched one hip onto its edge. "Like throwing a lamb to the wolves. I feared for my life in there."

She grinned. "You handled it very well. Like a true gentleman. You treated them like ladies, which they are unlikely to forget."

"You are a courageous woman to bring that lot into your home. You'd better keep an eye on the Crimson Ladies. And count the silver before they leave."

"Nonsense. They may be vulgar and illiterate—what an idiot I am for not realizing they could not read the descriptions—but they are not thieves. I only hope I can give them enough work so they will not have to work the streets. Or at least not so often. Oh, but what am I going to do about those prints? Flora will have an apoplexy when she sees they don't match her descriptions in the least."

"Bringing in those doxies was her idea, so she will have to live with it."

"I will tell you something," Edwina said, "that will no doubt demonstrate my complete ignorance of such things. Something I am certainly foolish to admit to a man of fashion like yourself. But I rather liked the way they colored the prints. Go ahead, laugh. But I prefer bright colors. I always have. I wish they were more popular."

"I have a feeling they will be, once this issue is distributed."

*   *   *

Two weeks later, a remarkable number of fashionable ladies were seen about town wearing bold shades of orange and green and purple in combinations never before attempted. And shoemakers had difficulty keeping up with an unusual number of requests for red-striped slippers.

Chapter 10

❦

"Hullo, Withers. I believe m'mother is expecting me."

"She is, Mr. Anthony. She will be pleased to see you, sir."

Tony handed his hat and walking stick to the butler, peeled off his gloves and dropped them into the hat. Withers handed it all over to a hovering footman Tony did not recognize, and led the way upstairs to his mother's sitting room.

He did not visit as often as he should, and this time he'd been summoned. His mother's note had not said what she wanted, but only that he should call upon her at this time.

He found her elegantly arranged upon a chaise with a mountain of lace pillows at her back and a book propped open on her lap. Two or three India muslin shawls were draped about her shoulders, and a fetching lace cap was perched upon her blonde curls and tied beneath her chin.

"Anthony! My dear boy. You have come at last."

She held out a hand to him, and he took it and kissed it, then bent and kissed her cheek as well.

"You're looking very pretty this morning, Mother."

"And you are turned out as fine as fivepence, as always. I am so glad you do not powder that lovely golden hair."

"No one powders anymore, Mother."

"Not among your generation, perhaps. Mine can't seem to get both feet over into the new century."

"You still have beautiful hair. You have no need of powder."

"One of the blessings of being fair, as you will learn for yourself one day, is that silver strands are less noticeable among the gold. But your father would not approve if I went out without powder in the evenings."

"He doesn't approve of anything I do, so I shall not concern myself over his objection to my un-powdered head." He ran his hands through his hair with casual indifference. "Your note was a bit vague, but I got the impression you had a specific purpose in wanting to see me."

"Yes, I do. Sit down, my boy."

He pulled up a chair and sank into it with languid ease. "What is it, Mother? Have I done something to put me in Father's black books again? Surely he's not upset about those turkeys in Green Park. It was a harmless wager, I assure you."

"This has nothing to do with your father, my dear, and I'm not even going to ask about turkeys in Green Park."

She sent him a gentle look of reproof that made him feel like a naughty schoolboy. Tony gave an insolent shrug and flashed a grin he knew his mother could not resist. He had almost always been able to charm her into taking his side whenever his father rang a peal over him.

She smiled. "Incorrigible boy. No, no, it is something else entirely. The most curious thing, actually." She shifted upon the pillows and sat up a bit straighter. "I was having tea with Mrs. Balcombe-Shinn yesterday. I detest the woman, you know, but I owed her an invitation and thought to get it out of the way. Anyway, she was wearing the most garish sash of bright orange, with matching orange and yellow ribbons on her hat. And she was going on and on about some magazine and its new fashion plates that had inspired her to brighten her wardrobe."

Oh, God.

"She finally pulled a copy out of her ridiculously large reticule and showed me. *The Ladies' Fashionable Cabinet.* I had seen it before, of course. It's been around for years. But Mrs. Balcombe-Shinn was exclaiming about recent changes, new fashion reports, and what not, so I flipped through it just to be polite. Before I handed it back to her, something on the cover happened to catch my eye. You will not credit it, my dear. At the bottom, in tiny print, it said 'Printed for A. Morehouse, Charles Street.' Well, you can imagine my surprise."

"Indeed."

She frowned. "At first I thought it must be some other A. Morehouse, but I am familiar with most of your father's family and could come up with no other possibility." She cocked her head to one side and regarded him thoughtfully. "It is you, is it not, my boy?"

"It is."

Her blue eyes widened slightly. "You are the proprietor of a ladies' magazine?"

"I am."

"But . . . but how?"

"I won it in a card game."

She stared at him for a moment, unblinking, and then quite astonished him by bursting into laughter. "Oh, my dear boy," she said at last, "you are a hopeless knave but always so thoroughly entertaining. How do you do it? Wait until your father hears about this."

"I would prefer he did not hear about it just yet, Mother."

"Why ever not?"

"He will only think it frivolous, a waste of time and money. Just one more mark against me."

"You cannot avoid it forever, love. He is bound to find out sooner or later."

"I'd prefer it to be later. Give me a little more time."

"Why? What is liable to happen to change things?"

"I am hoping to make it into a success." The words were out almost before he realized what he was saying.

He wasn't sure when the idea had begun to form in his mind. Perhaps it was that first time he'd seen his name on the cover listed as publisher. There had been a rush of pride when he saw it, to have his name associated with a successful business venture. He'd had many business successes over the years, of course, but as an investor or silent partner. This one actually had his name on it.

At least for now.

He found himself taking a more serious interest in the *Cabinet* and all that Edwina hoped to accomplish. He wanted it to be successful, whether he won the wager or not. Even if he lost, which he was making every effort to do, he planned to offer himself as an investor, infusing more capital to make the publication all that Edwina wanted. Perhaps she might even agree to having his name on the cover with hers: "Printed for E. Parrish and A. Morehouse."

For the first time in years, Tony was excited about something other than a high-stakes game or a risky investment scheme. Even if the *Cabinet* was a huge success, it would not make him rich. But it would make him proud.

What a novel experience that would be.

"I am so pleased to hear that," his mother said. "It's an odd venture, to be sure, but it is so nice to hear you take an interest in something other than cards for a change. Even a ladies' magazine. I'm so proud of you, love. And I think your father would be, too."

"I doubt it. But I'm glad you're pleased."

"Tell me everything, my boy. I want to hear how you have become a publisher."

And so he told her everything. About Croyden. About Edwina. About their wager.

"I sent Millie out to buy a copy for me," she said, "and I have to say I enjoyed it tremendously. The fashion report especially. It was great fun to try to guess whose dresses were being described, and those who were mentioned by name, or by suggestion, must be in high alt. What a clever idea that was. Oh, and the plates really were lovely, if a bit unusual. But I believe they've started quite a trend. Mrs. Balcombe-Shinn is not the only one I've seen in some of the new, bold colors. They are quite the rage."

"I had noticed. Shall I tell you how they came

about? I'm afraid you might find it rather shocking."

He told her about the Crimson Ladies, and she
laughed until tears ran down her cheeks.

"I believe I shall pay a visit to Mrs. Twigge tomorrow and see about having a pelisse made up in
one of the new colors." She flashed him a teasing
smile. "I would hate to appear out of step."

"And don't forget the red slippers."

"With stripes. Duly noted."

"Besides the fashion plates," he said, "what did
you think of the rest of the magazine?" Lady Octavia Morehouse was fairly typical of her class, the
very sort Edwina should be seeking as subscribers.
It might be useful to solicit her opinion.

"Well, let me think. The Busybody is entertaining. Are those letters genuine, by the way, or merely
made up so she can pen the advice she wants?"

"I believe they are genuine. I haven't yet met the
Busybody, but will be sure to ask her when I do.
What else?"

"The poetry was lovely, as I recall."

"Not too sentimental?"

"My dear boy, a woman never tires of romantic
poetry. You would do well to learn that if you are
going to publish a magazine for ladies."

"What about the essays and book reviews and
such?"

She shrugged her slim shoulders. "A bit on the

dry side for me, but you know I was never a scholar like you or your father. I'm afraid my tastes run rather shallow. Amusing, lighthearted entertainment suits me best."

"What about the fiction? You've always been an avid reader of novels." He indicated the book in her lap. "What do you think of the serialized stories in the *Cabinet*?"

"I adore a good serial. The more romantic and sentimental the better. I must confess that I have a weakness for the stories in the *Lady's Monthly Museum*. I always turn into a watering pot before they end."

"So you like their stories better?"

"Yours did not make me cry. I do enjoy a good cry."

"Well then, I shall just see what I can do to make them sadder for you. And now, I'm afraid I really must toddle off." He rose and shook out his coattails.

"So soon? But I haven't seen you in such an age. And there is so much else to catch up on." She waved him back to his chair.

"Is there? What have you been up to, then?"

"Nothing at all. It's deadly dull in town this time of year. But your father refuses to leave while Parliament is still in session, and it looks like it will never end this year. Something about a budget not yet passed and something about the war with France. I am not certain of the details, of course. I never pay much attention to such things. But so long as your uncle Cedric retains his seat, your father will be there beside him, whispering advice in his ear."

"Father should simply find a burrough and take his own seat."

"I wish he would do so. For some reason, though, he seems to prefer working quietly behind the scenes, helping Cedric build coalitions or whatever it is they do. Anyway, I suspect we will not see Handsley before Christmas."

"Really?"

Something important must be brewing. Tony had heard rumors of peace negotiations with Bonaparte but discounted them as wishful thinking on the part of a war-weary people. Addington had been preaching peace since he came into office and established his administration as a clear breach with the war ministry of Pitt. Tony had no particular faith in the man. He appeared colorless and mediocre compared to Pitt. But perhaps he had done as he'd claimed and found a way to negotiate a peace.

"But enough of that," his mother said. "Tell me about this Miss Parrish of yours."

"Edwina?"

His use of her Christian name brought a smile to his mother's lips. "Yes, tell me about Edwina. I vaguely remember her as a coltish young girl coming to visit her grandfather. What is she like now?"

Tony shrugged. "Bright. Quick-witted. Capable. Fiercely independent. Beautiful."

She raised her eyebrows slightly. "You're in love with her."

"Mother, you are such a romantic. I use a handful of words to describe a woman and somehow you deduce I am in love with her."

"It is not what you say about her. It is how you look when you say it."

Tony shook his head and said nothing. He didn't know how he looked when he spoke of Edwina. But he knew how he felt, and he was beginning to think his mother was right.

"Is she in love with you?"

"I don't know. I doubt it. I've wagered her for ownership of the magazine, you see."

"Oh, Anthony." Her eyes softened and she reached out a hand to him. "My dear boy, you may be risking too much this time. You could be in danger of losing more than you bargained for."

"Sometimes you have to risk it all, Mother, if the stakes are worth it."

"I think you should read this."

Edwina stared in anxious consternation at the latest copy of the *Lady's Monthly Museum* Anthony had just tossed on her desk. "Why?"

"I have it on unimpeachable authority that their fiction is better than ours."

Two trains of thought battled for prominence in

her brain: her total contempt for the *Museum* and its editors, and the fact the Anthony had taken to referring to the *Cabinet* as "ours."

"What authority?"

"My mother."

She couldn't suppress a smile. "Your mother is an authority on fiction?"

"So long as it is sentimental, romantic, and even a little gothic, there is no better authority. She is a voracious reader of novels, you see."

"And she prefers the fiction of the *Museum*?"

"Says it makes her cry."

"Well, of course it does." Her smile had dissolved into a frown of pure disgust. "Every single story in the *Museum* ends tragically, with death or madness or ruin or hopelessness. I get so angry when I think of how they manipulate their readers with sentiment and melodrama. It's what we've been fighting against for over four years now."

"Fighting?"

Oh, dear. She hadn't meant to say all that.

"What are we fighting, Edwina?"

We. How long ago had she given up all hopes that he would stay out of the business? And at what point had she decided she no longer cared that he did not?

She studied him for a long moment. Could she trust him, this reckless, impulsive, seductive man? He was also honorable, generous, and honest, yet she had been none of those things to him. Perhaps it was time to change that. It was time to trust him. A little.

"Perhaps you had better sit down," she said.

He gave her a wary look, but moved from his favorite perch on the edge of her desk and sat in the armchair opposite. His gray eyes regarded her frankly. "I'm listening."

"You know enough of my opinions on political and social issues not to be surprised at what I'm about to say."

He nodded for her to continue.

She held up the loathsome magazine. "Do you see what it says here on the cover? 'The Lady's Monthly Museum; or Polite Repository of Amusement and Instruction being an assemblage of whatever can tend to please the fancy, interest the mind, or exalt the character of The British Fair, by a Society of Ladies.'

"The 'instruction' is of a specific nature to encourage weakness and complaisance in all females. And the 'Society of Ladies' is not a group of women at all, but of very conservative men. You see, the *Museum* was started in reaction to all the republican ideals and rational philosophies that rose up in the last fifteen years or so."

"Anti-Jacobins?"

"Yes, and more. This group of men is part of the general conservative reaction in this country against the Revolution in France. They truly believe that education of the lower classes will lead to revolt—'poisoning the minds of the lower orders.' They fear an uprising here in England, especially with yet another year of bad harvests and economic hardship. These men, who may have other political outlets for all I know, decided to use a ladies' magazine as one vehicle for their reactionary messages."

"Seems an odd choice."

"It's likely one of many—antidotes to the 'poison' of rational debate. This one is aimed at keeping women in line."

"Ah. Protecting them against the venomous messages of women like Mary Wollstonecraft?"

"Mary, Thomas Paine, and others. These men believe that all the underclasses, and that certainly includes women, must be subjugated to the will of the government and traditional values in general. And so they have used the *Lady's Monthly Museum* as a means of reaching one of those worrisome groups, encouraging women to reject any ideas smacking of the rational, the radical, or the republican."

"You intrigue me. How do they do it?"

"By filling their pages with subtle messages calculated to subvert contrary views. Independent thinking is discouraged. For example, those maudlin tales your mother enjoys are loaded with messages of female subservience to male will. Whenever a girl is shown to disobey or disrespect the will of her father and runs away with the man she loves, she always comes to a tragic end. They throw themselves off cliffs. They fall into madness when their lovers desert them. They are murdered when they resort to living on the streets. They are rejected by family and society. Only hopelessness, despair, and regret await them."

"Terrifying!" He gave a theatrical shudder. "I have only read the one installment of a rather gothic tale in this issue," Anthony said, pointing to the magazine on the desk, "so I don't know how it ends. But it is indeed the tale of a willful daughter who falls into the hands of a villain."

"And will no doubt be clapped in a dungeon where she will go mad or die."

"Well, that is a popular genre these days, Edwina. Readers, especially female readers, delight in the horrible. Mrs. Radcliffe and others have been very successful with it."

"And the *Museum* editors play on that success by using a popular format to subtly persuade readers into their way of thinking. And not just with fiction. Their historical and biographical essays almost always feature a woman who devoted her life to the career and happiness of her husband. Females who glory in giving up their own wishes to those of a husband or father are held up as shining examples of womanhood. Truly outstanding women are either ignored or disparaged in some way, as when one essayist claimed Queen Elizabeth could not possibly have been a true female, and was at the very least a hermaphrodite."

He gave a little snort of laughter. "Well, that certainly is a novel concept."

"And you will notice the *Museum* includes no news or current events. No mention of politics or the war. Its editors do not believe those are fit topics for the frail sensibilities of its female readers. As if our lives are not affected. Every aspect of the *Museum* extols feminine weakness and encourages complete submission to male authority. Women are encouraged to receive, with gratitude, the protection of men, yet have no support if the protector becomes the aggressor. It is very devious, actually, the way they manipulate readers. When the *Cabinet* came into my hands, I decided to use the same devious tactics against them."

He lifted a brow. "Indeed? How so?"

"I gathered a group of writers and poets who shared my views and set them to work creating articles and stories that appear to be in the same vein as those in the *Museum*, but with a completely different set of messages."

"Such as Augusta Historica's recent biographical sketch exalting the extraordinary leadership of the very female Queen Elizabeth?"

"Exactly."

"And such as stories about young women who run away with their lovers and ultimately find true happiness?"

She smiled. "Yes. Simon Westover is one of the writers who pens our fiction, and there was never a greater romantic. He loves to show young women reaching for the moon and finding it."

"Simon Westover? A *man* writes your stories?"

In for a penny, in for a pound. "Yes, he is one of many contributors. He writes the Busybody column as well."

"The devil you say! I thought the Busybody was an old woman."

Edwina flashed a grin. "That is what you are meant to think. It had in fact been an old woman when I was given the editorial reins. But she wanted to retire and Simon took over the pseudonym. His advice, as you know if you have read the column, is always supportive of young women taking responsibility for their own decisions, their own lives." She chuckled softly. "In fact, he got into a bit of trouble a while back with his advice. A woman tracked him down and wanted his head on a platter."

"Egad. What did he do?"

"He married her."

Anthony gave a bark of laughter. "Seems his advice was a success after all. But tell me more, Edwina. Who else is involved that I should know about? Nicholas?"

"Yes. He pens most of the historical and biographical essays as Augusta Historica. Samuel Coleridge contributes from time to time, both in poetry and prose. William Godwin has submitted an essay. Helen Maria Williams and Mary Hays are frequent contributors. They know my objectives and do not preach rhetoric. I would not print it, in any case. But all of them have been able to couch their principles in uplifting, positive essays and stories and poems, extolling education, intellect, and independent thought. All using pseudonyms, of course. Some of their true names might discourage the more conservative readers. But without a recognized radical or republican name attached, you'd be surprised how palatable some of their views become."

"You have gathered a remarkable team of writers, my dear. Why didn't you tell me before?"

She hunched a shoulder. "I didn't know if you'd approve. I have not been under the impression that you share many of my views."

"Even though I was able to quote Wollstonecraft well enough to win a drive in the park with you?"

She smiled. "I simply presumed you were more well read than you let on. I never really believed you harbored republican ideals in your heart."

"I don't, in fact. Not entirely, anyway. But frankly, I rather admire what you're doing." He flashed a lopsided grin. "It's quite cheeky, actually. I like that you are using the *Museum*'s own tactics to combat their influence. Good for you, Edwina."

She sank back against her chair and expelled a pent-up breath in a long sigh. She had been right to trust him. "Oh, thank God," she said. "It is such a relief to have all this out in the open. You don't know what an effort it has been to keep it secret from Uncle Victor all these years."

"No, I can imagine he would not have approved."

"He would have shut us down. Several of his own publications are in direct opposition to our principles. He even owns shares of the *Anti-Jacobin Review*."

"Well then, it was a lucky day for you when I won the *Cabinet* from him."

She smiled. "It will be an even luckier day when I win it from you."

"There you go again, getting too confident."

Her smile faded, and twisted down into a grimace when he grinned at her. She hated when he taunted her about the wager. He seemed so determined to win, so damned certain that he would. He was determined to pay her back for all those lost wagers so many years ago.

His expression softened and his eyes shot her a look so warm it made her forget to be annoyed. "Just for the sake of argument—because, of course, I fully intend to retain my ownership and win back the Minerva—just what will you do *if* you win? Will you change the content to more directly reflect your opinions?"

She regarded him curiously. The question surprised her. And she really could not help but notice the hint of playfulness in his voice when he claimed he would win. Was he, after all, merely baiting her again? Did he, in fact, expect *her* to win?

Flora and Prudence believed he was trying his best to lose, that his insistence on increased fashion coverage, for example, was clearly meant to encourage new subscribers. Why would he bother, if not to insure Edwina won?

Edwina had never agreed with their assessment of his motives. She had believed he pushed Flora and fashion reports on her simply because it was contrary to her objectives, and his only motive was to annoy her.

Had she been wrong about him?

She studied his clear gray eyes and saw nothing but genuine interest in her answer. Had she misjudged him?

"No," she said, "I will not change content right away. I think we can reach more women, it is sad to admit, with the lure of fashion and entertainment. But once we have their attention, the other messages are there for them to absorb. So, no, I will not change the magazine, but I will take full advantage of its profits. There is so much to be done."

"To improve the publication?"

"No. The profits could be put to better use." She must be careful here. It was one thing to admit the guiding principles of her editorship, quite another to admit to other activities secretly supported by monies skimmed from the *Cabinet*'s profits. But perhaps it would not hurt to gauge his reaction to those causes. Just in case.

"So many people are in need of help," she said. "The appalling extravagance of Pitt's war with France has taken an enormous toll. Combine years of bad harvests with war taxes, and the result is that people are starving. I can't possibly help the masses, but perhaps one family at a time. I would use the profits to support factory reform and education for the poor. Just think of those poor women who are coloring our prints. If they had been given an education, even of the most rudimentary sort, they might not have had to support their families by selling themselves on the streets. I have some ideas for schools for these women."

In fact, profits siphoned from the *Cabinet* already supported one such school in St. Giles. But he need never know that. Once she'd won the wager, the profits would be hers to do with as she pleased.

"You humble me, Edwina, with your compassion and generosity. If you were to win our wager—which is, of course, not going to happen—I would happily salute your victory knowing the profits would be put to such good use."

"And if I lose?" She had no more intention of doing so than he did, but it couldn't hurt to ask about his plans.

"We shall discuss that when the time comes. In the meantime, perhaps you could show me the current subscriber lists." He flashed her a lopsided boyish grin. "Let us see how you stand in achieving this impossible dream."

As he drove back to Charles Street, Tony wondered how seriously she took his teasing about the wager. He had learned her competitive nature had not modified much over the years, so he figured his taunts only spurred her to work harder toward victory. That was precisely what had happened when they were children. Had he been astute enough to realize it, he would never have boasted so loudly that he could outrun, outride, and outclimb her. Nicholas had said the wager was a good thing, that it had pushed her in a positive way. So Tony continued to push.

He considered all she had told him about what she would do if the *Cabinet* were hers. His admiration of her had risen several notches. Her face— always a pleasure to look at in any case—had been so animated and alive as she spoke. It was another signal that considerable passion was buried beneath that all that control, passion he so wanted to expose and experience.

He was honestly impressed with what she'd accomplished, and admired her dedication to principle. He liked her all the more for it. But he had been quite truthful when he'd told her he was humbled. Again, she made him examine his own life, his selfish disregard for the plight of those less fortunate. He had a great deal of money, but he used it for little more than to make more money. Perhaps it was time to put it to better purpose.

But if he made some sort of grand charitable gesture, would it be for himself, or only to impress Edwina? He'd been trying to impress her since he was a boy, without much success. She would see right through an empty gesture, no matter how large or lavish it might appear.

Perhaps it was time to stop trying to impress her, or his father, or anyone else. He'd spent a lifetime failing to live up to the expectations of others. It was time to set his own goals and see about living up to them. For himself.

He turned the curricle away from Charles Street and toward the offices of his solicitor.

Chapter 11

～♽～

"**L**et's make all the accessories in shades of red and blue this time." Flora spoke to the eager Crimson Ladies gathered around Edwina's dining table and demonstrated what she wanted with a pair of completed prints. "In honor of the peace. Patriotic colors will be all the rage anyway, so let us be the first to embrace them."

"That's a wonderful idea," Edwina said.

"Cor luv yer, Flora, yer a bleedin' genius."

Edwina smiled at Madge and said, "Precisely what I was trying to say."

"C'mon then, girls," Madge said. "Let's git crackin'."

It was the second month of hand coloring, and the women were excited about the work. Though they tended to be bold in their use of color, the quality of their painting had been excellent. Polly, in particular, had shown remarkable talent. They were so pleased to have a legitimate source of income, however meager, that each of them took care to do a good job. They were not, however, the quietest of workers. Edwina and Flora left them to their work and chattering about the peace.

"Madge is an absolute marvel," Edwina said as they entered the study. "She keeps them all in line and makes sure they get as much work done as possible."

"She has a lot of experience keeping girls in line," Flora said. "It's been her business for years. That's why I suggested her for supervisor. And why I am giving her some other work, too. She is happy to take on some of the deliveries, to carry messages, and such."

"Well, I am very grateful to her. To all of them."

Edwina took a chair and stretched out her legs. Whenever they sat down for long chats, Flora insisted she come out from behind her desk. Friends, she had said, do not have barriers between them.

"Not as grateful," Flora said, "as they are to you for giving them a chance to earn honest money to feed their families. Most of their men, if they have any, are useless buggers who drink up any money that comes in and have no scruples about sending their women out to earn more on their backs. And it gets harder to earn much that way when your face is creased with lines and your flesh sags."

"The poor things. So long as I have any say in the matter, they will have work here. That was an inspired idea about the patriotic colors."

"I'm just hoping this peace takes. I've never had much faith in politicians, and I've heard talk this isn't the smartest treaty ever devised."

"It is merely preliminary. The formal negotiations will begin next month at Amiens. But this peace is a welcome respite. People are bled dry from so many years of war taxes. They were getting restless, with food riots and all, and I think the government was ready to do anything to prevent a Reign of Terror here in England."

Flora had taken the armchair and arranged her skirts in a perfect array of soft drapery. She regarded Edwina thoughtfully.

"You can't say those words without a hitch in your voice, can you?"

"Which words?"

" 'Reign of Terror.' I've noticed it before."

Edwina took a deep breath. Flora could be like a dog with a bone when a subject interested her. And this was not a subject Edwina wanted her to chew on.

"I asked your handsome brother about it," Flora said. "He told me something of what happened to you and your friends—arrest, imprisonment. But he was circumspect about the details and said I should ask you, that it was your story to tell."

Edwina turned away, unable to meet Flora's gaze.

"He said I should ask you about Gervaise."

Edwina's chest constricted with an old misery, long repressed. "No."

"Nicholas said you would not speak of it. But I got the feeling he thought you should. That it would do you good. So, I am here to listen, my dear. As a friend. As a woman. And nothing you say will leave this room."

Remembered grief rose up from the tightening in her chest and into her jaws. "I don't know if I can, Flora."

"Try, my dear. Tell me about Gervaise."

Edwina did not want to do this, despite what her interfering brother may think was best. It was not that she preferred to pretend it never happened, or that she locked those memories away in some deep, dark place never to be opened again. Gervaise and France were never far from her thoughts. What happened there informed every subsequent day of her life. From time to time she even spoke of it, with Prudence or Helen Williams or Nicholas. But rarely, and never without pain.

She looked up into Flora's kind eyes, however, and thought this wise, worldly woman might understand. She took a deep breath and let it out slowly—and again, and yet again—before she was able to force the tale from her lips.

"We went to France in August of '92," she began, a little shakily. "Nicholas, Simon, and me."

"Simon?"

"Simon Westover. He is a friend and writes for the *Cabinet*. He should be back in town soon and you will no doubt meet him."

"Was he your lover?"

Edwina gave a weak smile. Leave it to Flora to hone in on the really important details. "No, he was not. He was a little in love with me, but my heart was already given to someone else. I had met Gervaise de Champdivers when he came to London briefly that summer. He fired our blood with revolutionary fervor so that we all determined to go to France and be a part of this extraordinary undertaking. It was an exciting, exhilarating time. There were a lot of like-minded English in Paris then. John Hurtford Stone led the English Revolutionary Society. Helen Maria Williams held Sunday-afternoon teas that we all attended. I met and became friends with Mary Wollstonecraft there."

"And Gervaise?"

"I had fallen head-over-heels in love with him in London. We became lovers in Paris. He became my reason for living. He was everything: my life, my love, my passion. And he felt the same. He would have done anything for me."

"Except marry you?"

Edwina frowned. She had not expected such conventional concerns from Flora. "We spoke of it. But we were so busy with other more serious issues, and it never seemed nearly as important as the work we were doing. Gervaise was a Girondin, one of many who were outspoken in their support of a federal republic based on the American model. I acted as his secretary, writing letters and speeches and pamphlets. We attended Madame Roland's salons together and mingled with all the great philosophers and writers who had gathered in Paris. It was a heady time, Flora. I was in love and fired with republican fever. I never felt more alive. Those were the best days of my life."

Flora smiled but her eyes were soft with concern. "And then the Terror," she said.

"Yes. Factions had already begun to splinter the various groups. When the king was killed in January, divisions multiplied. The more moderate Girondins, who objected to the king's execution, were cast aside and the fiery rhetoric of Marat held the day. By June, most members of the Gironde were imprisoned, including Gervaise."

Her voice had become quivery and the tightening in her chest had grown stronger. She paused a moment to compose herself. Flora moved her chair closer and took Edwina's hand. She said nothing, but gave an encouraging little squeeze.

"I was beside myself with worry," Edwina con-

tinued. "Feelings were running high against for-
eigners, and most English fled Paris—were urged to
do so, in fact. But I could not leave with Gervaise in
prison. I could not."

"Of course you couldn't. What happened, my
dear?"

"Nicholas and Simon stayed behind with me. I
believe they would have fled but for my determination not to desert Gervaise. It was a terrible time—
we could never be sure who to trust, and we were
watched closely. When Marat was assassinated by
a pro-Girondiste, I went almost mad with fear for
Gervaise. And then Robespierre's inexorable rise to
power brought about a national unity more terrible
than anything we had dared envision. The Terror
began."

She stopped again, the pain of remembrance almost too much to bear. Flora sat with her in silence,
holding her hand, waiting until she could continue.

"In early October, I was arrested under the new
machinery of the Terror, along with other English
who had remained behind. I was sent to Luxem-
bourg prison along with Helen Maria Williams and
other women. Two weeks later, we could hear the
cheering of crowds in the streets after twenty-one
Girondins were executed. Gervaise was one of
them. They cheered his death. A martyr for liberty."

She reached up with her free hand to wipe away
a tear. Memories of that day were still sharp—the
raucous shouting heard through the high windows

of the prison, the scramble among the prisoners to climb atop one another to try to see outside the bars, the bellowed list of names of the "enemies of the people" who'd been brought to justice, Gervaise's name called out as one who had met Madame Guillotine.

They might as well have killed Edwina, too. She had wanted to die. Even eight years later, in her darkest moments of grief, she sometimes still did.

She took a deep breath, composed herself, and continued. "I fell quite ill with grief. Dreams of personal happiness as well as that greater noble cause had been shattered. All those whom Robespierre put to death that day had represented everything that was fine and good about the Revolution. Eloquence and idealism, youth and grand aspiration. I couldn't bear it. If Helen Williams had not been with me, I surely would have died."

"Oh, my poor child." Flora linked her fingers with Edwina's and held on tightly. "How long were you kept in prison?"

"Helen was able to manipulate her own release in November, and took me with her. Nicholas and Simon had escaped imprisonment through a complicated intrigue involving false papers and a series of hideaways. Helen got word to them somehow, and they made plans to get us all back to England. I remember little of being hustled out of Paris. I was so ill, my whole body ached with the pain of loss. I wanted to die, but my brother and Simon, bless their hearts, would not allow it. They could not save my spirit, though, which was entirely broken." She gave a shuddery sigh of relief that she had got through the whole tale, however abbreviated. "I was a long time recovering."

Flora gave Edwina's hand one last squeeze and released it. She fumbled in her reticule and pulled out a linen square, which she handed to Edwina, who took it gratefully and wiped her eyes. She hated to be seen so discomposed and made an effort to bring herself under control.

"But you have recovered," Flora said, "and gone on to make a life for yourself."

"It was never the same again, though. My heart had been crushed from so many directions, it seemed. But I learned several important lessons. Twice in my life I have lost someone I loved when passion spun out of control into chaos and tragedy. Never again will I act upon passion of any kind."

"Never? Oh, don't say such a thing, my dear."

"Moderation has served me well in the years since France, and I am perfectly content. My ideals have not changed, but I have tempered my expectations. I will never, never again support revolution of any kind. Careful, steady reform is my only objective."

"And to influence opinion through your magazine."

"Yes, of course. But I am not advocating revolt. Only an open mind toward acceptance of wise, rational progress, especially as it relates to women. We have no one else representing our interests. We must do it ourselves. But it is a quiet passion for me now, not a fervor gone mad."

"And what of passion of the heart? Have you forsaken that as well?"

"Gervaise was the one true love of my heart. I have had my Grand Passion."

Those somewhat hyperbolic words were exactly how she thought of him now. In fact, during the years since his death, her memories of Gervaise had taken on the qualities of high romance. Or high tragedy. Sometimes the everyday, commonplace details of their months together faded in her memory. Worse still, sometimes she could not call to mind a vivid image of his face. But her heart and her body never forgot how she felt when she was with him, or when she lost him. The physical joys and pains had remained bright, while the visual images faded.

Flora's eyebrows rose sharply. "And where is it written that you are allowed only one Grand Passion? My dear girl, I have had more of them than I care to admit."

"But I am not like you, Flora. Forgive me, but I am not the sort to flit from man to man."

"I have indeed done my share of flitting. A woman has to survive, after all. But I am not talking about sex. I am talking about true, deep, emotional passion. Love, if you will. It doesn't happen so often, of course, but when it does, you must embrace it."

"I did embrace it. I gave myself totally to Gervaise—body and soul."

"But he is dead eight years now. And you are not. Do not waste any more years, my dear, repining what has been lost. Reach out and grasp what is now found."

"You are speaking of Anthony, are you not?"

"Perhaps. That is for you to discover."

"Was he one of your Grand Passions?"

Flora laughed. "Heavens, no. Nor was I his, in case you are wondering. No, he was merely an extremely pleasant diversion who ended up being a great friend."

"Oh."

"So you must never think there is any competition between us for his heart."

"But I am not after his heart."

"You should be. He is most certainly after yours."

"Oh, Flora, I don't think so. Everything is a game with him, even—especially—seduction. But he is a handsome, charming gentleman and, if you must know, I have considered the possibility of . . . I don't know. Of something."

"Of entering the game yourself?"

Edwina gave a sheepish smile. "Perhaps. I'm not sure I remember how to play, though. It's been so long. But for the first time since Gervaise, I confess I am tempted."

Flora placed a hand dramatically at her breast. "Thanks be to God," she said. "I was so worried you would not allow yourself to feel again. Welcome back to the world, my dear. Who knows? Perhaps another Grand Passion awaits."

"Not that, Flora. I don't want that again." It was too frightening even to consider. The singular obsession. The breathless passion. The intense highs and desperate lows. The very idea of being possessed by that madness again made her pulse race. "Nothing like that," Edwina continued. "A little flirtation, a little dalliance. A . . . a casual affair, perhaps."

"Bah! Anthony is not casual in his affairs. And neither are you. It will be something more grand between you, when and if it happens."

"Casual or grand, it would still be foolish to get involved with him. Do not forget that wager. He holds my future in his hands."

"I rather think it is in your hands, my dear. How are the subscription numbers coming?"

"We are getting closer. But with less than a month to go, I begin to fear it is an impossible goal."

"Do not give up, my girl." Flora rose gracefully and shook out her skirts, then bent to kiss Edwina on the cheek. "Thank you for trusting me with your story. Now you must trust me when I tell you not to allow an old and painful grief to own your heart. I am an expert, you know, in these matters. You must allow yourself to be free to love again, my dear."

She turned to leave, but stopped when something on a worktable caught her eye. "Ah, more proofs for me to review? I am so pleased you have given me more tasks to do for the magazine. I don't know when I have enjoyed myself so much."

Edwina had indeed delegated several tasks to Flora, just as she had hoped to do when she requested an additional assistant. In particular, Flora had taken on most of the aspects of working with the printer, including proofing, scheduling, managing deliveries back and forth, and so on. It had allowed Edwina to spend more time writing, which she preferred.

"Hold on," Flora said. "What's this?"

Edwina sucked in a sharp breath when she saw what Flora had picked up.

Flora turned to her and frowned. "Still pamphleteering, Edwina?" She held up proofs for a pamphlet Nicholas had written on Catholic emancipation.

Edwina cleared her throat. "On occasion."

"How frequent an occasion?"

"I couldn't say."

"These are printed by Daniel Imber?"

"Yes."

"Side by side, in the same print run with *The Ladies Fashionable Cabinet*?"

Edwina sighed. "Yes."

Flora shook her head and studied the proofs. "Dare I ask how you are financing these little side projects?"

"No."

"Ah. I thought as much. It is a deep game you are playing, my girl. I don't suppose Anthony knows where his profits are going?"

"No."

"Nor your uncle before him?"

"No." Edwina rose to stand beside Flora. "But it is not much. Not enough to be noticed. As long as the account books are not scrutinized too closely. And it supports a good cause."

"You'd better hope Anthony doesn't see this one." Flora looked up from the proofs, disappointment clear in her eyes. "Did you write this?"

"No. Nicholas did. He writes most of the pamphlets we sponsor. He is still more political than I am."

"He has skewered Cedric Quayle in this one."

"Quayle is one of the most vocal opponents to Catholic emancipation. He only barely supported the union with Ireland, but he refuses to allow their Catholic representatives to sit in Parliament. He claims only loyalty to the king on this issue. But it is more personal. His arguments in the House have demonstrated despicable personal prejudice. Nicholas is right to attack him."

"Did you know Cedric Quayle is Anthony's uncle?"

Edwina gasped. "What?"

"Anthony's mother is Quayle's sister. And his father is Quayle's closest advisor."

"Good Lord." Edwina placed both hands on the worktable and leaned on them for support. "I had no idea."

"I do not believe Anthony is close to his uncle, and I think you know of his shaky relationship with his father. You need not worry that he shares their views on this matter."

"No, I doubt he does." Edwina's mind was racing.

"But this pamphlet would embarrass him, nonetheless. Especially if it was discovered he is even peripherally involved."

"No. No, we must stop it." Edwina's stomach tied itself into knots just thinking what would happen if Anthony found out. She suspected all game playing would come to an end. He would do everything within his power to win their wager. And she would never have the *Cabinet* for her own. "I shall speak to Nicholas and have him modify the proofs or submit a new version entirely."

"Good girl. Now, have him give the corrected proofs to me and I will make sure Imber gets them. There is no point in making two trips. As long as you want me to manage everything with the printer, I might as well include your brother's pamphlets. Don't worry, I will be discreet. I don't entirely disagree with his opinions, you know. Just take care not to offend Anthony."

"That would be the worst possible thing I could do, considering our wager. Thank you for alerting me, Flora. And for everything else. I am so pleased to have you involved in the *Cabinet*. And very grateful for your friendship."

She surprised herself when, quite uncharacteristically, she put her arms around Flora and hugged her tight.

Finally. He had been waiting for the perfect opportunity. These were the slow months in terms of social activity—but now there was the peace, and celebrations aplenty. She could not possibly refuse.

Tony spent several days making calls—and nights making deals at the tables—in an effort to get everything in order before paying a visit to Golden Square late one afternoon. He was rewarded for his patience by finding Edwina alone.

She was not in the library office, but in an informal parlor upstairs, a cozy room he'd never seen. A pair of paned windows overlooking the back garden flanked a small fireplace. A worn Turkish carpet covered the floor. Above the mantel hung a large painting of classical figures in a landscape. Her mother's?

Tony was so accustomed to finding Edwina behind the mighty bulk of her desk that he was delighted to find her ensconced in a large wing chair on one side of the hearth. She looked perfectly charming with her feet tucked up under her as she read a book. She wore a simple muslin gown and was wrapped in a paisley shawl. A pair of slippers on the floor looked to have been casually kicked off. Tony was pleased she did not shift into a more ladylike posture when Lucy announced him.

"You look comfortably snug," he said. "May I join you?"

At her nod, he took a seat in the matching chair on the opposite side of the fire. She closed her book and tucked it into the seat cushion.

"We haven't seen much of you lately," she said.

He grinned. "Have you missed me, then?"

"I had become accustomed to having you constantly underfoot, that is all. Have you found some other enterprise to interfere with?"

"I have been rather busy, as it happens. But I come bearing good will and an invitation."

"An invitation? Driving again?"

"Only a short drive, and in the evening this time. I have secured a box at Covent Garden for a special performance of *Artaxerxes* with Mrs. Billington on Friday. I would be honored if you would accompany me."

Her brows lifted slightly. "I had thought it impossible to get tickets for Mrs. Billington's performances. Or so I read in the *Morning Chronicle* today."

"It is to be a benefit performance for the widows and orphans of the late war, in honor of the peace, and only just announced yesterday."

"Mrs. Billington has agreed to perform without pay? The most expensive singer in all of London?"

"She is donating her fee, I understand. The reviews of her performance as Mandane have been outstanding. I'm sure you would enjoy it. Will you go with me, Edwina?"

The expression on her face hinted at an internal struggle, as though she wanted to go but thought she should not.

"Please, Edwina. Say yes."

"Why are you so determined to take me? There must be any number of others whom you could invite."

"Perhaps I am courting you."

A speculative glint came into her eyes. "Perhaps you are simply wooing me as a prelude to seduction."

"Courtship, seduction, cajolery. Whatever works, my dear."

"So long as you have designs on my magazine and my Minerva, I do not believe I should trust you in whatever it is you want to call it."

"I remind you that it is *my* magazine and my father's Minerva by rights, but I think you are merely grasping at excuses to refuse me. Probably because you have nothing pretty enough to wear to such an occasion."

She bristled. "I do so."

"I'll bet you don't."

"Another wager?"

"All right. I'll wager you don't have a single fashionable gown to wear—and I shall be the judge for I know more about what is fashionable than you."

She flinched and he knew he had her. No woman, even one as enlightened as Edwina, wants to be told she is unfashionable. It was all right for *her* to joke about it, which she had done on more than one occasion. But to have someone else, especially a man, actually agree with her, was more than she was willing to endure. What she did not realize—or did she?—was that no matter how plainly she dressed, she would always outshine any other woman in the room.

"Unfair," she said. "You would not be an objective judge."

"All right. We'll let others be the judge. If your dress makes at least one woman glare at you with envy, you win. It must be a genuine sneer of contempt, though."

"Why not a look of admiration?"

"Not good enough. What might appear to be a lady's admiration could just as well be politeness.

No, a truly splendid dress will inspire genuine jealousy, the type that will drive a woman to make a great show of ignoring you. I'm betting you cannot come up with something to inspire that jealousy."

"What about a look of admiration from a man?"

"My dear, you would receive admiring looks from men if you wore nothing at all."

Her brows shot up and a smile teased the corners of her mouth.

Tony laughed at his blunder. "Yes, well, of course you would. What I meant to say was that you would receive male admiration regardless of what you wear. Besides, you will have my admiration in any case, and I am definitely male. No, it must be a woman's contempt. That will tell the tale."

"So if I wear something that causes at least one woman to glare at me with chilly disdain, I win the wager?"

He wondered if she realized she had as good as accepted his invitation? She was no longer dithering about whether to accompany him, but about what to wear when she did. Edwina was more like him than she would admit. She was as susceptible to a good wager as he was.

Lord, what a thrilling ride life with her would be.

There was still one concern he needed to deal with before they came to terms. He knew she had little money. He did not want her feeling obliged to go out and spend what she could not afford on a new opera dress.

"Let us rather put it this way," he said. "You must wear something currently in your wardrobe upstairs. You may not go to one of the fashionable modistes and have something new made up. Nor may you borrow something—from Flora or anyone else."

"Nothing borrowed, nothing new?"

"Correct."

"I must concoct something fabulous from my current wardrobe? Something to make at least one other woman green with envy?"

"Well, my dear, if you think it is such an impossible task—"

"No, no. I am prepared to accept those terms."

The look on her face spoke otherwise. But Tony had no doubt she would win this wager regardless of the modishness of her costume. She was bound to elicit more than one jealous sneer just because of her extraordinary beauty. And because every male eye would be on her, to the supreme annoyance of every female in the theater.

"All right, then," he said. "We are agreed on the terms. Now, as to the stakes, I think whoever wins should get a boon of his, or her, choosing. Something personal. Something not related to the *Cabinet*."

"For example?"

"Oh, I think we should designate the stakes as a winner's choice, a boon which can be named at the time of claiming."

"Seems a bit risky. What if my boon was to ask you to jump off Westminster Bridge? Or throw yourself in front of a speeding mail coach?"

He laughed at the wicked gleam in her eye. "Let us say the loser has reasonable right of refusal. And the winner may not choose a boon that is life-threatening, expensive, or illegal. Does that suffice?"

She pretended to consider it for a moment. Finally, she said, "I believe it will."

"Splendid. Then I shall come by for you Friday evening and we shall see if you can twist any grande dame noses out of place."

"Should we not record it properly?" she asked. "In your little red book?"

He nodded and pulled the betting book from his pocket. "We will need a pen," he said.

Edwina uncurled herself from the wing chair, and her toes, clad in white stockings, searched out and found the slippers. She rose, leaving the shawl on the chair, and shook out her ubiquitous white muslin skirts. Tony followed her to a tiny writing desk in one corner. She dipped a quill into the ink pot and handed it to him. He recorded the wager and signed it, then passed the book to Edwina. She read what he'd written and initialed it.

After replacing the quill, she held out the betting

book for him to take. Instead, he took her hand and pulled her close.

"This is how we seal things properly between us, Edwina."

He lowered his mouth to hers and kissed her.

Chapter 12

⁓⁓⁓

"Thank God you've come, Flora. You've got to help me."

"Good heavens," Flora said as she stepped inside the entry hall. "What on earth has happened?"

"Come upstairs with me and I'll explain."

Edwina did not give Flora even a moment to remove her bonnet and pelisse. She took her by the elbow and hurried her up the two flights of stairs to her bedchamber. When Flora saw where she was, she offered a brilliant triumphal smile.

"So, you have done it, my girl. You have taken Anthony to bed."

"No!"

"Then you are seriously considering it. Good

girl. Now, how can I help you? I am, of course, an expert in these matters."

Edwina could not contain the little snort of exasperation that erupted, unladylike, from her lips. "I need your expertise in other matters, Flora. I need to put together something smashing to wear tomorrow night."

"Well, that is simple enough." She gave a dismissive little wave. "Come, let me take you to my modiste, Madame Lancaster. She is a wonder."

"No, no, it must be something I already have, not something new. But look at this." She flung open her clothes press. "It's pathetically bare. What *is* there is dull and outdated. And I never know what goes with what. Oh God, it's hopeless. What am I going to do?"

Flora narrowed her eyes. "What are you up to, my girl?"

"Anthony has invited me to attend the opera tomorrow night—"

"Excellent!"

"—but I have nothing to wear."

Flora eyed the clothes press and nodded in agreement. "And you cannot purchase something new?"

"No, it has to be something here. But there's *nothing* here."

"Hold on a moment. Do I sense another wager afoot?"

"Yes, yes, yes. You must help me, Flora. *Please.*"

The hint of desperation that had crept into her voice was mortifying. She must get hold of herself. She was being ridiculous. It was only a small wager, after all. It was not that important.

Oh, but it was. She wanted, desperately wanted, in the most uncharacteristically shallow feminine way, to look beautiful for him tomorrow night. Not to win the wager. Or not only that, though she already knew what boon she'd ask if—when!—she did win. She simply wanted for him to think she looked beautiful.

It was all because of that kiss, the one that had sealed the bargain of this latest wager. It had not been elaborate and searing hot like the one that afternoon in the drawing room when she had proven she knew how to please a man. But it had been soft and slow and somehow terribly intimate. And where the other, more passionate, kiss had almost frightened her in the way it made her feel, this one had the opposite effect entirely. It had made her want more. And strangely enough, that thought didn't frighten her at all.

After much soul-searching and a long, sleepless night, she was finally able to admit the truth. It was more than just her treacherous body reacting to his practiced seduction. She wanted Anthony More-house. And she wanted to be beautiful for him.

"Let me get this straight." Flora began to smile. "You are to show up tomorrow night looking fabulous using only what you have at hand?"

"That's it. But just look at this. There is so little to work with. I was hoping . . . well, you have such a flare for putting just the right things together. Perhaps you can see some potential in this jumble that escapes me."

Flora eyed the various garments neatly laid out in the press—most of them white, most of them old, none of them fabulous—and tapped a finger against her lips. "This is a serious challenge, indeed. But have no fear, my dear. A good showing is not all in the gown, though it certainly must flatter in its line and color. But a direct smile, an air of confidence will always make others believe one is far more beautiful than one actually is. Believe me, I know this from experience. In your case, however, there is no need to suggest beauty. It is already there in abundance."

"You are very sweet to say so, Flora. But I still need something to wear."

"Not to worry, my dear. We will contrive something. It's all in the way you put it together. Now, let's have the whole lot out and take a look."

Edwina shrieked when Flora scooped up an entire shelf of dresses and flung them unceremoniously onto the bed. She had emptied the top section of shelves in less than a minute, creating an enormous billowing heap.

"While I sort through these," Flora said, "you round up the trimmings and accessories."

"Like what?" Edwina felt decidedly out of her element.

"Anything. Any little bits and scraps of things that might be used to adorn a dress or your hair. Thankfully, you seem to know how to manage your hair, so we won't have to worry about that. But your clothes are another matter. You'd think someone who'd lived in France for a time would have more to work with. But never mind, my dear, this will be fun. Toss anything useful over on that chaise and we'll see what we can put together."

And so while Flora began organizing the dresses in piles that must have made some sort of sense to her, Edwina began rummaging through the drawers of the clothes press and another small chest where she kept her undergarments and a few accessories. She heaped the chaise with bits of ribbon and lace, lengths of embroidered India muslin, handkerchiefs, scarves, shawls, tuckers, and fichus.

"What about this?" she asked, holding up a length of silver cord.

"Add it to the pile," Flora said.

Edwina received the same response for each item she found, until she stopped asking and simply tossed anything and everything on the chaise. Bits of fringe, silk flowers, feathers, plumes, tassels.

"And don't forget jewelry," Flora said.

Edwina dragged out every bit of trumpery she could find and laid it out on her dressing table. A coral parure, a cameo, a silver-and-paste crescent-shaped wig pin that had been her mother's, tortoiseshell combs, brooches, earrings, lace pins, a gold mesh bracelet with enamel clasps, a pearl necklace, a paste aigrette, a gold quizzing glass.

"This is it, then?" Flora stood in the center of the room, hands on hips, and surveyed the scope of the problem at hand.

Edwina looked at the maddening disarray and swallowed hard. "A sorry state of affairs, is it not? I've never cared much for fashion, never could keep straight the changes each season, and never liked wasting time getting pinned and measured by some dressmaker with a mercenary glint in her eye. I did buy a few nice things in Paris—actually, Gervaise bought them for me. I'm sure they're horribly outdated, but perhaps—"

"Edwina, Lucy said you were—oh, my!" Prudence stood in the doorway and gaped open-mouthed at the untidy mess that had once been Edwina's neat little bedchamber. Her voice held a note of alarm. "What's happened? Are you going away?"

"She's going to the opera," Flora said, "and we're trying to find her something to wear."

"Oh." Prudence covered her mouth and actually giggled. "Oh, my."

Lord, it really was pathetic when even mousy little Prudence recognized the futility of the task.

"Come on in, Pru," Edwina said. "Three heads are better than two, especially when one of the two is completely useless. As you see, we have practically my entire wardrobe arrayed about the room. Surely there is *something* appropriate."

"Strip down to your chemise, my girl," Flora said. "We have work to do."

And so for the next hour Edwina stood like a mannequin while Flora dressed her in gown after gown, draping scarves and sashes artfully this way and that, tying bits of ribbon here and tucking in lace there—all in ways that would never have occurred to Edwina. It was positively dizzying. Flora kept to the whites, eschewing most of the bolder-colored accessories Edwina preferred. Prudence made a suggestion or two, but primarily watched Flora at work and gave a thumbs up or a thumbs down to each variation.

"This one is the best for an underdress," Flora said, eyeing a petticoat of white crepe with fine silver embroidery along the hem that had always been a favorite. Edwina hadn't thought there was any hope of using it, since it was at least five years old. "The fabric is excellent and very becoming," Flora continued. "It's a bit too full in the back, but you are slender enough to get away with it, so we shan't worry. But we shall have to put something else over it to bring it up to date."

"Like a robe?" Prudence asked.

"No, more like a tunic," Flora said as she rifled through the mountain of dresses. "Tunics are all the rage. There must be *something* here we can use."

"What about this?" Prudence held up an enormous shawl of white crepe shot with silver and trimmed with silver spangles along the edges. "It would complement the underdress nicely."

Flora took it from her and fingered the soft fabric. "My girl, you surprise me. This is perfect. How attached are you to this shawl, Edwina?"

"Well, I've always loved it. I bought it all those years ago in Paris, so it is quite old."

"Then you won't mind if we cut it up a bit?"

"Cut it up? No, I suppose not."

Flora went to work. When she was done, she had transformed the old shawl into a short Grecian tunic held in place by an attractive criss-crossing of braided silver cord. The tassels at the ends of the cord were allowed to hang long in front. The sides of the tunic were gathered up over the longer sleeves of the underdress in deep drapes fastened at the shoulders with tiny lace pins of clear paste in the shape of stars.

Prudence, to Edwina's astonishment, fashioned a wonderful bandeau of white silk twisted with more of the silver cording to be woven through her hair. She was working on an arrangement of small plumes to be attached to the bandeau with the paste aigrette, when Flora suggested no plumes and the crescent wig pin instead.

It was perfect.

"You look like the goddess of the moon," Prudence said in an awestruck voice.

"You do look quite lovely, my dear." Flora circled her and admired the final results. "There is still work to be done, of course. This neckline must be finished off. But it should be easy enough, a simple hem will do." When Edwina frowned, Flora added, "You do know how to stitch a hem, do you not?"

"Yes, I suppose so. But I'm not very good at it."

"I am," Prudence said.

They both turned to look at her. "I like to sew. I can create a decent neckline for you quite easily. Here, let me show you."

She pulled out a packet of pins from her reticule and began to cut and pin until it looked like a true bodice, so long as the silver cords were in place. Flora was ecstatic with the results and Edwina was simply amazed.

"Now, do you have a good pair of white slippers?" Flora asked. "Good. And decent gloves? Oh, and I think the paste earrings. There you are. Fit to turn every head at the theater."

Edwina grabbed both women and hugged them to her. "You have saved my life, both of you. I could not have done it without you. And that is a problem, in fact. I do not know if I could re-create this again without you. Do you think . . . Is it asking too much . . . Could you both come back tomorrow and help me to get ready?"

"Of course, my dear."

"I'd love to."

"Thank you, thank you, thank you. Both of you. I am forever in your debt."

"It was fun," Prudence said.

"You have a good eye, girl," Flora said. "We'll have to see what we can do about you next. Then maybe that handsome brother of Edwina's will take note."

"Flora!" Prudence blushed scarlet but would not meet Edwina's eyes.

Was it true, then? Did Prudence have a tendre for Nicholas? If so, she would need every bit of help Flora could give her, poor thing. Nicholas flirted with almost every woman he met, as though it were the most natural thing in the world. He'd had a grand time teasing the Crimson Ladies, once he got over the aggravation of "tripping over old bawds every time I come home." But Edwina was fairly certain he'd never flirted with Prudence. She would be surprised if he ever even noticed her.

"But first things first," Flora said. "We must help Edwina win yet another wager with that rogue Anthony. You are certain to make him very proud to have you on his arm, my dear. Especially on that particular night."

"Oh? What is so special about tomorrow night? Except, of course, that it is a special benefit performance?"

"Do you know what it benefits?"

"Anthony mentioned something about widows and orphans of soldiers in the late wars."

"Yes, it is a new benevolent society, recently created. The benefit is more to call attention to its cause than to actually raise money. There is apparently a great deal of money already endowed."

"That's wonderful," Edwina said as she fiddled with the tassels on the silver cord at her waist.

"It is Anthony's endowment."

"What?" Edwina's head jerked up.

"Mr. Morehouse has endowed a charity for war widows and orphans?" Prudence asked.

"He has indeed, though he has done a fine job of keeping his name out of it and staying in the background. But I do have my sources, of course. It was through his efforts alone that Mrs. Billington agreed to perform."

Anthony had done all that?

"And she is said to command the highest fees in London, if not all of Europe," Prudence said. "It must have been difficult to get her to do a free benefit performance."

"She may not be," Flora said. "I have my suspicions that Anthony is paying her full fee himself."

"Oh, my."

Edwina could not keep a smile from her face. She was bursting with pride on Anthony's behalf. He had said nothing about his endowment, and she suspected he never would, unless she directly confronted him about it. She had known all along, deep inside, that he was not merely the reckless gambler who lived for his own pleasure and nothing more. She had so wanted to believe the sweet, young boy she had once loved had not been entirely crushed and corrupted. He was still there, and she still cared for him.

Suddenly, very quietly and without hesitation or fear, a tiny corner of her heart unlocked for the first time in eight years.

"Well, what do you know?" she said.

"And what, may I ask, are you doing here, Flora?" Tony stood in the entry hall where he awaited Edwina's appearance with eager anticipation. He could hardly wait to see what his wager had challenged her to accomplish. "I had better not see anything I recognize from your wardrobe when she comes down."

"You should know her better than that, my dear. I wanted to take her to Madame Lancaster. After all, how would you know whether or not it was something new? When have you ever seen her in evening dress? But no, she would honor the terms of your idiot wager."

"I am happy to hear it. Buy why, then, are you here? A little moral support?"

"Prudence and I have some work to do for the *Cabinet*," she said, "so you may mind your own business, if you please."

"Work?" He looked up at the sound of movement on the stairs. "What sort of—"

The vision that met his eyes caught him somewhere beneath the ribs and stole the breath right out of him. Edwina descended the stairs looking for all the world like an ethereal deity coming down from the heavens to grace the humble earth with her magnificence. Tony could only stare. He couldn't speak. He could barely breathe. He was marginally aware that his mouth hung open, but he did not care.

She was quite simply glorious.

Every movement sent light shimmering in all directions, as though she were wrapped in moonbeams. Silver glistened everywhere, from embroidery and spangles and cording and paste to a cunning little crescent moon in her hair. And all that brilliant white was set off to perfection by the black hair and brows and eyes.

He held out a hand to her as she reached the lower steps. When she took it, he was sorely tempted to pull her forward and straight into his arms, to wrap himself around all that silvery whiteness.

Later. He hoped.

She stood on the bottom step and arched a brow. Tony managed to find his voice. "Madam, I am ravished by your beauty." Keeping hold of her hand, he swept her an elegant bow with the other. "You are magnificent."

Edwina looked him straight in the eye, studied him for a moment, then gave him a smile that shot right through him and out the other side, leaving him breathless.

"Thank you, Anthony. You look quite splendid yourself."

A soft sigh from above had him looking toward the top of the stairs, where Prudence stood with hands clasped to her breast and a dreamy look in her eye.

"Anthony is the perfect foil for you," Flora said. "He is all golden to your silver, the sun to your moon. The pair of you will dazzle the crowd."

Tony had taken care to look as fine as he could, but then one always felt a bit fine in evening dress. Although men's fashion had become more conservative in the last few years, Tony still liked to add a bit of flash. His blue coat and white breeches were standard wear, but his gold-embroidered waistcoat, white silk under-waistcoat, and frilled shirt added a certain dash. And, of course, there were the fobs. Rather elaborate ones tonight, with diamonds and sapphires set in gleaming gold.

But his own radiance paled next to Edwina.

He helped her with her wrap, a shawl of fine Indian pongee silk in emerald green woven with silver dots. It looked like it had once been part of an Indian sari. Very clever, and very becoming against the white dress.

"Oh, there is one more thing," Flora said. "You must take these, my dear."

She handed Edwina a tiny ivory notebook with matching pencil, and a collapsible pair of gold opera glasses. Edwina looked up in question.

"You must get a good look at everyone," Flora went on, "and take notes on the fashions. I will work it into the next report."

"You want *me* to take notes on the fashions? *Me?*"

"Of course, my dear. It is sure to be a grand occasion with every woman there dressed to the nines. Anthony can tell you their names, if you do not know who they are. Then just make brief notes about their dresses, their jewels, their headdresses. That sort of thing."

Edwina looked at the notebook as though it were something slimy and unpleasant, but she dutifully put it into her reticule.

When they were finally in his carriage and on their way, Tony couldn't take his eyes off her. And in the close confines of the carriage, he became aware of her perfume, a slightly exotic, spicy scent with a musky undercurrent that suited her well. And was liable to drive him to madness.

He could not wait to see the stir she would cause at the theater.

"You're staring," she said.

He grinned. "I can't help it. You look so beautiful. I am ready to concede our wager right now, for I have no doubt you will stoke the flames of jealousy in the hearts of every woman in attendance. Not to mention earning the admiration of every gentleman."

"You are very gallant to say so. But I fear we may

never find out if this traffic does not let up. We are barely moving."

Tony didn't care if they ever got to the theater. He would be happy to spend the entire evening inside the carriage with Edwina. And he knew just how he would use that time.

"But Flora will never forgive you," he said, "if you don't come back with notes for her fashion report."

She gave a contemptuous little snort. "She will be even sorrier when she sees what I give her."

"What's this? Defeated before you begin? Can this be the Edwina I know, the one who rises to every challenge, who never says no?"

"Well . . ."

"The Edwina I know would never give up before she'd begun. And I'll bet she would do a fine job."

"Yes, but it is well known that you will bet on anything."

"And just as well known that you will never reject a challenge."

"Are you suggesting yet another wager, sir?"

"Yes, I believe I am. I will wager that you can provide Flora with a creditable set of notes on the fashions seen at tonight's performance."

"But I am sure to lose. Why should I accept such a wager?"

"Perhaps to even out the results. I am just as sure to lose the wager about your dress."

"And what stakes this time?"

"Oh, the same, I think. A boon of the winner's choice, to be named at claiming. Same restrictions."

"So, if by some odd chance I win both wagers—"

"You get two boons of your own choosing. Or I could win two boons—unlikely, considering the success you made of your supposedly paltry wardrobe—or we could each win a boon. Whatever the results, it should be an interesting evening, don't you think?"

They locked gazes, and he could swear she was thinking exactly what he was, that the personal boons could prove more than merely interesting. He knew what his boon would be. Would hers be the same?

"Yes," she said at last, her voice a notch huskier than usual, and he wondered if she was responding to his silent question. "Very interesting. All right, I accept. If I am able to make decent notes for Flora, then I win a boon. If not, you win. Shall we record it in your little book?"

"Oh, I don't think that is necessary." He took her chin in his hand. "We can simply seal our bargain in the usual manner." He leaned forward and kissed her.

Her lips met his softly and with a small sigh. That sigh, almost his undoing, sent a surge of desire rushing through his blood as fiery and sweet as a shot of brandy. But now was not the time to lose control. Instead, he kept it unhurried, soft, and delicate.

They savored each other slowly and deliberately,

without hunger or urgency. It was a kiss of exploration and wonder, each testing and tasting and relishing the other in ways unlike their other kisses, as though a new kind of acceptance had evolved between them. Tony dined on her lush mouth for long moments before leaving it, to skate his lips along her jaw and down the elegant length of her throat. At the base of her neck he found a tantalizing pulse beneath the fine white skin and pressed a kiss against it.

He had made his way back to her mouth, deepening the kiss, when the carriage lurched forward and brought them both to their senses. Tony pulled back, reluctantly, and set her away from him. It was one of the most difficult things he'd ever done.

"As much as I would like to continue such delightful activity," he said, "I fear for your beautiful dress and your charming coiffure. It would be a shame if you were to lose your wager—the first one, that is—because your gown is hanging askew and your headdress is listing westward."

She smiled and checked her dress, making slight adjustments. "Thank you," she said.

"For kissing you, or for stopping kissing you?"

"Both."

"Ah. Well, I do feel as if I may have claimed my boon before it was earned. Forgive me. You are simply irresistible this evening. At any time, actually, but the closed carriage emboldened me."

She smiled again, but said nothing. Her eyes

seemed to have grown even darker, however.

"Once again," he said, "you have convinced me that you know how to please a man. I find myself wondering who taught you. You said you'd been in love before."

"Yes, a long time ago."

"Tell me about him."

He felt her stiffen slightly beside him. Perhaps he should not have broached so personal a subject, but he really wanted to know. If there was some ideal he was being measured against, he wanted to know what, or who, it was.

"He was a Frenchman," she said at last. "I met him in London and followed him to France. He was one of the leaders of the Gironde, and I had hoped to be involved in bringing about the republic they envisioned. Of course, that was not to be."

Tony's gut tensed up into a tight knot. This was not what he'd expected. He ought not to have asked.

"He was among the Girondins sent to the guillotine?"

"Yes."

Tony took her hand and held it between both of his. "I'm so sorry, Edwina. It must be very painful for you still. It was very intrusive of me to ask."

"It's all right," she said, and gave him a weak smile. "It was a long time ago."

"What a dreadful way to lose someone you love."

"I do not suppose there is any easy way, but yes, it was quite dreadful."

"What was it like to be in Paris then?" he asked, genuinely curious.

And she told him—with some reticence at first, but she grew more voluble as he asked specific questions about events and people and politics. He tried to keep the conversation away from the topic of Gervaise de Champdivers, the man she'd loved. But he had been an integral part of the events and climate of the time, so it was impossible to avoid mention of him. Yet Edwina seemed composed as she spoke of him, almost serene. Tony was not made to feel as though he intruded. She spoke to him as a friend, and that warmed his heart.

He was stunned to learn she'd been imprisoned. And his heart ached for what she must have felt when the cheering crowds outside the prison announced her lover's death. She had not, of course, admitted they had been lovers, only that they had planned to marry one day but had been too involved in more important matters to get around to it. But Tony knew. Gervaise had been her lover and the great love of her life, and she'd lost him in the most cruel manner imaginable.

He wanted to enfold her in his arms when she spoke of that frightful October, but she didn't need his arms. She was strong and she had survived, despite a broken heart and broken dreams. He didn't know another woman, except perhaps Flora, who could have endured as much and risen above it. Edwina Parrish was quite a remarkable woman, and he could no longer deny he was falling in love with her.

He understood now her need for restraint and control in her life, after seeing what havoc could be wreaked when passions turned to unbridled chaos. He was more determined than ever to help her break free of those restraints, to see the caged bird fly again.

And he wanted to fly with her when she did.

"I am sorry your dreams were shattered so violently," he said. "But I also hope you have not stopped dreaming. Life goes on."

"Yes, it does. I do not often indulge in dreams anymore." She gazed at him with sharp interest in her fine dark eyes, as though seeing him in some way for the first time. "But sometimes something new and unexpected comes along to give me hope to dream again."

His heart soared to think he was the new and unexpected thing in her life.

"There is the peace, for example."

And his heart plummeted back to earth with a thud. He ought to have known her dreams would be selfless and on a grand scale. He looked away so she would not see the disappointment in his eyes, and pretended to flick a bit of lint from his coat sleeve.

"You think it will last?" he asked. "This new peace? You trust this Bonaparte fellow?"

"I hope it will last. We have been too long at war and our people have suffered too much for it. As for Bonaparte, he has at least brought stability to a nation that had almost destroyed itself."

"I don't trust the little blackguard for one moment," Tony said, "and think he duped the government into signing a treaty favorable only to himself. But I, too, am weary of war and ready to celebrate peace. Ah, and here we are."

The carriage had finally made its way to the front of the line and come to a stop at the Bow Street entrance of the Covent Garden Theatre. The columned portico was filled with a fashionable crowd of people waiting to go inside. There was an air of excitement in the din of voices heard above the clatter of carriages.

"Let us begin tonight's celebration."

Chapter 13

Anthony handed her out of the carriage. She made a quick adjustment to the cording that held her tunic in place, flicked the tasseled ends, and was ready to face the crowd. The first thing to meet her eye was a woman swathed in pink silk, with a head wrapped in a complicated turban sporting a huge topaz brooch. She stood only a few feet away and scowled at Edwina as though she were some loathsome swamp creature who'd just slithered ashore. She made a great show of lifting her chin in haughty disdain and tugged on the arm of the gentleman at her side. As they walked up the few steps to the portico, the gentleman turned. When he saw Edwina, his brows lifted and his lips curved up into a smile. The woman spoke sharply

274

to him and he turned back to her and led her inside.

"Now, I would call that a clear win," Anthony said. "Congratulations, my dear. I owe you a boon. What shall it be?"

"I think it best that we wait until after the performance to discuss boons."

He gave her a seductive grin and offered his arm to lead her inside. "How shall I bear the wait? That was Lady Craig, by the way. If you're taking notes."

"Oh. Please remind me when we're seated. Lady Craig wearing pink silk."

"It was a rose crepe Russian tunic. I shall remind you."

They jostled their way through the crowd into the large vestibule, where stoves were lit against the chill autumn air and several large groups mingled before making their way to boxes or galleries. Anthony discreetly pointed out several women of note as they headed toward the grand double staircase leading to the upper boxes. Edwina tried to commit to memory every name and dress style, but heavens, there were so many. It was a splendid occasion that boasted almost every member of the *ton* who was in Town. She wondered how Anthony had managed it. Perhaps they had all lost wagers to him and this was his payment.

But that was not fair. From what Flora had said, he had kept his name out of the endowment and the benefit. He was doing it to please himself, because it was a fine and generous thing to do, not to publicly flaunt a grand charitable gesture. He must be very proud.

And so was she. It warmed her heart to know he had done all this in support of a class of people so often overlooked. The widows and orphans of soldiers were frequently left in the most desperate levels of poverty. He could not have chosen a more deserving group in need of a charitable endowment. At some point, she would like to know more about it, to understand exactly what services the endowment monies would provide, and to know how she might be of help. But she would first wait to see if he admitted his involvement.

It was the least he could do, after all she had admitted to him.

Edwina could still not believe how easy it had been to tell him about France and about Gervaise. Easier even than telling Flora. She had felt so close to him in that moment, after that lovely long interlude when they had kissed and kissed. Something had changed between them during that kiss. It was as if they had each laid themselves bare before the other in an act of mutual revelation. How odd that such a seemingly momentous thing should happen during a kiss, or series of kisses, that was more gentle than passionate.

Without fanfare or upheaval, he had unlocked yet another little piece of her heart. She feared it would not be long before he had taken full possession of it, and that notion shook her to the core.

"Edwina!"

The familiar voice pulled her from her reverie. "Simon! And Eleanor. Oh, how wonderful to see you."

She threw her arms around both her friends, then stood back holding a hand of each. "You both look radiant. Marriage certainly agrees with you. When did you get back?"

"Only yesterday, in fact," Simon said. "We've not even had a chance to come by and see you and Nick. But my father had secured a box for this performance and asked us to come along."

"And I have never heard Mrs. Billington," Eleanor said, "so here we are at the theater before we've even unpacked. I am looking forward to it. My goodness, don't you look stunning."

"I am sure I cannot compare to the newly wedded radiance that glows all about you. Oh! Heavens, how rude of me." She turned to Anthony and brought him forward with a touch on his sleeve. "Allow me to introduce Mr. Anthony Morehouse. Anthony, these are my very good friends, Simon and Eleanor Westover."

Anthony took Eleanor's outstretched hand and kissed it. "Your servant, madam." Then he took Simon's hand and gave it a quick, manly shake.

"Morehouse?" Simon asked. "Could you be the same Morehouse—"

"—who now owns the *Cabinet*," Edwina said. "Yes, Simon, this is my new employer."

"And I believe," Anthony said, "that I am addressing the infamous Busybody?"

Simon cast a questioning look at Edwina. At her nod, he smiled. "Egad, keep your voice down, sir. I should not like the whole audience to know that little secret."

"Don't worry, Westover, it serves no one to have it known that the old woman they hold dear is really a very tall young man."

"Morehouse! You dog!"

A voice from the crowd beckoned Anthony, and he rolled his eyes. "If you will excuse me a moment, Edwina, I shall be right back."

He edged his way through the crowd to stand by a fair-haired gentleman who was eyeing Edwina through his quizzing glass. Eleanor, unaware of the man's brazen scrutiny, grabbed Edwina by the arm and lowered her voice.

"My dear, he's gorgeous!" At a significant look from her husband, she added, "I'm sorry, Simon, but just because we're married doesn't mean I'm blind. The man is a golden idol, Edwina. Not at all the ogre I expected when I heard the magazine had a new owner."

"Nick wrote me about the wager," Simon said. "I'm surprised to see you with him. I'd have thought you'd be scratching his eyes out at every opportunity. But you look to be getting along . . . rather well."

Edwina felt her cheeks color. "We've become good friends, that's all. And I still intend to win the wager and have the *Cabinet* all to myself."

Simon cupped Edwina's cheek and said, "My God, you are blushing. Do not tell me you have finally fallen in love again after all these years?"

Edwina shrugged, unwilling to commit one way or the other.

"Oh, Edwina. How marvelous." Eleanor bent closer and lowered her voice to a whisper. "And I can tell you from personal experience that when you find someone to love, someone who loves you in return, don't waste another moment grieving over the past. Carpe diem, and all that."

"It is time," Simon said. "Long past time. Gervaise would agree, my dear, that you have kept to yourself long enough. It is time you started living again."

"My sentiments exactly."

Edwina jumped at Anthony's voice. She had not seen him come up behind her and was mortified to think how much he'd heard.

"That is why I invited her this evening," he said. "She spends much too much time cooped up in that house working on the *Cabinet*. Now, however, I think we must make our way to our box. It is an honor to meet you both."

"A moment, please." Edwina looked at Simon. "Can you have the next installment of 'The Hermitage' ready next week? I need five thousand words, if possible."

"Yes, ma'am," Simon said and gave her a wink.

"And one more thing," she said. "Eleanor, how would you describe the dress you are wearing?"

Eleanor gave her a puzzled look. "My dress?"

"Yes. What do you call that style with the drapery over one shoulder?"

"Oh. It's called a mantle of Venus. It's just a long piece of lutestring pinned up here—see?—and twisted around the back. It's very simple. My cousin, Mrs. Poole, showed me how to do it. She is passionate for the antique look."

"Very clever. Remind me to tell you one day how my own dress came to be."

"Oh, you must. It's one of the most beautiful things I've ever seen."

"And what do you call that sort of sawtooth border along the underdress and the edge of the sleeves?"

"Vandyke trimming."

"And the band twisted in your hair?"

"A fillet."

"And the feather thing?"

"An esprit."

"Come, Eleanor," Simon said, "You two can talk fashion some other time. My parents are waiting.

I'll come by and drop off 'The Hermitage' in a few days, Ed. Good to meet you, Morehouse."

"Now, that was very well done," Anthony said, as he led her up the stairs to his box. "You can mention your friend in the fashion report, and you have the accurate description as well. Very smart, my dear."

"Let's hurry, Anthony, so I can write down my notes before I forget everything. And by the way, who was that man staring at me through his quizzing glass?"

"That was Lord Skiffington. He had apparently wagered against you showing up."

"So, I am now the object of wagers other than your own? That is rather unsettling, if you must know."

"It is to me, too. And so I told Skiffy, in no uncertain terms. Look to your right, my dear. That is the Viscountess Downe—wearing a petticoat of Italian gauze under a rose satin robe trimmed in festoons of lace."

Edwina stopped and stared at him. "How do you *know* these things?"

"I read *The Ladies' Fashionable Cabinet.*"

Edwina laughed aloud, causing more than a few withering glances to be cast in her direction. Anthony tucked her arm under his and hurried up the stairs.

When they were finally settled in their box near

the stage, Edwina took only a moment to admire her surroundings, all white and gilt with beautiful plasterwork above the stage. She loved the opera, but had never had the pleasure of such an excellent vantage.

She wasted no time, though, in retrieving the little notebook Flora had given her. She dashed off a few lines about Lady Craig, Lady Downe, and Mrs. Simon Westover before turning her attention to the fashionably dressed people filling the three tiers of boxes. Plumed heads bobbed and jewels glittered in the candlelight of small chandeliers placed at intervals along the box circles.

"Oh, look," she said. "There is the Duchess of Devonshire in the box opposite. And Lady Bessborough."

"Flora will be pleased to have them mentioned in her report."

"Let me see. The duchess appears to be wearing a white dress—oh, dear. I can't tell what sort of fabric it is. Is it muslin?"

"Worked muslin."

Edwina turned to find Anthony peering through Flora's opera glasses straight at the duchess.

"Put those down," she hissed.

"Why? Everyone else is doing the same. She is accustomed to it, probably expects it. And just for your information, there are quite a few glasses turned on you at the moment."

"Me?" Edwina looked about the three circles of

boxes, the galleries above, and the pit below. He was right. Several gentlemen, and a few ladies, were frankly staring at her, with and without opera glasses.

"I must be some sort of novelty," she said.

"They are drawn to your beauty, my dear. You outshine everyone here, and they are all dying to know who you are. Does it make you uncomfortable?"

"A little. But I have been stared at most of my life, so I am somewhat used to it. I just never could understand the sheer brazenness of the way it is done at the theater. But it makes it easier for me to justify staring back, if I need to see a dress close up. Now, back to the duchess. A worked muslin dress and a brown sash."

"Not brown, my dear. It's Egyptian earth. Last year it was *feuille morte*, dead leaves. But never, never simply brown."

"All right, then. An Egyptian earth sash crossed in the back and hanging loose in the front."

"A fine girdle of Egyptian earth sarsnet worn in an elegant cross behind and tied with a graceful negligence in front."

She stared at him again. "And a white cap with pink feathers."

"A capote of white satin with a spray of small pink ostrich feathers inclining to the right."

"Heavens." She quickly scribbled Anthony's description. "How do you *do* that?"

"It's all in the language, my dear. You see that woman over there in the turban with its tail dangling down? That's Mrs. Whitney-Legge, by the way. Well, to my mind, that turban is a mess. Looks like it would fall apart if you jostled her. But you might easily describe it as twisted with stylish carelessness and finished off with a long end draped boldly over one shoulder. You see?"

"I think so. Let me try with the woman in the next box over. She is wearing a yellow dress—"

"Jonquil."

"—with a decorated hem."

"A narrow flounce."

"She is wearing a sort of turban—"

"A demi-turban."

"—made of the same *jonquil* fabric twisted with a shiny silver fabric—"

"Silver tissue."

"—adorned with short white feathers."

"A plumette of white heron feathers."

Edwina looked at him and grinned. "You have missed your calling, sir. I ought to have asked you to write the fashion reports."

"No, thank you. I am only showing you how it can be done. Once you have a few basic terms. Try again. There, in the third box over, second tier, are Colonel and Mrs. Hamilton. Have a go at her hat."

"All right." She lifted the glasses and studied the woman. "It's a cap of beige satin—"

"Buff."

"—buff satin covered in lace. The crown is full and confined with a white ribbon, and adorned with a cunning little white rosette at the side."

"Perfect. See how easy it is? Now, across from us and up one box is Lady Julia Howard. She's the dark-haired one on the left. Tell me about her dress."

Edwina held up the glasses and found the lady in question. "It's a petticoat of white satin under a robe of clear striped muslin. Plaiting at the sleeves. The bodice trimmed in ribbons of bright red . . . no, ribbons of coquelicot." She turned to Anthony and beamed in triumph. "What do you think of that?"

"I think I am going to lose another wager."

Edwina hummed softly as she sat beside him in the carriage. He could not be sure, but he thought the tune was meant to be Mandane's great aria, "The Soldier Tir'd of War's Alarms," sung with such passion earlier by Mrs. Billington. Unfortunately, Edwina's musical ear was somewhat less developed than Mrs. Billington's.

When Tony had first met her again after all those years, he had been so blinded by Edwina's beauty he thought she might be as nearly perfect as a woman could be. But he loved learning of her little imperfections and shortcomings. She had a tiny scar on the underside of her chin from a fall out of a tree that he remembered well. She had no fashion sense. She claimed not to be able to sew a straight seam. And she couldn't carry a tune.

He was smiling when she turned to look at him. She stopped humming and smiled in return.

"It was wonderful, wasn't it? I don't know when I've seen such a splendid performance."

"And on top of all that splendor, you have won two wagers this evening. What a triumph for you."

She hunched a shoulder and looked a bit sheepish. "It doesn't seem altogether fair. I could not have won the first without Flora's help, nor the second without yours."

"Are you forfeiting your two boons?"

She grinned. "Oh, no. I intend to have them both. In fact, I think I will name one of them now and save the other for later."

"I am all agog, madam. Tell me what boon you will have? And remember, it cannot be anything to do with the *Cabinet*."

"No engravers or colorists or binders?"

"No. It must be something personal. Something for you only, not for all the unfortunates of the world."

"Because you have done more than your share for them tonight."

"What?" Damn. She knew.

"I'm sorry. I realize you didn't want anyone to know. But I do. And I'm very proud of you, Anthony."

He looked down at the hands in his lap. He was

pleased—hell, he was over the moon—that she was proud of him. He was pretty damned proud of himself for once. Even his father, who shared the same solicitor and so knew what he'd done, had written a note congratulating him on finding something noble to do with his life. That note had almost undone him. But he really, really had not wanted Edwina to know.

"Thank you," he said softly. "But I don't want you to think—"

"That you did it for me?"

He looked up at her. "I did it for me, Edwina. To assuage my guilt, I suppose, over wasting my life and my resources. To give a little back for a change. To do something worthwhile. I did not do it *for* you, but I did it because of you. You taught me to look beyond myself to the greater good. You humbled me with your selfless devotion to causes and principles. You opened my eyes to the rest of the world. So, anyone who is helped by what I do owes it all to you."

The moonlight slanting through the carriage window fell across Edwina and glinted off her watery eyes. She chewed on her lower lip. "Oh, Anthony," she said. "What a perfectly lovely thing to say. You make me want to cry."

He took her hand in his. "Don't do that. I am useless in the face of tears. You will show me up to be a cad. Let us return instead to that other matter at hand. Your boon."

"Oh, yes." She gave a little sniff, blinked a few times, and composed herself. "My boon. I was actually hoping you would tell me about your endowment so I could perhaps be of help."

"Some other time I will be happy to do so. But this boon is for you. What will you have, Edwina?"

A little air pocket of silence opened up between them. She met his gaze squarely, but it was a long moment before she spoke.

"There is one thing I would like very much."

"Yes?"

"I would like you to kiss me again."

His heart did a little flip-flop in his chest, but he kept his eyes steadily on hers. "That is what you want from me?"

"Yes."

He lifted a hand to her face and stroked his thumb along the line of her jaw. "Never have I faced a more pleasant forfeit, madam. Allow me to oblige you."

He bent his head to hers and kissed her.

It began slowly and gently, just as it had earlier before the opera. He started with her eyes, kissing the corners, which were still slightly damp with unshed tears. He trailed butterfly soft kisses along her jaw and cheekbones to the delicate hollow beneath her ear, and downward to the vulnerable skin of her throat.

Her breathing became shallow and stirred the hair at his temple, and stirred his desire to a fever pitch. He moved up to take her mouth, and something instant and volatile flared between them. Wild and torrid and unbridled. He ravished her mouth, plundering its mysteries and sweetness. He pressed her close, felt her breasts crushed against his chest. Her arms had wrapped around his neck, encircling his shoulders, enveloping him in the spicy fragrance she wore. One hand worked its way up his neck and into his hair, and giving turned to taking. The assault became hers. He let her take what she wanted, opened his mouth wide and offered his tongue. And she sucked and pulled on it in imitation of a more intimate act, and he thought he might go mad with wanting more.

Instead he wrenched back control and pulled her more tightly against him, sliding his hand over the soft fabric of her dress, tracing the elegant curve of her spine and hip. He pressed her hip against him so she could feel his desire, and reached his hand down to cup her breast.

They kissed and kissed until the blood was roaring in his head. He was ready to lay her down on the bench when the carriage came to a halt.

They had reached Golden Square.

He broke the kiss with small nips to her neck and throat and jaw. "You're home," he murmured against her ear and then forced himself to pull away.

"So I am," she said somewhat breathlessly. She sat up straight, then laid a hand on his arm. "Thank you, Anthony. That is one of the nicest boons I have ever received."

He took her hand and kissed it. "It was my pleasure, madam."

They both began putting themselves to rights, adjusting clothing and hair and jewelry. There would be no mistaking what had just happened if anyone were to see them now, no matter how hard they tried to make themselves presentable. It was always worse for women, of course, with their elaborate hairdos and dresses that were often literally pinned together. Fortunately, he had only to get Edwina inside the door and hope that Nicholas wasn't waiting there.

And if he wasn't? Would Edwina ask him in? Would she take him upstairs so they could finish what they started in the carriage?

He hoped and hoped that was precisely what would happen, but he really wasn't sure what to expect yet from her. She had obviously decided to let down her normal defenses and let him get at least one foot in the door. Was she ready for the next step?

He leaped out of the carriage and held out a hand to Edwina. She stopped in the door and a strange look came over her face.

"Something's wrong." She all but lurched out of the carriage, almost knocking Tony off his feet.

He took her elbows and steadied her. "What do you mean?"

"Look." She gestured toward the house. "The rooms are lit, there are shadows at the windows, and carriages here in the street."

"That's Flora's carriage," Tony said, recognizing one of the two. The other was a hackney.

Edwina made a dash for the front door, but it was flung open by a frantic-looking Prudence, who called over her shoulder, "They're here."

Tony followed Edwina into the entry hall, and was taken aback to find its narrow confines crowded with Prudence, Flora, Nicholas, and— most astonishing of all—Madge of the Crimson Ladies, all talking at once.

"The worst thing . . ."

"A stupid mixup . . ."

"I din't know . . ."

". . . not Madge's fault . . ."

". . . have to be reprinted . . ."

". . . should have checked . . ."

"I dunno what . . ."

"But they're already . . ."

"We'll have to retrieve them."

"Stop!" Edwina held up a hand and shouted above the group to get their attention. When everyone had finally gone quiet, she said, "I can't make any sense of what you're all saying. One at a time, please. Prudence?"

"All right." Prudence took a deep breath. "There was a bit of a mixup with the proofs for the next issue. They accidentally . . ." She paused and darted a glance toward Anthony, then sent a plaintive look to Edwina. "The magazine page proofs became mixed up with . . . some other proofs for something else."

"Ow, Gawd, it be all my fault," Madge wailed as tears ran down her face. "I dropped 'em, see. I din't know they was differ't things. I musta put 'em back wrong, like. But I din't know. I din't mean to do nuffink wrong."

"It's all right, Madge," Flora said, and moved to put an arm around her. "It's not your fault. I shouldn't have asked you to do my job for me, especially knowing you could not read the pages."

"So the pages got mixed up," Edwina said, her voice tight and contained, "and printed out of order?"

"Something like that," Nicholas said. He stepped forward to add his piece to the narrative. "The long and the short of it is, one of my projects got bound in with the magazine."

"Oh, no." Edwina's face paled and she brought a hand to her forehead.

"And they've already been distributed," Prudence added. "Just tonight, in time for sales tomorrow. Thank goodness we were here. Flora and I stayed late to go over some of the advertising contracts. We were a bit behind schedule because of—" She paused and seemed to notice for the first time the less-than-perfect state of Edwina's dress. A quizzical look came into her eyes, and then they widened suddenly as she obviously realized what it meant. A flush spread over her cheeks and down her neck. "We . . . we had been busy with other things. Anyway, when your copies were dropped off, we decided to check them over and discovered the mistake. We knew we had to act fast."

"They knew you were at the opera," Nicholas said, "so they got a message to me at the coffee-house where I was meeting with William Thurgood. Pru's note indicated we would need all the help we could get, so I stopped by and picked up Madge since I knew . . . um, that is, she . . . I was . . . Oh, hell, I knew where to find her, all right? We were just beginning to discuss how best to rescue the situation when you walked in."

"Oh God." Edwina's naturally pale face was drained of all color. "What time were they delivered?"

"It was around half past nine," Prudence said.

"Thank God for that, then," Edwina said. "We can hold out some hope that the packets didn't reach the main post offices in time for the night coaches to pick them up."

"That's what we were hoping as well," Prudence said. "Otherwise . . ."

"Yes, otherwise we will be in a terrible fix. So, let's assume they haven't been picked up. We must see about getting them back."

"That's what we were just discussing before you arrived." Flora's eyes took in Edwina's slight dishevelment and sent Tony a speaking glance.

Tony felt he was missing something. There was too much anguish in the air over a few misbound pages. Something else was going on here. "Let me see if I understand what has happened," he said. "Nicholas had some sort of project destined for the printer, unrelated to the *Cabinet*, and the pages accidentally got bound in with the next issue?"

"That's right," Nicholas said.

"And what exactly is it that got bound in by mistake?" Tony asked.

Nicholas cleared his throat. "Actually, it was a political pamphlet."

He might have guessed as much. "On what topic?"

"On, um, Catholic emancipation."

Edwina made a strangled sound behind him. Tony caught a look passing between her and Flora, then Flora frowned and nodded her head.

"Bloody hell."

Everyone turned to look at Edwina, who never swore. She was red with fury. "We must retrieve every single copy of the *Cabinet*. All three thousand four hundred and twenty-two. Every one of them. Now. Tonight."

So much for his more amorous plans for the rest of the evening.

Tony was not entirely certain he understood the

level of Edwina's anger. He sensed it was the topic more than the printing error that worried her. It was a volatile issue. His own father and uncle were outspoken opponents of Catholic emancipation. Edwina must be concerned about possibly alienating certain readers so soon after wooing them with fashion.

"It is a controversial topic, to be sure," he said. "You are right, Edwina, that it should not be in the pages of the *Cabinet*."

"It most certainly should not." Her dark eyes were black with anger and her oddly stiff posture revealed her impatience. "But we have no time to stand around and discuss it," she continued. "Come into the study with me, all of you, and I will tell you what we are going to do."

Chapter 14

***

"Here it is."

Anthony held up the package from Daniel Imber marked LFC Oct 30 copies.

"Hurry up," Edwina whispered. "I hear someone coming."

He tucked the package under one arm, grabbed her hand, and dashed up the stairs from the service yard to the street. Edwina crashed into his back when he came to a sudden halt.

"Evening," he said in an odd voice.

Edwina's heart raced as she pressed up close behind him, trying to be invisible.

"'Ere now, wotcher doin' down in Jackman's yard at 'is time o' noight?"

Anthony began to chuckle and he staggered

slightly on the stair. "Jus' having a bit of fun, don-cha know?" His voice was thick and slurred. He pulled Edwina forward and turned her into his shoulder. He rubbed his hands along her spine and gave her bottom a little pat. "Man's allowed to have hish fun, ishn't he?" He bent his head and gave Edwina a sloppy kiss.

The man laughed. "Right yer are, guvner. Nice little piece yer got there. Would't mind 'avin a go at 'er meself."

It was no wonder the man thought her Anthony's lightskirt. Though he was still in evening clothes, she had changed into more comfortable garments and looked positively drab next to his golden splendor.

Anthony wrapped his arm around her more tightly. "Get your own woman, man. Thish one's mine."

"A'right, a'right. No need ter git inter an 'uff about it."

He walked away, but Anthony kept a close hold on her until the sound of the man's boot heels had faded. Then his chest began to shake and she realized he was laughing. He released her from his embrace, grabbed her by the elbow, and hurried her down the street and around the corner to where his carriage waited. He flung open the door and practically tossed her inside. He said a few words to his coachman, threw the packets in the boot with the others, and joined her in the carriage.

The moonlight shimmered in his golden hair and enhanced the twinkle of laughter in his silvery eyes. "Well, my little doxy, that was another close call."

"And that was quick thinking, sir."

They locked gazes for a moment, and simultaneously burst into laughter. She fell against him, helpless with mirth. His arm came around her and they laughed and laughed.

Edwina finally came to her senses. "We must not dawdle. There are several more booksellers on the list."

It really was no laughing matter, even though it had turned into a rather fun adventure. Edwina had determined to retrieve every single copy of the *Cabinet* before any of them fell into the hands of a reader. She, and all of her cohorts, had also been very careful that none of the misbound issues got into Anthony's hands. They kept him busy with other distractions so that he never got an opportunity to actually read the offending pages.

Later, Edwina was going to throttle her brother for not correcting those pamphlet proofs and removing the attack on Anthony's uncle.

Thankfully, her meticulous attention to detail meant that she had the precise list of all booksellers in town who received copies. There were over three hundred booksellers in London, but only about fifty, thank heaven, carried the magazine. The bulk of the issues were mailed to individual subscribers, and those had been delivered to one of the two main post offices for distribution via the Royal Mail. They had been exceedingly fortunate that the packets had been delivered too late for the night coaches, and so they actually had until morning to retrieve them.

But Edwina wanted to deal with those first. She and Anthony went to the Lombard Street Post Office where, as owner and editor they had the right to reclaim the magazines before they were distributed. The night guards had not questioned her and Anthony's authority; the only difficulty had been in locating all the packets, which were already being sorted. But they had managed to find them all, with Edwina checking off each one on the long list of subscriber names. The whole business had taken an inordinate amount of time, though, and she was glad she had anticipated as much and had only taken on the task of going to booksellers in the near vicinity, beginning at Cheapside.

Edwina had assigned each team of two—Nicholas with Prudence and Flora with Madge—to go to every bookseller who'd received a delivery of the magazine and retrieve them. She had divided up the list geographically, with each pair assigned fifteen to twenty shops. It was a thoroughly improper and clandestine operation, resulting in outright thievery in most cases, since the magazines had been paid for.

Before leaving Golden Square, she insisted that all of them, with the exception of Madge, help write out notes to each bookseller confessing to re-claiming the delivery and promising a new delivery as soon as the issue was reprinted.

She and Anthony had left notes in service yards and slid them under doors and tacked them to doorframes. So far they had found every delivery, clearly marked and ready to be unpacked and sold in the morning.

"Where to next?" Anthony asked.

Edwina looked at the list again. "Ludgate Hill. Two shops. Then one in the Strand, and we're finished." She looked at him and smiled. "I can hardly believe we've done it. I hope the others have been as successful."

"As a gambling man, I ought to have put money on you tracking down every single copy. I'd say it was a sure bet from the beginning, since I had known you wouldn't rest until it was done."

"Too bad there was no one around to take that bet. You might have made a tidy profit tonight. Assuming the others are doing as well as were are."

He rapped on the ceiling, and the coachman slid open the tiny communicating window at his feet. Anthony gave him the direction, and they were on their way again.

"You made a pretty little doxy back there," he said. "That fellow wanted to get his hands on you, the cur."

"Ah, but you become very possessive in your cups, sir. It was actually rather thrilling to have you claim me as yours in such a manly fashion. You might have a future on the stage. You played the role to perfection."

He opened his mouth to say something, then did not. Instead, the amusement faded from his eyes as he gazed at her intently. "It was not a difficult part to play," he said.

A sudden yearning fluttered in her breast so fiercely she could barely breathe. Did he want her for his own? After their passionate interlude in the carriage earlier, it was clear he wanted her physically. But he'd never made a secret of that. And she wanted him, too. She had been considering the wisdom of inviting him into her bed when they had arrived at Golden Square to find pandemonium in the entry hall. But then she had become so angry, and so anxious Anthony might discover what had really happened, that all thoughts of such an important decision had been put aside. She thought of it now, though, and wondered if she would regret it if she gave in to her desire for him.

It was rather more likely she would regret it if she did not.

She was saved from contriving a response when the carriage came to a halt. It had been only a short distance from St. Pauls Church Yard, so it was just as well they had not embarked on a serious discussion about whatever this was that drew them to each other. There was no time.

The first shop had an easily accessible service

yard and they found the "LFC" package without difficulty. The next shop was only a few doors down. It had a service entrance on the side with a short stairway to the door. There was only a tiny area in front of the door, where night deliveries had been stacked. Anthony started down the stair, with Edwina close behind, when a cacophony of barking erupted from a large and ferocious-looking beast guarding the door.

"Damnation." Anthony stepped back, almost tripping her. "The thing's a monster."

They stared down at the very large and very loud dog at the bottom of the stairs. He looked determined to keep them out.

"I'm fairly good with dogs," she said. "Let me try."

"I don't think that's a good idea."

She ignored Anthony and inched down the steps holding out a hand, palm down, cooing, "Good dog," over and over as she approached. He stopped barking and she thought she'd won him over, when he bared his teeth and lunged.

A strong arm grabbed her around the waist and lifted her back to the top of the stairway.

"Damn it, Edwina, that thing might have killed you. Thank God he is on a short chain."

"But we have to get those magazines. Perhaps if we went down together . . ."

"I suppose you want me to fight off that beast while you search through the deliveries."

"We could try."

And so they made another attempt. Anthony took each stair ever so slowly, keeping Edwina at his back. The dog growled and tugged at his chain, but was no longer barking. He watched them with a baleful eye as they descended to his domain. When they reached the last stair, he started barking again. Loudly. Continuously.

Neighbors began to shout out their windows for quiet.

Anthony grabbed the dog's chain and held him at bay while Edwina moved cautiously toward the deliveries.

"Hurry," he said. "I don't know how long I can hold him off before he decides to rip my throat out."

There was a mountain of packages in the tiny space. She had to move several heavy boxes before she saw the distinctive "LFC" marking on a small package in the far corner. All this effort for only a dozen copies.

"Got it," she said, and tucked it under her arm.

She moved around Anthony, watching the still-barking dog the whole time. When she was in front of him at last, she dashed up the stairs. . . .

And found herself staring down the barrel of a very large gun. Held by a very large man in a night-shirt and cap.

Anthony collided with her and swore beneath his breath.

"I'll take that package, madam," the gunman said.

"No, please, let me explain."

"Hand it over." He poked her shoulder with the gun. "Now."

She could see no other choice, so she held it out to him. He kept the gun steady on her while he examined the package. He looked up and his face was pinched into a puzzled, exasperated expression.

"What is this? Some kind of joke? You confronted Lucifer for a bunch of ladies' magazines?"

"We can explain," Anthony said.

"I should hope you can. I'd be very interested to know what the bloody hell you're doing in my service porch in the middle of the bleeding night, pinching my merchandise."

"Are you Mr. Pritchard, then?" Edwina asked.

"Who wants to know?"

"My name is Edwina Parrish and I am the editor of *The Ladies' Fashionable Cabinet*. And this is Mr. Anthony Morehouse, the publisher."

The bookseller frowned. "You're stealing your own magazines?"

"As ridiculous as it sounds," Anthony said, "that is precisely what we are doing."

"But we have a note we were going to leave at the front door," Edwina added. She rummaged through her reticule and retrieved the note. "It explains everything. You see, there was a rather, er, embarrassing error in the printing which was not discovered until the magazines had already been distributed. We did not want to chance even a single issue being sold before we could pull them."

Pritchard lowered the gun and took the note. "That bad an error, was it?"

"Yes, it was."

"Well, it seems like a damn fool way to rectify it, scaring the life out of Lucifer and waking the whole bloody neighborhood. Here." He held out the package and Edwina grabbed it before he could change his mind. "Now get the hell out of here so I can get some sleep."

They were very quiet when they returned to the carriage. Edwina thought Anthony was angry over what had happened, but when she looked over at him, he was smiling.

"Come here," he said and held out an arm.

She curled up against him and he wrapped his arm around her.

"You are surely the most intrepid, tenacious, pig-headed woman I have ever met. And I adore you."

He kissed the top of her head and she thought it might have been the most purely contented moment she'd experienced in over eight years. He kept her close until they reached their next and final stop. The bookseller on the Strand had a large fenced-in delivery dock. It was simple enough to get inside, find the package, and remove it. No challenge at all. A rather pedestrian end to their night's adventure.

The sky had already begun to show the purple shades of predawn by the time they arrived at Golden Square. They were the last to return. The other four had experienced equal success, and equal adventure. The retrieved packages were spread out on the dining-room table. Edwina and Prudence set out to open them up and make a count.

When it was found that they had recovered all three thousand four hundred and twenty-two copies, wild cheering and shouting broke out. Edwina, too giddy and tired to be inhibited, threw her arms around Anthony and kissed him. Out of the corner of her eye, she saw Nicholas sweep Prudence off her feet to swing her around in celebration. The look in Prudence's eye left no doubt about her feelings for Nicholas. Did he know she loved him?

There was no time to ponder such questions. There was celebrating to be done. Nicholas led them upstairs to the drawing room and brought out the French brandy. He poured a small glass for everyone, and they traded stories of their adventures.

Flora and Madge, who had covered Shoreditch, Bishopsgate, and Snow Hill had been accosted more than once by men seeking their favors.

"But I knows how ter deal wiv them rotters. Crikey, I bin dealin' wiv 'em all me life."

"She was a marvel," Flora said. "Knows how to

get in and out of a place without being seen, I can tell you."

"Bin doin' that all me life, too."

Nicholas and Prudence, who covered St. James, Piccadilly, and New Bond Street, had been chased by the night watch.

"Were almost caught, too," Nicholas said. "The damned fellow thought we were thieves and set up a howl such as you've never heard. But we led him a grand chase through courts and alleys and finally lost him."

They had all encountered wily street urchins and would-be footpads, nosey neighbors and curious passers-by, and variations of Lucifer, but no one else had faced a gun, thank goodness.

Flora was the first to call it a night, claiming she was asleep on her feet. The others agreed, and everyone rose to leave.

"I'll take Pru home," Nicholas said.

"That is very kind of you," Prudence said, "but Papa would have my head if he saw me coming home at this hour with a gentleman, alone."

She had a disappointed look in her eye, as though she would like to defy her father this once.

"I'll take Pru," Flora said. "Come along, girl, before I collapse with fatigue."

Nicholas turned to Madge. "Then I shall do myself the honor of escorting you home. Assuming you have no irate father waiting at the door."

Madge gave a shriek of laughter. "First off, I ain't seen my pa fer years. And if I did, he ain't likely ter grouse 'bout a fine gentl'mun drivin' me home at any hour. More like ter try an' nap a bob orff yer."

Prudence followed Flora, but turned toward Nicholas briefly and looked as if she were about to say something, but shook her head and walked out of the room. Nicholas and Madge followed.

Edwina had noted a distinctly dreamy glint in Prudence's eye. She had a terrible feeling that the girl was going to have her heart broken. Perhaps she should have a word with Nicholas. Not to encourage anything between them, but just to warn him to deal cautiously with her. He would not deliberately hurt Prudence, but Edwina could not imagine he would ever return her affection. They had known each other too long, and Nicholas had never shown the least interest.

"What has put a frown on your face?" Anthony asked.

"I was just thinking about broken hearts."

He arched a brow. "Yours?"

"No."

"Egad, not mine, I hope. Are you going to break my heart, Edwina?"

"I don't think so. I hope not."

He came to sit beside her on the settee. "Good. But you do tend to set it racing, you know. Tonight especially. It's rather astounding that I have not fallen into an apoplexy."

"Is it racing now?"

"It is."

"So is mine."

He pulled her into his arms and kissed her. Instant desire flared white hot in her veins and she let it take her. She was prepared for her response this time, as she had not been earlier when it had almost overwhelmed her. She kept her guard high as ripples of sensation spiraled through her, but an unfulfilled longing grew deep inside her.

When they finally broke apart, they were both breathless and wrapped around each other like clematis vines.

"I should go," he said.

"Not yet."

He raised his brows in question.

"I am still owed a boon," she said.

He smiled. "Indeed you are. What shall it be, Edwina?"

She untangled herself from him, rose, and held out her hand. He placed his hand in hers, and she led him upstairs.

He held her naked in his arms at last.

Clothes were puddled at their feet and flung willy-nilly about the room; hairpins littered the floor. He had wanted to prolong the undressing, to savor the slow, erotic removal of each garment. But an urgent hunger overwhelmed them both and they had pulled off each other's clothes in wild abandon.

But now that they were naked, the fury had eased while they gazed and admired and explored. Edwina was every bit as perfect as he'd imagined. Beautifully made, softly curved, smooth, white, and flawless, but for the tiny scar on her chin and a mole on her left shoulder.

He wanted to touch her everywhere. While he gently kissed her, his hands roved up and down her spine, over the gentle curve of her hip, down to her firm bottom, up her ribs, and over her breasts. She moaned softly and he deepened the kiss, plundering her mouth with tongue and teeth.

And she ravished him in return, taking his tongue, pulling, sucking, biting. Her hands explored the muscles of his shoulders and back and buttocks, pressing him closer, putting every possible inch of her body in contact with his, as though she could not get close enough.

A wild euphoria almost overcame him. The knowledge that she wanted him as much as he wanted her was more intoxicating than good whiskey.

When he could stand the assault no longer, and was so drunk with desire he could barely stand at all, he lifted her in his arms and laid her on the bed. He sat beside her but took a moment simply to gaze upon her. The room was shuttered and dark—in their ardor they had not taken time to light a candle—and he wanted to see her.

He rose, went to a window, and pulled back the shutters. The pale light of dawn flowed into the room and over the bed, limning Edwina in a soft glow. He sat down beside her again and drank in the sight of her. Pale skin, luminescent now in the dawn's light. Black hair fanned out to one side like a raven's wing. Dark red mouth with lips slightly parted. Equally dark nipples, peaked and pebbled. A black triangle of hair at the apex of her thighs.

If he were an artist, he would paint her just so, in all her naked splendor.

He ran a finger gently from her throat, over the valley between her breasts, down her belly, and finally into the dark hair beneath. She shivered under his touch. He reversed direction and brought the flat of his hand over her stomach and up to the soft undersides of her breasts.

"I am honored to touch you," he said. "You are so fine, so beautiful."

She pulled him down beside her and kissed him. Hot and sweet, her tongue laid siege to his mouth, insistent and demanding, almost painful in its soul-stealing intensity. She was passion unleashed. No modesty. No taboos. Her hands and mouth explored every inch of his body with frank interest and wild demand. She took his mouth again in a potent kiss, and rubbed against him in a sensual, erotic undulation that was an exquisite torment.

He followed her lead for long, lush moments, then urged her to slow the kiss, and finally broke away. She was panting and her eyes were wide with frantic need.

He stroked her cheek and said, "Relax, my love. There is no challenge between us here. No competition. Let us not fight for control. Let us simply enjoy each other. Let go, Edwina." His fingers trailed to her neck. "Let go."

She gave a shuddery sigh and he felt her relax slightly. He bent to kiss her mouth, but kept it soft and slow and gentle. After a long, sweet moment, she seemed to will her body into pliancy.

He kissed her mouth and her cheek and her jaw and her throat, all while his hand gently fondled her breast, circling, cupping, teasing the taut nipple. She undulated beneath him, but with less urgency than before, then arched her back, thrusting her breast against his hand.

His lips trailed lower, over her collar bone and to the upper curve of her breast, then lower still until finally, inevitably, he took the dark nipple into his mouth and circled it with his tongue.

She gave a small cry and placed her hand against his head, pressing him to her, her head thrown back against the pillow. It was a moment of exquisite surrender, as explicit as the shudder that ran through her body.

He paid equal homage to her other breast, then dipped his mouth to its underside. He shifted his body over hers and buried his face between her breasts, pressing them against his cheeks. He eased down her torso, his knees forcing hers apart. He trailed kisses around her stomach, circling her navel and finally dipping his tongue into its tiny well. Her muscles tensed as his mouth moved lower, lower, until his tongue parted the soft, wet folds of her sex.

She cried out and her pelvis bucked beneath his mouth. His tongue tweaked the tiny bud of pleasure, and she almost instantly climaxed.

Edwina thought her heart would burst. She did not regret her surrender. Indeed, she blessed him for it. She had never thought to experience such physical release again. She had buried her sexuality with Gervaise, deliberately, almost as a memorial to the love they'd shared.

But Anthony had brought it to life again. He had taught her she was still vibrant, still alive. She could feel again. She could love again.

All barriers between them crumbled. Lips, tongues, hands went wherever they wanted, each giving and taking equally. First one led the way, then handed off to the other, with no struggle for command.

He pulled her on top of him and she kissed his neck and shoulder and chest. She suckled his nipple as he had done hers, and savored his gasp of pleasure. He ran his hands over her hips and buttocks, down to her thighs, and gently urged her knees up so that she straddled him. She eased her body down slightly until she felt his erection against her swollen, tender sex.

He shifted his hips and nudged against her and she sat up, hands flat upon his chest. She pressed her knees into his sides, eased down, and took him inside. She gave a soft groan and sat unmoving for a moment, savoring the sheer pleasure of being filled by him.

And then she rode him. Taking it slow at first, sliding down upon him and rising slowly. He allowed her full control. He lifted his hands to her breasts, caressing them as she moved over him. His eyes never left hers, but held her locked in a gaze gone dark with pleasure.

He shifted beneath her, half rising to meet her with his own thrusts. The tempo built and built until the sounds of their joining created a raucous, steady beat. Tension coiled inside her, building with each thrust, sending shafts of heat darting through her body, causing her skin, even her scalp, to tingle with anticipation.

When she thought she could bear no more, the knot of tension peaked and shattered into a thousand bits of sensation and wonder.

"Ah, my God. Anthony!" She threw her head back and cried out as the release shook her to the core of her soul.

He watched the climax flow through her, entranced by her uninhibited response. All that she felt played itself out on her face. Now twisted into a grimace, she opened her mouth wide in a silent scream, as though she were in pain. But as the spasms subsided, the muscles in her face relaxed, and a perfect joy suffused her beautiful features.

She was a woman who'd given everything of herself, and she had given it to him. It was one of the sweetest moments of his life. A pure, bright moment of dazzling clarity.

He loved her.

He held her fast while the tension drained from her body, and clasped her to him when she slumped to his chest. Then he rolled her onto her back, and pressed himself deep inside her. She looked up at him and smiled. He moved within her, and she was roused again, pushing up to meet each powerful thrust.

He found her mouth and kissed her, and they moved together in perfect, age-old harmony. When she wrapped her legs around his waist, he groaned and drove deep.

And the fire within him exploded. He called out her name and buried his face in her black hair as the primitive ecstasy of release gripped him.

They lay still a moment, breathless, panting,

damp. He lifted his head to look at her. She had never looked more beautiful. Lips parted in a smile of pure wonder. Splendid dark eyes, sleepy-lidded and glassy with slaked desire. He kissed her.

Anthony disengaged himself from her warm body, rolled to his side, and took her with him. She curled up against him like a kitten, her head nestled on his shoulder.

"Anthony?"

"Yes, my love?"

"Thank you."

And she fell asleep in his arms.

Chapter 15

Edwina woke to a feeling of such languor, such pure and joyful satisfaction, that she thought for an instant it had been a dream. But her body ached in ways and in places that told her it had been quite real.

When she reached out, though, she found the bed empty. She rose up on her elbows and saw him. He had not abandoned her, but was sitting at her writing desk. Perhaps he was penning a note to leave behind after he made a discreet exit.

But he was not writing. He was holding the Minerva.

The small gilt bronze head fit in the palm of his hand. He cupped her cautiously, as if she were a tiny bird, and stroked the length of her nose with a gentle fingertip. For one irrational moment, Edwina wondered if that was all he'd ever wanted from her. That damned Roman head.

But no. There had been much more between them than merely the Minerva or the wager. She would swear it had been more for him than simple, uncomplicated pleasure-taking. She would not have given herself so completely otherwise.

Edwina had not wanted this. She would have preferred the uncomplicated pleasure, had hoped she had reached a new level of maturity in allowing herself to take it. She ought to have known better. She could never be casual in her passions.

But she did not want to be in love again. Love was a wild, disordered state of mind and she hated chaos above all things. As she watched Anthony studying the Minerva, however, she thought he might be worth a little disorder in her life. He was shirtless, though he had donned his breeches, and the morning sun sculpted the smooth planes of his chest in bright white-gold relief. His hair, tousled and hanging over his forehead, glinted yellow gold in the sunlight. He was beautiful.

And her heart swelled with affection for him. For he had brought her back to life.

Perhaps the Minerva had acted as her talisman, her good-luck charm, once again. For it had brought Anthony to her. Back to her, after almost twenty years. There was a lovely symmetry to it.

"She is beautiful, is she not?" she said.

He turned to look at her, and the fury in his eyes struck her like a slap across the face. Dear God, what had happened? She sat up straight, clutching the sheet to her breasts.

"She is beautiful and cold and dead," he said, and put the little head back on its stand. "When were you going to tell me about *this*, Edwina?"

He held up a copy of the misbound *Cabinet* and her heart sank like a stone. She had forgotten it was there. She had brought it with her when she had come upstairs to change out of her evening dress before going out to retrieve the deliveries. She had wanted to see exactly what it said, in case some copies slipped through into readers' hands. And she had left it there, forgotten, in plain sight.

He had not been admiring the Minerva. He had been reading Nicholas's pamphlet.

She wanted to die. She wanted the earth to open up and swallow her whole. She wanted to shrivel up like a dead leaf and float away on the wind. Anything but this.

"Do you know," he said, his voice tight with anger, "that one of the men your brother so scathingly attacks here is my uncle? And that my father is his closest advisor?"

She swallowed hard. "Yes."

His eyes grew wide and his nostrils flared. "You *knew*? Bloody hell. You knew he was my uncle and went ahead with this diatribe anyway?" He opened and closed his fist convulsively. "Damn. Damn.

Damn! And it almost ended up distributed to over three thousand people with my name on it. *My* name, Edwina. Not yours. Not your brother's. My name. For my father to see. For all the world to see. Bloody hell!"

"But we stopped it." Edwina crawled to the end of the bed, keeping the covers over her bare breasts. She wanted to explain. She had to make him understand. "Why do you think I was so anxious to retrieve all the copies last night?"

He turned to look at her, and his eyes were cold and hard as polished steel. "But even if it had not been accidentally bound in with the *Cabinet*, the pamphlet would still have been financed by me, would it not?"

Her stomach seized up. "What?"

"Yes, my dear, I have discovered your little secret." He gave a sneering smile. "Not only have I been reading your brother's vitriol. You were unwise enough to leave one of the account books here on your desk."

"Oh, God."

"Indeed. You have been stealing money for years, first from your uncle, then from me, to finance radical publications and pamphlets." He narrowed his eyes and leaned toward her menacingly. "Well? Do you deny it?"

She lifted her chin. "No."

"You could have asked, you know. I would have

refused, of course, but then you knew that. You knew I would not want my name associated with politics I don't happen to support. So you didn't ask. You just skimmed a bit off the profits and kept them for your own use."

She swung her legs over the side of the bed and stood, taking the sheet with her. She would stand proud, but she would not stand naked.

"I admit we've been using some of the revenue for other activities. But it was never much, never enough to make even a small dent in Uncle Victor's profits, or yours. The money was not stolen. It was redirected. And not for anything personal or frivolous. The money was always used to support a worthy cause."

"Like Catholic emancipation?"

"In this case, yes."

"No matter who you hurt in the process?"

She took a step closer. "There was never any intent to hurt anyone. It was an opinion piece, that is all."

"In which my uncle was named and attacked for *his* opinion."

She straightened her shoulders. "Are you suggesting we should keep our views private, never daring to disagree with the government?"

"I am suggesting you did wrong to *steal* money from someone else to support your damned causes—"

"For God's sake, Anthony, we used a tiny bit of the profits from a frivolous ladies' magazine to do some good."

"—and you did very wrong to steal from *me* in order to attack a member of my family."

Edwina gripped the sheet and tried to curb her temper. "I have apologized for that. And I have worked hard to make sure no harm was done, that your name was not associated with an attack on your uncle's public views. Should I not at least be given credit for trying to make things right?"

He gave her a look of such withering scorn she felt as if he'd physically struck her. She stared at him, at the end of another dream. She ought to have followed her initial instincts and stayed away from him. She ought to have known they were fated to cross swords, not hearts.

He rose and pulled his shirt over his head. "You know what, Edwina? I thought I was in love with you. Can you imagine? And I thought you cared for me, too. I was ready to risk everything for you." He tucked his shirt into his breeches and looked about for the rest of his clothes. "Me, the gambler who never bets it all was about to stake everything—*everything*!—on you. What a fool I was. It was a sucker's bet and I fell for it. You don't care about me. You don't care about individual people, only those great faceless masses you think to help with your bloody reforms." He sat back down and began to pull on his stockings. "It's all causes with you. Causes that make you feel important, that make you think you're smarter than everyone else because *you* understand what people need. But you don't know what the poor want or need. You are a privileged woman playing at politics, condescending to think you know what is good for the unwashed masses."

"That's not true."

"It is. You *think* you know what is best for your displaced farmers and factory workers and street women. You support them with words, and a little money that isn't yours, but I don't see you spending time in the streets getting to understand their lives." He bent to buckle his shoes. "Hell, I'm willing to bet—yes, I believe I'd wager a monkey—that even in France you never left the salons to march in the streets with the people. You have no real experience or understanding of the lives you intend to change. You're nothing but a sham republican."

"No! You're wrong, Anthony."

"You believe your way of thinking is the only right way, and you don't care who you hurt in your noble quest to achieve some grand democratic scheme."

"No."

"It should not surprise me, of course. You were like that as a child. Always had to be right. Always had to win. You never cared even then how much you hurt someone with your arrogance."

She continued to stand tall, wrapped in her sheet, but inside, her heart ached that he should think such things of her. She was not a sham. She was not.

"Your damned politics are all that matter to you," he said. "How could I have believed you could lower yourself to love just one man? You're too busy loving the masses. Burke's swinish multitudes. You don't have time to care for me or anyone else."

No, he was wrong. She did care. She watched him shrug into his waistcoat and knew in that moment that she cared a great deal. Good God. It came to her in an instant of a startling clarity. She loved him. Despite his hateful words, which were surely thrown out in anger, she loved him.

The knowledge almost knocked her off her feet.

"No, Anthony, that's not true." Her voice rose more than she'd intended, and she lowered it deliberately. "I *do* care."

He glared at her for a moment with cold contempt, then worked his arms into the tight-fitting evening coat. "People don't publicly attack the loved ones of those they care about. Yes, you didn't allow the tract to be distributed in the *Cabinet*, but you would have allowed it to be distributed separately. Paid for with my money. *My* money used to hurt *my* family."

"I tried to stop it. I told Nicholas—"

"I knew something smoky was going on with you people, but I thought I could trust you." He picked up the rest of his clothes and tossed them over his shoulder. "I ought to have known better.

You are not a woman who can love a man. And don't tell me about your French lover. I don't believe you could have loved him either, but only his Great Cause, which you wanted for yourself. You loved the idea of him and what he represented. But I doubt you are capable of loving a single individual for himself alone."

"No!" How could he say such a thing?

He walked to the door with no regard for his *déshabillé*—an open shirt and loose waistcoat, a creased neckcloth hanging over his shoulder.

"Well, I leave you to your causes, my dear. And to your own devices. You shall not finance your seditious activities with my money again."

He turned at the bedchamber door. "I do thank you for a night of pleasure. There was that, at least."

And he left.

Edwina did not move for several minutes. A single tear fell down her cheek and onto the arm that held the sheets across her breasts. She could not have said for certain whether it was a tear of anger or disappointment or heartache.

She was angry, to be sure. Because he'd discovered her deceit. Because he was too stubborn to listen to an explanation. Because of the hateful accusations he'd made. And she was disappointed in his reaction, his intransigence, his descent into insult. And she was most definitely sore of heart. For she had discovered she loved him at almost the same moment it became clear they could never be together. Never.

She had feared an involvement because she had not wanted emotional chaos. Her fears were confirmed. Nothing could be more chaotic than the emotions roiling in her breast at the moment.

Not again. Not again!

She turned, stiffly walked to the bed, and sat down on its edge. A wave of weariness swept over her, and she lay back, turned on her side, and curled her knees up to her chest.

And as quickly jerked back up. His smell still clung to the pillows. She flung off the sheet, walked to her clothes press, and retrieved a dressing gown. She wrapped it about her, sank onto the chaise, and stretched out on its length. The light of morning spilled into the room. She rolled onto her side away from the window. A wool throw sat at the end of the chaise, and she pulled it over her feet and legs.

Edwina lay there for some time and simply allowed all the emotions churning within her to come to the surface. She wanted them out. Gone. Over with. Not held inside to erupt at any moment. She did not even fight the tears that inevitably came.

Her world wanted to spin out of control again, but she would not allow it. Not again. She would indulge in one brief bout of emotional release, then pick herself up and get on with life.

But what sort of life would that be? Would she continue at the *Cabinet* in her foolish attempt to enlighten readers with rational prose, when all they really wanted was a good fashion report? It all sounded so frivolous now. So naïve.

She could not let go of Anthony's accusation that she was a sham republican. Was she?

It was true that she had not marched in the streets of Paris. She had been swept up in the grand talk that had gone on in the salon of Madame Roland and others. Great thinkers, strategists, men and women of ideas had talked and talked and talked, but had done . . . what? Very little, as it happened. The doers had been the likes of Marat and Robespierre, and no matter how heinous their deeds, the talkers had not been strong enough to combat them.

In retrospect, none of them had trusted the masses to truly understand their purpose, even though it would have been to their advantage. They had not walked among the people. It had not been thought necessary, when right was on their side.

Anthony had said she merely condescended to think she knew what those less privileged needed. As she lay there, miserable on her chaise, it shamed her to consider that he might be right. She was still a talker and not a doer.

At least that was something she could change. She ought to be grateful to him for shining that light on her arrogance.

But there was one thing about which Anthony was dead wrong. She was indeed capable of love. Just now, she rather wished she were not.

* * *

"You look terrible."

Nicholas stood in the doorway of the back parlor, where Edwina had taken refuge. She glared at him, picked up the nearest thing at hand, which happened to be a large volume of poetry tucked between the seat cushions, and threw it at him.

He ducked.

"What the devil is wrong with you?" he said, and came into the room, even though any sensible person would have run screaming in the other direction.

"Go away, Nickie. I'm too angry with you right now to talk rationally."

He ignored her, of course, and took a seat. "Then don't talk," he said. "Let me do all the talking. But look at me, first, Ed. No, don't turn away. Look at me."

She lifted her eyes to his and glared.

"You've been crying."

She snorted and looked away.

"Look, Ed, I don't like to see you unhappy like this. You've never thrown a book at me before. I'm assuming it has to do with Morehouse. I saw him storming out of the house this morning, half dressed."

"Don't scold me about that, Nickie. It's none of your business."

"I know. And I wasn't going to scold. It's just that I assumed things were going rather well between you two. You could hardly keep your eyes off each other last night, and I can only suppose that the hour and state of his departure means you took him to bed."

"I repeat, it's none of your business. I'm a grown woman. I can make my own decisions."

"Of course you can. Come on, Ed. You know I've never interfered with your personal life. But something went wrong. And because I love you, I want to help."

"You've already helped quite enough, thank you. It was your blasted pamphlet that sent him storming out of here. I *told* you to pull the Quayle portions out, Nickie. What the devil happened?"

He pulled a face. "I forgot. Plain and simple. I meant to do it, but before I thought to get around to it, Madge had taken the proofs to Imber. I'm so sorry, Ed."

"He read it, you know. Can you imagine how he felt? To think that his uncle might be vilified in a publication with his name on the cover? But it's worse than that."

"Oh, God. What else?"

"I had left one of the account books on my writing desk. He found it. He knows what we've been doing. He was furious, Nickie. And now . . ." She thought of the things he'd said, that she couldn't love, that she hadn't loved Gervaise. There was only one reason why he would say such horrible things to her. "And now he hates me."

She looked away and blinked hard. She would not give in to tears again. She had spent her share. She heard Nicholas rise and crouch down before her. He pressed a hand to her cheek and turned her face toward him.

"He does not hate you, Ed." His voice was gentle and he took hold of her hands.

"You didn't hear the things he said. I know he was provoked, he was angry. But he couldn't have spun those notions out of the moment. He must have thought them all along. He was just angry enough to speak them aloud."

"What did he say?"

"Among other things, that I can't love a person. That I can only love a cause."

Nicholas tugged on her hands and pulled her to her feet, then wrapped his arms around her. "He is wrong. You most definitely know how to love. You love me. You love Simon. You love Pru. You loved Gervaise." He stroked the back of her hair. "And you love Morehouse. Don't you?"

"I thought I did," she said, her words muffled against his shoulder. "After last night, I thought I did. But I never wanted to, Nickie. I never wanted that again. You know I didn't."

"Yes, I do know." He nudged her away from his shoulder and looked into her eyes. "And I cannot tell you how pleased I have been that you were ready to let a man love you again. It has pained me to see you so closed up, so alone, for so long."

Edwina shrugged out of his embrace and walked to the window overlooking the garden. She wasn't closed up. She was simply disciplined. But she had allowed that discipline to slip, and see where it got her?

"Let me go to Morehouse and explain," Nicholas said. "I will tell him how you asked me to change the proofs when you learned Cedric Quayle was his uncle. You begged me to drop the attack on him. But I didn't. It is me he should be angry with, not you. Good Lord, if it weren't for you, all those copies might not have been retrieved."

"There's no need for you to do that, Nickie."

"But I want to help make things right between you."

"You can't." She turned to face him. "It was never going to be right between us. There was the wager to begin with. Which, by the way, I am not going to win. There are only two weeks to go and we are almost six hundred subscriptions short. There is no way to make that number, hard as we tried."

"You don't know that."

"And there is the fact that I work for him, if I continue on at the *Cabinet*."

"If?"

"I have begun to realize how trivial the magazine is in the overall scheme of things. It will never make any sort of a difference in the world."

"My God, Edwina, how can you say that? You are reaching thousands of women. How can that be trivial?"

"I have been thinking that I'd like to do something more . . . direct."

"What do you mean?"

"Anthony said I do not have any true understanding of the poor and their needs. He is right. I stay here in Golden Square and spin words. It is time I did something more useful."

"Have a care, my dear. Do not let a bruised heart push you into rash action. Morehouse certainly lashed out in anger. Let him cool down a while, Ed. He will regret what he's said, I'm sure of it."

"It doesn't matter. It would never have worked between us. We are too different. He scoffs at my ideals and my 'causes' and yet they are vitally important to me. He doesn't understand me. And I don't understand him. I don't know how a person goes through life as a gambler. He likes to be reckless. I prefer order." She sighed. "We would never suit."

Nicholas moved to stand beside her. "There is such a thing as too much order, you know."

"No, there isn't. Order is predictable, clean, unambiguous." She looked out the window. "It's like my little garden. I never have to worry about it going wild because I keep it under control."

"Ah, but your garden is an unnatural thing, Ed. It is nature pruned and clipped and trained into something artificial. A little disorder is natural, my dear. And welcome. Don't be as ruthless with your emotions as you are with your garden. Don't prune away all that is honest and human."

Tony stormed around with a wad of anger in his throat for more than a day. He was still furious. With Edwina, with Nicholas, with Prudence, with the whole bloody lot of them and their righteous causes and their pilfered profits. When he thought about how close a call it had been, to have that attack on Uncle Cedric published under his name, his blood ran cold. It wasn't as though he agreed with his uncle. In fact, he disagreed with him on most things. But for once in his life he was on the brink of actually making his father proud of him. It still stunned him to think of that note congratulating him on the endowment. It was the first positive word he'd had from the man in twenty years.

He hadn't realized how much he'd craved those few words of praise.

It might all have been lost if that damned magazine had been distributed. At least he had Edwina to thank, he supposed, for insuring that hadn't happened.

How could he have been so wrong about her? How could he have fallen in love with a woman ready to plunge a knife in his back? The time they'd spent in each other's arms had been so special it had shaken him to the core. Why did she have to turn it into something he could now only regret?

The thing was to simply put her out of his life. Completely. He would not seek out her laughter, her face, her voice, her body. He did not need her. He could find all of those things elsewhere. The pleasures of London awaited him. Good wine. Good food. Good play. Good women. London teemed with them, everything he could desire.

And yet somehow it all seemed so empty.

How was he to put her out of his mind?

He was trying to do so in a small gaming hell off Jermyn Street when he looked up to find Nicholas Parrish at his side. Bloody hell.

"Did she send you to find me?" Tony glared at Nicholas and wondered how the fellow had managed to track him down.

"No, of course not. I need to speak to you in private, if you please."

"Now? While I am having such a streak of luck?"

Nicholas surveyed the hazard table and the pile of winnings in front of Tony. "If you please."

Tony sighed and nodded to the other gentlemen at the table. "It seems I must call it a night. Please excuse me."

He gathered his winnings, rose, and indicated that Nicholas should follow him into another parlor. He found two empty chairs near the fire and took one. Nicholas sank into the other.

"What may I do for you, Parrish?"

"Edwina told me what happened."

Tony arched a brow and wondered precisely how much she had told her brother.

"You have a right to be angry," Nicholas said. "But not at her."

He did not wish to listen to Edwina's apologist. She had defended her position well enough and he had no desire to hear it all again. He made to rise. "If you will excuse me, I have no desire to continue this conversation."

"Sit down and hear me out, Morehouse."

Taken aback by the man's sharp tone, Tony resumed his seat. He glared at Nicholas and said nothing. He would let the fellow have his say, and be done with it.

"The mixup with the magazine was entirely my fault," Nicholas said. "When Edwina learned that Cedric Quayle is your uncle, she came to me at once and asked me to remove all references to him from my pamphlet. I simply never got around to doing it."

Tony gave an indelicate snort. "Indeed."

"It was not a malicious oversight, Morehouse. I simply forgot. The proofs were delivered to Imber before I had corrected them. It was all mischance, a foolish series of errors. I wanted to make sure you understood that."

"Your sister had much the same excuse."

"It is no excuse. It is merely the truth. I know you

are still angry, Morehouse. But at least the error was caught in time."

"How fortunate for everyone. Now, is that all?"

Nicholas studied him for a moment, then said, "No, that is not all. I am extremely fond of my sister and you have made her very unhappy. That doesn't set well with me."

Tony shrugged. The protective big brother was back.

"I don't know all that happened between the two of you and I do not want to know. You apparently said some rather vile things to her, though. Hurtful things. One in particular that I must set you straight on."

"Oh? What is that?"

"You told her she was not a woman who could love. I am here to tell you that nothing could be further from the truth. She has loved. She does love. So much so that her heart is easily broken."

Had Tony broken her heart? He didn't believe so. She kept it locked up too tight to allow it to be touched, much less broken.

"She is a very strong woman of great character," Nicholas went on. "She likes to be in command of every situation, does not like to feel vulnerable in any way. But do not mistake that for an inability to love. She has a great capacity for love, but she fears it because when she does love, it consumes her. Losing Gervaise made her even more afraid. But that was a long time ago, and I had thought she was let-

ting go of her fear at last." He gave Tony a significant look. "Instead, I believe she is more afraid
than ever."

None of this was a revelation. Tony had recognized Edwina's vulnerability for some time. It was
not so long ago, only yesterday, in fact, when his
heart had soared to think she had got beyond her
fears to let him into her heart. But everything had
changed when he'd read that pamphlet and the account book. How could he trust her after that?

"I'm sorry, Parrish. I had frankly hoped there
was something between us. But she deceived me.
You all deceived me."

"And you cannot forgive her?"

Could he? His anger was still so fresh and hot it
was impossible to see beyond it.

"She believes you hate her," Nicholas added.
"Do you?"

"Of course I do not hate her. I am just . . . angry."

"Then perhaps you will eventually be able to forgive her?"

"I cannot think clearly just yet," Tony said.
"Give me a little time."

"Your wager comes to an end in two weeks."

Lord, so soon? "Give me until then."

Chapter 16

"**Y**er don't mean it?"

Edwina smiled at Madge's incredulous expression. "I do mean it. I want to have a look around St. Giles, and since I know you come from that area, I was hoping you could come along with me."

"I think yer must be daft, Miz Parrish. No one goes ter the rookeries jus' ter 'ave a look round. 'Tain't safe. Specially fer a lady like yerself."

"That is why I want you to come with me, Madge. I shall feel quite safe with you."

"Dunno why. Yer needs a big strappin' man, not the likes o' me."

"I believe we shall be fine together. I would not go at night—"

338

"Gawd, I should 'ope not."

"—and I am sure it must be less dangerous in broad daylight. Besides, I want to see the school."

"Oh." Madge made several musical syllables out of the word. "Yer never seen it, then?"

"No."

"Then 'ow come yer knows about it? I figgered yer been there, even though yer a lady an' all, seeing as how 'twere yer what told me to go." Madge stood before Edwina's desk and stared at her with sharp interest.

Edwina, and the *Cabinet*, had been funding the school in St. Giles ever since she'd learned of it. She knew it taught prostitutes and other unfortunates how to read and write, along with some other basic skills, in hopes it would help them to find better employment. The stated objectives had been enough for Edwina to lend her support, but she had never once visited the school, to see for herself if it was successful. It was past time she did so.

Anthony's accusations had struck home.

"I learned about the school a few years ago," she said, "and have since been providing a small amount—a very small amount—of financial support to help pay the rent, buy books and materials and such. And since Flora has been entrusting you with more duties, I thought it would be helpful if you learned to read."

Madge colored slightly and cast her eyes down. "So I wouldn't make no more mistakes."

"It was not your fault, Madge. We all had a hand in that one. But it can only serve you well in all aspects of your life to be literate. And I thought the St. Giles school would be the perfect place for you to learn."

" 'Tis a fine thing ter be able ter read." She stood up a bit straighter and a look of sheer wonder gathered in her eyes. "I still be learnin' me letters, but I can make some sense o' signs and such. I be most grateful to yer, miss. Din't know 'bout that school, an' it right under me nose."

"Its existence is not trumpeted about. Too many of the men—factory wardens, brothel owners, pimps—do not want their women to be educated."

" 'Fraid we'll be able ter get better work somewheres else, I 'spect."

"Exactly. Just as you have done here at the *Cabinet*. I hope that by working for us you will no longer have to earn your living on the streets."

Madge shrugged. "Gettin' too old fer that any'ow."

Edwina would be surprised to learn that Madge was even thirty-five, though she looked ten years older. "But you are never too old to learn to read and write."

"Cor lumme, I wish I'd learnt sooner. But there weren't never any time. An', o' course, me old man wanted me out at night bringin' in the dibs so 'e could spend it in gin shops."

"Does he know you are going to the school?"

"No, an' I ain't tellin' 'im. Long as I bring 'ome the blunt, 'e don't need ter know nuffink. So, why'd yer wanta go to the school for?"

"I just want to see if I could be of any help. I don't have more money to give, but I could help teach."

Madge's eyes grew round as saucers. "In St. Giles? Yer'd come down to the rooks to teach girls ter read?"

"I don't see why not."

"Well, I do. Yer a lady wot'll stick out like a rose in the ragweed. An' yer'd be lucky if yer met up wiv no worse'n a cutpurse. There's bad folk in them alleys."

"What about your teacher at the school? She apparently does not worry about her safety."

"That's cuz Miz Jakes lived nearby most 'er life. Grew up in Seven Dials, but married 'erself a brewery foreman an' got all respectable, like."

"And so she is trying to help other girls better themselves, as she did. How remarkable. It will be a pleasure to meet her. Shall we go?"

Madge rolled her eyes but said, "Whatever yer wants, miss. But yer'd best change outa that dress."

They set off on foot, for St. Giles and Seven Dials, two of the worst areas of London, were only a mile or so from Golden Square. The atmosphere changed abruptly when Oxford Street met Tottenham Court Road. The sound of carriage wheels faded as the streets narrowed and fed into a network of dingy courts and alleys, grimy rabbit warrens of closely packed buildings.

Shadows hovered and disappeared. Dark, ragged mounds stirred. Drunkards slumped in doorways. Piles of rubbish were heaped against walls. Open gutters, full and filthy, ran down the middle of cobbled lanes. The occasional rat skittered along the gutter edge. A putrid smell of decay filled the air, along with a sick-making sweetness from the nearby breweries. Edwina covered her mouth and tried not to inhale too deeply.

So much squalor so close to home caused Anthony's words to ring loudly in her ears. While Edwina sat in her comfortable house beside a warm fire, real human misery was barely a step away. She penned passionate pleas about the plight of the impoverished masses, and yet never once walked the few blocks to face that poverty head-on.

She kept close to Madge, who would not allow her to dawdle by drinking in every detail or stopping to offer help to every miserable creature.

"Walk brisk, like yer got business 'ere. Lallygaggin'll mark yer fer sure, an' every knuckler and buzman'll be all over yer like fleas on a dog."

Madge had insisted she wear dark, simple clothes that showed wear and dirt, the easier to blend in. She wore no jewelry and carried no reticule or pocketbook, though she did carry a few small coins in her pocket with the intent of handing them out to the most needy. But she soon discovered there were too many wretched urchins and too few coins. She would save them for Mrs. Jakes.

At street level, many buildings housed businesses: fish sellers, costermongers, gin shops, picked clothing. The upper levels housed families and, Madge told her, a variety of illegal operations, prostitution being the most prevalent. Few windows retained their glass, and those that did were black with grime. Many were filled with straw as the only barrier against the cold. Some were open with laundry hanging on the sills. One woman leaned out an open window and tossed the contents of a slop bucket into the street. Through another window, a dark figure lifted a jug to his mouth.

Most of the men of the district who were employed worked at one of the breweries. Some worked at the timber yard, others worked as stone cutters in the mason's yard. But a great many did not have any employment at all, due to illness, disability, or drunkenness. These men relied on their wives and daughters to pay the rent by walking the streets at night.

Almost every idle woman who leaned out a window, sat on a stoop, or huddled in a doorway was, according to Madge, a prostitute. Hundreds of them. Some looked as young as twelve or thirteen. Skinny, ragged, sickly—they made the Crimson Ladies look the picture of health and prosperity.

As she walked beside Madge, Edwina's fists clenched and swung stiffly at her sides like bell clappers. It angered her that she had been so oblivious to the true nature of poverty and despair. She had read, and penned, thousand of words on the plight of the poor. But walking through St. Giles gave a new meaning to those words. And stirred her to a new purpose.

Madge stopped at a nondescript door of a grimy brick building on a dark alley. She entered without knocking and Edwina followed close behind. They walked up a narrow staircase and turned into a long corridor. Madge halted before a door that stood slightly ajar. The soft chatter of female voices could be heard within.

"They're 'avin' a lesson," Madge said.

"Perhaps we should wait."

"Naw. We'll be quiet as mice an' Miz Jakes won't mind. Come on."

She pushed open the door and they stepped inside. It was a small room with one small window high on the far wall. Three long benches were lined up like church pews. A motley group of women and girls filled every available space—young, old, fat, thin, all of them scruffy, tattered, and dirty. Each had a small scrap of paper on her lap and a stubby pencil in her hand. They were practicing their letters.

A tall, fair-haired woman stood before them, holding a large notebook with a few words written in big, bold print. A small stack of paper and a box of pencils stood on a table at her side. She was younger than Edwina had expected—no older than herself. She turned and smiled.

"Ah, Madge. Come for an extra lesson, have you? And you've brought a friend. Wonderful! Ladies, make room if you will."

Tony sat at the breakfast table and tried to read the morning newspapers. But he couldn't keep his mind off Edwina. The growing bond between them. The laughter. The lovemaking. The deceit.

He wasn't quite finished being angry with her. He wanted to be angry with her. She deserved his anger. And yet he was almost ready to forgive her. He'd even begun to regret some of the things he'd said to her. Especially about not being able to love. That had been an inexcusable insult. He had not needed Nicholas Parrish to tell him so.

He could not decide what his next move should be. They had hurt each other, but he wanted to believe they could get beyond the hurt and back to where they'd been before he had crept out of her bed and into a sinkhole of anger and disappointment. He had been on the brink of a declaration, perhaps even an offer. Surely they could salvage something that had led them into each other's arms.

He had been the worse injured, after all. If he was willing to forgive her, she would certainly find it in her heart to forgive regretful words he'd flung out in anger. Wouldn't she?

It was a delicate situation, to be sure. And there

was the wager to consider. She was close to winning. He had seen exactly how many subscribers she had the night they had chased down every copy in town. The issue had been reprinted—he had seen a copy at a local bookseller—and the patriotic prints and added fashion reports would be sure to lure even more subscribers. He was certain she would win the game.

And then what? Would she want him out of the business, and her life, entirely? Or would she be willing to let him back into her life, back into her bed? She could not ignore what had happened between them there, the passion and desire—and love?—that had swept them up like a tidal wave. It was not an experience easily forgotten. Surely it had been as momentous for her?

And so he must contrive a way to make things right between them. As right as they could be.

"I beg your pardon, sir."

Anthony looked up from the paper he wasn't reading. "What is it, Brinkley?"

"A package has arrived for you, sir." He held a small square box tied with brown paper and string. "Shall I put it here?"

"Yes, just put it right there. Who is it from, do you know?"

"No, sir. It arrived by special messenger."

"All right. Thank you, Brinkley." His tone was one of dismissal, to which Brinkley apparently objected if one were to judge by the sudden stiffness of his spine and the clicking of his heels as he gave a quick bow. He had hoped to see what was inside the box, no doubt.

When he'd gone, Anthony took a paper knife to the string, and ripped away the paper. He wasn't sure what he had expected, if he had expected anything, but it wasn't what met his eyes when he opened the box.

The Minerva sat in a pile of fine protective tissue. *Oh, God.*

He lifted it out with fingers that were oddly unsteady. There was a note. Of course there was a note. It was folded in a neat square underneath the little bronze head. He didn't need to read it. He knew what it would say. He held the paper in his hand for a long moment before gathering the courage to unfold it.

Anthony,

I have decided to concede our wager early. Not because I do not believe I could win. I concede because I no longer want the magazine. It is no longer of any importance to me. I have found more worthwhile uses for my time. I am therefore returning the Minerva to you as part of our bargain. I find that I am unable to continue as editor of the Cabinet. I believe it would be unwise to do so, and I daresay you will not wish my continued in-

*volvement. I will stay on through the end of
the month in order to finish up the next issue.
After that, you must make plans to find a new
editor.*

*Yours,
Edwina Parrish*

He dropped the note and pressed a hand to his
temple. Hell and damnation. What had she done?

She could not give up the *Cabinet*. How could
she even think of doing so? It was the pride of her
life, the center of all her passions. What could possibly be more worthwhile to her?

A myriad of remembered conversations played
out in his head. How it had come to her. How she
had quietly changed its direction to be something
more than frivolous entertainment. How she had
recruited important contributors. How she wanted
to make a difference in her readers' lives. How
proud she was of her work. How important it was
to her.

She was ready to throw away all of that?

Tony picked up the Minerva and unconsciously
ran his fingers over the soft ridges where gilt had
worn down to smooth polished bronze. He had
done this to her. Edwina was ready to walk away
from the work that had defined her life all because
of some brutal accusations he'd made in a pique of
anger.

She had stood up to him, magnificent in her draped sheet, and defended her actions, refuted his indictment of her principles. He had assumed those words, at least, had not touched her.

He had been wrong.

She must have taken his words to heart, else why would she do something as rash as quitting the magazine?

Well, he wouldn't let her do it. He loved her too much—yes, even her deceit had not changed that—to allow her to do this. It was unthinkable. Her spirit would be killed. She *had* to continue with the *Cabinet*. Edwina *was* the *Cabinet*.

He didn't want the bloody magazine. It was hers. He'd intended her to have it all along. The wager had just been a game to fuel the competition between them. He was willing to give it to her outright, but she would be too proud to take it.

Yet it was not too late for her to win it fair and square. If she won it, surely she would not walk away from it. There were still two weeks left in the wager. Perhaps he would simply ignore her concession and see what he could do to insure her victory.

"Did you see this, Edwina?"

Prudence handed her a copy of the *Morning Chronicle* and pointed to an advertisement at the top of the front page, alongside announcements of new book publications. Edwina blinked when she saw the name of her own publication in the ad.

The Publisher of *THE LADIES' FASHION-ABLE CABINET* wishes to call attention to the recent improvements and enhancements in regard to reports of current fashions, accompanied by excellent colored engravings of those fashions drawn from life by Mr. Lionel Raisbeck, R.A. In honor of these enhancements, and to commemorate the late Peace, the Publisher wishes to announce that for every new subscription received within the next two weeks, all subscription fees will be donated to the LONDON BENEVOLENT SOCIETY FOR WAR WIDOWS AND ORPHANS. The Publisher expects all fashionable ladies of a charitable nature will want to enter the subscription lists.

She looked at Prudence, who was grinning from ear to ear. "You see?" she said. "He is trying to help you win."

"It is too late. I have already conceded."

Prudence's mouth dropped open. "You what?"

"I conceded. There was no hope of winning."

"But there *is*. Look what he's done." She jabbed her finger at the advertisement.

"Even that won't bring in six hundred subscribers in less than two weeks. It doesn't matter, Pru. I've decided I don't want the *Cabinet*."

"What? You can't mean it."

"I do. It was never anything more than a piece of

light entertainment with a few subtle messages buried inside. Those messages would never reach enough readers to make a difference. In the meantime, people are starving less than a mile from here. The *Cabinet* isn't helping them."

Prudence frowned. "What has got into you, Edwina? You have always admitted the magazine was not a true political forum, but only a convenient vehicle for those subtle messages. I cannot count the number of times you told me how even that was important in its own small way, and how proud you were to be involved. And now you're saying you no longer care about it? You've conceded the wager?"

"Yes, I have. I already sent him the Minerva as a forfeit."

"You didn't!"

Edwina shrugged. "And I resigned as editor. I've decided to find other ways to make a difference. Besides, after our quarrel—an inadequate word for what happened—he will have no wish even to see me again. I daresay it would be awkward for both of us if I stayed on."

Prudence placed both hands flat on the desk and leaned forward. "You have always been an inspiration to me, Edwina. I have respected you, admired you, even envied you. But how can I continue to do so if you behave so foolishly?"

"Pru, I—"

"Yes, Mr. Morehouse was angry, and rightly so.

And yes, he may have said things that hurt you. But this ad shows he still cares. He wants you to win. He *loves* you."

Lord, how she wished she could believe Prudence. She had tried desperately to quell her feelings for Anthony. She had tried to convince herself she did not love him. She did not want to love him. She thought she had cried him out of her system, that she was over him, that she could banish him from her mind.

But it had been impossible to do. When she closed her eyes sometimes, she could still feel his mouth on hers, his hands on her skin, could smell the musky male scent of him, could feel the strong muscles of his back and shoulders and legs, could hear the sounds of his pleasure.

It would be a very hard thing to forget.

"Nicholas had a talk with him, you know."

Edwina groaned. "No, I did not know. How do *you* know?"

"He told me. He felt badly about that mixup with the pamphlet. It was his fault, he said, and he went to Mr. Morehouse and told him so."

"Damn it, I wished he had just stayed out of this. He has only made it more difficult. Anthony will think I sent him."

"Don't be a fool," Prudence said. "Mr. Morehouse knows you would be too proud to do such a thing. But please, Edwina, don't allow one mistake to ruin the love between you. Accept the peace offering of his advertisement. Accept this implied apology, and give him a chance to accept yours."

And at that moment Nicholas burst into the room. "You won't believe this," he said, and slapped on the desk a copy of the *Times*.

"My dear boy, have you gone mad?"

"It's quite possible, Mother, but indulge me, if you please. You made dozens of those little Union wreaths earlier in the year. Only this time they will be Peace wreaths."

"But Anthony, *five hundred* of them?"

"I know it's a lot, but I've brought all the ribbons, hundreds of yards of ribbons. And I have helpers for you. All you need to do is show them how the wreaths are woven and give them a place to work. I've put them in the breakfast room."

"Helpers? In the breakfast room?"

"Yes. You see, I've thought of everything. So, will you do it, Mother? Please?"

"Five hundred peace wreaths to give away with magazine subscriptions. It would be a formidable project." Lady Morehouse smiled and rose to her feet. "But I never could refuse you, as you well know. I shall do it. I only hope it brings you what you want."

"I haven't told you what I want."

"It is easy enough to guess. All right, my boy. Let's get started."

Anthony led her downstairs to the breakfast

room, but they were halted by the great bellowing roar that could only be Sir Frederick in a temper.

"Octavia!"

They rounded the corner to find Anthony's father, red-faced and fuming. His wife went to him.

"What is it, dear?"

"What in blue blazes are six doxies doing in my breakfast room?"

Chapter 17

P rudence hovered over the desk while Edwina counted the huge pile of subscriptions.

"Four hundred and seventeen."

"How marvelous!" Prudence said. "In only one week. Those advertisements worked beautifully. You're going to win this wager, Edwina."

"But I've already conceded."

"Well, you can just unconcede as soon as all the numbers are in. Imagine it, Edwina. The *Cabinet* will be yours. All yours. Did you ever think it would happen?"

A week ago she had decided she didn't care if it happened. She was truly convinced that she preferred to spend her energies on more direct action, such as Mrs. Jakes was taking in St. Giles.

But the *Cabinet* was in her blood, she supposed, for the closer the subscription numbers came to the wager's goal, the more she realized how difficult it would be to give it up. And now it appeared there was a real chance for her to win, for the *Cabinet* to be hers at last.

"Before Uncle Victor lost it in a card game," she said, "I never hoped to see the day when it would be mine. Since then, since the wager with Anthony, I have dreamed. Oh, how I have dreamed. But I will tell you frankly, Pru, I didn't think we could do it."

"And we could not have, without Mr. Morehouse's help. He has certainly done a great deal to lose his own wager. It seems rather strange for a gambling man, does it not?"

"You are a fine champion for him, Pru. But don't push too hard. I know you have romantic notions about the two of us, but it simply is not going to happen. He may be trying to deliberately lose the wager simply because he really and truly doesn't want the magazine. He never wanted it, remember. He thought it was a piece of furniture."

Prudence giggled. "But he has worked hard to make it a success, by bringing in Flora, by allowing you to hire Mr. Raisbeck for the drawings and Mr. Jarvis for the engravings. And the Crimson Ladies, of course. And now the advertisements. You can see the results of his efforts right there on your desk." She indicated the pile of subscriptions. "And he's doing it all for you."

"I don't know what to think, Pru."

It did not make sense that Anthony would be doing this for her. She had betrayed his trust—irrevocably, she had thought—and had sent him the Minerva in concession. Despite the pull of her heart, she had been quite certain whatever had begun between them was over. She did not believe he would be able to forgive her.

So, why was he doing this? Why had he placed those advertisements? If he did it for her, what did that mean?

She folded her hands and leaned her chin upon them. "To tell you the truth, Pru," she said, "I've never been so confused in all my life."

"Do you love him?"

"Probably."

"Do you think he loves you?"

"I thought he might, until he discovered the truth. I have thought since then that he must surely hate me. If you could have heard the things he said to me, you would understand."

"But he doesn't hate you. Nicholas said so."

"What?"

"When Nicholas went to talk to him, Mr. Morehouse said he did not hate you. He was angry and disappointed. But he doesn't hate you."

"Well, that is something, I suppose."

"It certainly is! It means there is hope for reconciliation. Hope for the future."

"You are too much like Simon, my dear. Always spinning romantic dreams."

"Simon's dreams came true."

Edwina smiled. "They did indeed."

"Don't you have dreams, Edwina?"

She shrugged. "I stopped believing in dreams long ago. But I confess . . . I had hoped . . ." She was reluctant to put into words what she had in fact dreamed. What hopes she had cherished in her heart after Anthony had made such sweet love to her. She had made an effort, a Herculean effort, to put those hopes and dreams out of her mind.

"What had you hoped?" Prudence asked. "Tell me."

Edwina heaved a deep sigh. "I had only hoped . . . that he might love me. He made me feel so alive, so whole again."

"Then you must honor him for that, whatever else happens. I have always thought your grief had become like a suit of armor, that you used it to keep life at arm's length. This is the first time since I've known you that you have allowed a man close to you. For such a beautiful woman who could have anyone at all, I have never understood it. If I had a man like that interested in me . . ."

She flushed and shook her head.

"If you had been in France, Pru, you would know why I am the way I am."

"What nonsense."

Edwina's brows lifted. "I beg your pardon?"

"Other people were in France, too. Other people suffered great loss. Entire families were lost. But those left behind survived. They carried on. They built new lives."

"I did all of that."

"Yes, but you locked up the best part of you. You closed off your heart. And that is the real tragedy of your time in France."

"I tried to unlock my heart very recently, and had it shattered in my breast."

"Oh, Edwina. I am so glad to hear you say that."

"That he broke my heart?"

"That you unlocked it far enough to allow him to chip it a little. Don't lock it up again. He is trying so hard to repair it."

Edwina laughed. "He is certainly up to something. I shall just have to wait and see what it is."

"Miss Parrish?" Lucy popped her head in the door. "There's a lady to see you. Mrs. Westover."

"Eleanor! Send her in."

Eleanor bounced in looking bright-eyed and happy, wearing a light blue muslin round gown with short frock sleeves, a double plaiting of lace around the neck, and a cashmere shawl woven in shades of red and blue. Edwina smiled that she could recognize such details now.

"So this is where the *Cabinet* comes together?"

"Eleanor, how nice of you to come by. This is my

friend Prudence Armitage. She is our assistant editor. Pru, this is Simon's wife, Eleanor Westover."

"I am pleased to meet you, Miss Armitage. But I am afraid I must take Edwina away for a while."

"Take me away? Where?"

"Grab your bonnet and shawl, Edwina. There's something I want you to see. We won't be long, I promise you. Oh, and here's the next Busybody column from Simon. He sends his love."

Eleanor would brook no objection or delay, and so Edwina, intrigued, did as she asked.

When they were settled in Eleanor's barouche—a wedding present from Simon, she was told—Edwina turned to her. "Are you going to tell me what the mystery is? Or must I wait?"

"It is no mystery. It is simply a remarkable phenomenon I thought you should see."

Edwina narrowed her eyes in suspicion. "Does this involve Anthony somehow?"

Eleanor adjusted her shawl. "Why would you guess that?"

"Because everyone seems to want to patch things up between us."

"I had heard of what happened, of course." She reached over and touched Edwina's hand briefly. "Nicholas came by to commiserate with Simon. He felt wretched about it. And of course Simon told me. I have wanted to come and chat with you about it, to offer the same support you once gave me when Simon walked out of my life. But as I was driving in the park today with Simon's mother, I saw something that made me think I could wait no longer to speak to you."

"Anthony was in Hyde Park?"

"Yes."

Her heart gave a tiny lurch. "With someone else?"

"Not exactly. Or at least, not in the way you mean. You will see. Ah, here we are at the gates. Slow down, please, Hibbert, and pull over to the edge of the road."

"Why are we stopping? I don't see Anthony."

"I thought you might not want him to see you just yet, so I didn't want to go any closer. Do you see that little cluster of ladies over there near the Serpentine?"

"Yes, but I can't see—Oh, wait. Is that . . . is that . . . *What* is he doing?"

Eleanor laughed. "I believe, my dear, you have found yourself a true entrepreneur. Either that or the man loves you to the point of idiocy. He has set up a table and is soliciting subscriptions to the *Cabinet*."

"You're joking."

"I'm not. He's parked himself smack in the midst of Hyde Park at the most fashionable hour and is selling subscriptions."

Edwina laughed uncertainly. "Now why didn't *I* think of that?"

"If you will allow me, I should like to walk over

there and see just exactly how's he's doing it. Then I can report back to you. But you can stay here, out of sight, if you like."

"Oh, yes, please do go. I'm dying to know what he's up to."

"Wait here, then. I shall be right back."

The coachman helped Eleanor down, and she walked down the long, straight path to the table where Anthony had set up shop. Edwina watched as Eleanor approached. There were several other women crowded around the table. She saw Eleanor speak to Anthony. He handed her something that looked like a flower, but she couldn't be sure from that distance. Eleanor offered her hand and Anthony kissed it, looked briefly in Edwina's direction, then went back to whatever he was doing.

Had he seen her? Had Eleanor said something to let him know she was there?

The walk coming back seemed to take twice as long as the walk going. Edwina's nerves were tied in knots by the time Eleanor was lifted back into the barouche. "Well?"

Eleanor smiled and handed her a small wreath made of red, white, and blue ribbons with a tiny red bow at the top and a pin stuck through the back. It was charming, but . . .

"What is it?"

"It's a peace wreath. Anthony has five hundred of them. Or had. He is giving one to every woman who signs her name to the subscription list. It is a very long list."

"They are tokens for subscribers? How very clever."

"And popular. Everyone wants to acknowledge the peace. Almost every woman I passed was wearing one. See there?"

A curricle passed with two women on the seat, both wearing the little patriotic wreaths pinned to their bodices.

"And that's not all," Eleanor said. "He is asking them to put their subscription fees in a large jar and says all the money in the jar will go to the London Benevolent Society for War Widows and Orphans. Some are stuffing the jar with much more than the annual subscription fee. The jar is filled to bursting with notes."

"Oh, Anthony," Edwina whispered.

"That is the charity he endowed, is it not?"

"Yes."

"He gave me an extra wreath for my friend. He told me to tell her he has collected over two hundred subscriptions."

Edwina's jaw dropped. "Two hundred? Eleanor, I only needed one hundred sixty-one to win the wager."

"Congratulations, my dear. I believe you have yourself a magazine."

* * *

He came the next day.

She looked up from her desk to see him standing in the doorway, and her heart was thrown into wild, undisciplined, chaotic disorder. He was holding a box.

"I have brought your Minerva back," he said. His voice was flat, without expression. "You have won the wager."

"But I conceded."

"I reject your concession." He walked into the room and placed the box on the desk. "You won it fair and square. I have also brought papers for you to sign, transferring full ownership of the *Cabinet* to you."

She stood and brought a hand to her mouth. She thought she might cry, and she hated to cry. But the *Cabinet* was hers! It was a dream come true.

"I don't believe it was at all fair and square," she said. "It was due to your efforts, not mine, that the subscription numbers doubled. Even though I told you I no longer wanted the *Cabinet*."

"I chose not to believe you."

How had he known? She had fooled herself for a short time. Did he know her so well? Better than she knew herself?

"Besides," he said, "I only helped a bit at the last minute. The rest you did on your own. With your crack editorial staff, of course."

"But your recent methods have been most ingenious. The peace wreaths were very clever. I thank you for your efforts on my behalf."

"Not only your behalf. A good *cause* was served through all the new subscriptions."

"Your benevolent society."

He nodded, then took a set of folded documents out of his inside pocket and placed them on the desk. "Sign these, Edwina, and the *Cabinet* is yours. My solicitor drew them up. You can take time to read through them, of course, so you will understand precisely what you're getting. I would advise you to do so. Or you can have your own solicitor review them, but—"

Edwina pulled them toward her, dipped a quill in the inkwell, and signed. Then, without hesitation or forethought, she walked out from behind the desk, put her arms around him, and laid her head on his shoulder.

His arms came up to wrap around her and he held her tight.

"Edwina, I—"

She pulled away slightly and placed a finger over his lips. "No, let me. First, I want to apologize for taking your profits and using them for my own ends."

"Apology accepted."

"That easily?"

"Well, I was angry as fire at first. But it was the principle of the thing, not the actual expenditures. I saw where the money was going. The school in St. Giles, for example. The charity hospital in Derby. I did not object to what you were doing, only to how you were doing it. But you can do as you please now, without hiding anything from anyone."

"Second," she said, "I want to apologize for not making sure Nickie removed that attack on Cedric Quayle as soon as I found out he is your uncle."

"Apology accepted. And I have already accepted your brother's apology. He told me what happened. He took full responsibility."

"Third, I want to apologize for not trusting you. I should have told you everything from the start."

"Apology accepted. But you had no reason to trust me after I placed a wager on you the first day."

"And fourth . . ." She looked deep into his eyes, trying to judge whether or not she was about to fall off a cliff, or fly.

"Fourth?"

"And fourth, I love you, Anthony Morehouse."

He closed his eyes and rested his forehead against hers. "Oh, Edwina, I don't deserve that. I said hateful things to you. Horrible things."

"Apology accepted."

He lifted his head, tilted her chin, and kissed her. Softly and with such tenderness it made her want to cry. He kissed her lips and eyes and temple and jaw, then gently held her away from him, taking both her hands in his.

"Now it is my turn. I have a few things to say to you, Edwina. I was *so* angry with you. I thought you had betrayed me and it hurt. But when your note said you were giving up the *Cabinet*, my anger was overtaken by concern. It had been my words that had driven you from the most important thing in your life, and I could not bear it. I could not bear to see you lose your passion. The anger was momentary, you see. The love is forever. And I do love you, Edwina."

How could she have believed she never wanted to hear those words again? Her heart took flight and soared. She had not fallen off a cliff. She was flying.

"I want you," he said. "I want to claim you for my own, just as I did that night when I pretended you were my lightskirt. I think we could be good together, you and I. I need you to keep me grounded, to temper my reckless nature, to help me keep my focus outward rather than inward. I need you to teach me to be unselfish and generous and thoughtful, to find my place in the world."

"Oh, Anthony."

"And you need me to keep you from being too earthbound, too selfless, too controlled. You need me to show you how to take risks, to reach for the moon. Just as I am risking everything right now to bare my heart to you."

He squeezed her hands and pulled her slightly

closer. She might have buckled at the knees if he hadn't been holding her upright. His words were so beautiful to her ears, it was almost beyond bearing.

"We need each other," he said. "I suspect we shall each spin off into our own private directions without the other, and dissipate in the wind without a trace. We complete each other. At least, I know you complete me. Without you I am unfinished and unfulfilled. I don't want to live like that. Complete me, Edwina."

She could bear no more and flung her arms around his neck. "Nothing would make me happier. To complete you. To be completed by you. I do need you, Anthony. For all the reasons you have said. I need you—in my life, in my heart, and in my bed."

"I was hoping you would say that." She could hear the smile in his voice. "I want to spend every night making glorious, breathtaking, earth-shattering love to you. I do have one more question, though."

"Yes?"

"You are a most unusual and unconventional woman, Edwina, and we have often been at war with each other. Dare I hope that you will agree to live in love and peace with me in a horribly conventional arrangement like marriage?"

He must surely have seen all the joy shining from her eyes for she was filled with it, flooded with it, almost overwhelmed by it.

"I have some doubts about peacefulness between us," she said, "but I will wager we can make a success of such an age-old convention."

"I will take that wager," he said. "I will bet my life on it."

And he kissed her to seal the bargain.

Epilogue

have since clothes should perhaps dress differently," she said, "but I will grow on make-up.

"I will approve of..." he said, "I will try to talk on it.

And he kissed her on the lips, on their...

She woke to the sensation of Anthony's lips on hers. He was teasing her awake, and she rolled into his kiss.

"Hmm. What a lovely way to wake up."

"Good morning, Mrs. Morehouse."

She smiled. "That is a lovely way to wake up, too. I like the sound of it, Mr. Morehouse."

"You are as beautiful as ever in the morning. I had been worried, you know."

"About what?"

"That your incredible beauty was merely a façade of cosmetics and wigs. One never can be too sure about those things, you know."

She laughed. "And now you know. You are very

370

beautiful yourself, Mr. Morehouse. In the morning. Anytime."

He placed a hand on his chest. "You humble me, wife."

"It was a very fine wedding, Anthony. Your mother was so sweet."

"She cried all over my neckcloth."

"And I like your father, despite how less than supportive he has been to you over the years. I thought he was going to burst into tears when you gave him the Minerva."

"It was good of you to allow me to give it to him. It had been his, after all. He was the one who unearthed it. It was wrong of me to use it as a stake all those years ago."

"And so now she is back where she belongs."

"Right you are. And so, my love, are you ready for our wedding trip?"

"Almost. Just a few more things to pack."

"Are you certain about going to Paris again? It won't bring back bad memories?"

"It might. But you will help me banish them. Besides, this is the first time Paris has been open to travel in years. Since I was last there, in fact. I will be interested to see what reforms Bonaparte has implemented. And perhaps . . . I am almost embarrassed to say it."

"What?"

"Perhaps I will do a little shopping. My wardrobe

is sadly out of date. I should hate to appear a dowd next to my fashionable husband."

Anthony ran a finger over her breast, teasing the nipple into a peak. "I like what you're wearing now just fine."

She gave a little shiver and closed her eyes. "It will be strange to be away for so long."

"Are you worried about the magazine?"

"It's grown so. I am a bit concerned leaving Prudence in charge for several months."

"Nicholas will be there to help her."

"That is one of the things that concerns me. But never mind. I am going to put everything else out of my head while I enjoy a full and lusty wedding trip with my handsome new husband."

"Lusty, you say?"

"Wild, uncontrolled, unbridled lust."

"Ha! I knew you were a Modern Woman. Come here."

He rolled on top of her and began the first full day of their marriage with a passionate promise for the future.

Author's Note

When Edwina accepted the challenge to expand her magazine's subscription base to four thousand, some readers may wonder why such a small number seemed like such a big deal. In fact, it was a very big deal.

Periodicals in the late eighteenth and early nineteenth centuries did not have the circulation in the hundreds of thousands we expect today. The most popular and widely circulated periodical of the time was the *Gentleman's Magazine*, which had a subscription base of around ten thousand, a number that far outstripped other periodicals of the day. A typical monthly periodical printed around 2,500 copies, and these generally did not include colored prints. Heideloff's *Gallery of Fashion*, the most expensive and exclusive of the early fashion magazines, had an annual subscription list of only around four hundred.

To give *The Ladies' Fashionable Cabinet* an initial circulation of two thousand, and a final circulation of four thousand is in fact stretching credibility to the limit. It is much more likely that such a magazine would have had an annual subscription list closer to a thousand. But I have used a bit of literary license in establishing the number slightly higher for the sake of twenty-first-century sensibilities.

With the exception of *The Ladies' Fashionable Cabinet*, all magazines mentioned in the text did exist in 1801. The political and social agenda behind the *Lady's Monthly Museum* existed as described.

The preliminary peace between Britain and France, the London Treaty, was signed on October 1, 1801. It was a prelude to the more formal Treaty of Amiens signed on March 25, 1802. It lasted less than a year. War between Britain and France resumed in May 1803 and continued until the Battle of Waterloo in June 1815.